THE FAIRHAVEN CHRONICLES
BOOK 3

THROUGH CLOUD
& SUNSHINE

D0066782

THE FAIRHAVEN
CHRONICLES
BOOK 3

THROUGH CLOUD
& SUNSHINE

SHARON DOWNING JARVIS

DESERET
BOOK

Salt Lake City, Utah

This book is a work of fiction. The characters, places, and incidents in it are the product of the author's imagination or are represented fictitiously.

Library of Congress Cataloging-in-Publication Data

Jarvis, Sharon Downing, 1940–
   Through cloud and sunshine / Sharon Downing Jarvis.
     p. cm. — (The Fairhaven chronicles ; bk. 3)
   ISBN 1-59038-433-4 (pbk.)
  1. Mormons—Fiction. 2. Bishops—Fiction. 3. Alabama—Fiction. I. Title.
   PS3560.A64T48 2005
   813'.54—dc22   2005000482

Printed in the United States of America   54459
Malloy Lithographing Incorporated, Ann Arbor, MI

10   9   8   7   6   5   4   3   2   1

For Wesley and Josephine Jarvis,
the kindest and best of in-laws

CHAPTER ONE

" . . . ON A COLD WINTER'S NIGHT THAT WAS SO DEEP"

Christmas was essentially over; now at nine forty-five on Christmas night. With their two younger children tucked in bed and their eldest in her room reading one of her new books, Bishop James Shepherd and his wife, Trish, could finally relax. They sat in the living room with the lights dimmed except for those on the tree—small white stars that beamed their steady radiance from within the mysterious dark branches of a fragrant pine. The children preferred the other tree, the one in the family room, with its racing, multi-colored lights and ornaments that represented peppermints and gingerbread men and drums and sleds and rocking horses and snowmen. The more formal living room tree held Trish's cherished crystal ornaments and tiny velvet-backed books in shades of rose and green. There were miniature editions of Dickens, the Gospels, Shakespeare's *Twelfth Night,* and "The Night before Christmas," as well as others, most of which the bishop didn't recognize. Trish had been collecting the ornaments for this tree from before they were married.

She was curled in a corner of the sofa now, gazing at the tree while a Tabernacle Choir Christmas collection softly played. The bishop was sprawled in a nearby chair, his slippered feet stretched out before him, watching his wife in a rare moment of repose— rare, at least, this season of the year. *Christmas Eve had been good,* he reflected. They'd had Muzzie and her children over, and Buddy Osborne, and Melody and Andrea Padgett. Trish had per- suaded the children to act out the Christmas story—both the New Testament version and the Book of Mormon counterpart, in which the faithful were nearly put to death while waiting for the sign of Christ's birth to be given. Jamie had been especially enthusiastic acting the part of an unbelieving priest anxious to slay the believers, while Buddy Osborne had been a patient, if embarrassed, Joseph, kneeling beside Tiffani as Mary at the side of the sleeping Baby Jesus (Mallory's doll—Mallory had cam- paigned to have the cat, Samantha, wrapped up as the holy child, but her mother had firmly quashed that idea). The other children took the parts of shepherds and wise men and as believ- ing Nephites in the Book of Mormon version, after which a sup- per of soups and varied breads, crackers and cheeses, followed by hot fudge and peppermint ice cream sundaes, had been happily consumed.

Christmas morning had been fun, too—always is, the bishop mused—watching his children open their gifts and exclaim over them, and then presenting Trish with his gift for her—a gold and pearl charm bracelet with a custom-engraved charm that read "Number-one Trooper and Helpmeet." He also gave her a James Christensen jigsaw puzzle entitled "The Responsible Woman," showing that good lady burdened every which way with the trap- pings of her varied responsibilities. Trish had laughed and kissed him and then handed him her gifts—a cell phone and a new bathrobe and pajama set. He had mixed feelings about the cell phone—never had wanted one, in fact—but he tried to be grateful, and she persuaded him that in his position, with so many people clamoring for his attention at all hours, he needed one. *Now,* he mused, *if I can only learn to use the dang thing properly, it might be as much of a help as an annoyance.*

The cat, Samantha, seemed to partake of their post-Christmas relaxation as she lolled beneath the tree, stretching in the incredibly elastic way she had, then rolling onto her back and batting half-heartedly at a dangling crystal icicle.

Trish wagged a finger at her. "Don't even think about it," she warned. Samantha began to lick her side as though she had no other thought in mind. "Jim," Trish said, turning her attention to him, "have I told you lately how happy I am?"

He grinned. "Tell me again."

"I'm very, very, very, very happy."

"I'm just exactly that glad."

"I honestly can't think of a single thing missing in my life. I'm perfectly content."

He went to sit beside her, and she nestled into his arms. He nuzzled her shiny dark hair, which was one of his favorite things about her and which always seemed to smell like sunlight and flowers. "You make me happy, too, Trish," he told her. "You're my anchor and my rudder and the wind in my sails."

She pulled back and gave him a playfully narrow-eyed look. "I'm a *ship?*" she inquired.

"You're a sailboat, babe—the fastest, sleekest, most gorgeous kind."

"Oh. Well, then."

They were quiet for a few moments. Then she said, "The only thing I ever wonder about is whether there might be another child for us. Sometimes I think there is."

He kissed her hair. "We're not as young as we used to be."

"That's true." She sighed. "And my track record in producing children is not the best. Still—I wonder. It's the only thing in my whole life that I would change if I could. To have a couple more children."

"I know. But we've got three great ones, and they seem to keep you pretty busy."

"They do, and they're great kids. I adore each of them. I don't know—maybe it's because there were four of us in my family, and I'm programmed in that direction. It's no big deal. Just a thought."

"We aren't doing anything to prevent it, sweetheart, so if it happens, it happens. I just want you to be safe and well."

"I know. Thanks, Jim, for being you. I love you so much."

He held her to him, savoring the moment. "Don't know how to be anybody else. And I love you, Trish. With all my heart."

"This has been a wonderful Christmas, hasn't it?"

"The best ever."

"Do you really hate your phone?"

"Oh, hey—I hardly know it, yet. Give us a chance to get acquainted before I pass judgment. It's a very thoughtful gift, I can tell you that."

"Just not what you wanted."

"I didn't want anything in particular. I'm always happy with whatever you give me."

"I love my bracelet. It's gorgeous, and it makes me feel—um—elegant, and cherished."

"Would you rather have had a new food processor?"

"Are you kidding me? I can process food just fine."

"You sure can. Dinner was great."

"Thanks. It was lovely, having your mother here. I'm glad she felt well enough to come, and I'm grateful that the good weather held out long enough so that Paula and Travis could bring her. In fact, it held out just long enough, sounds like. Listen to that wind kicking up!"

The wind was, indeed, howling outside, whipping in gusts around the eaves and keening at the windows.

"Bet we'll get snow before morning," he commented.

"Snow's fine—I just hope it won't be an ice-storm. I hate those. They're gorgeous, but treacherous."

"Like some women, huh?"

"Oh—well, I, of course, wouldn't know about that." She giggled softly.

He hugged her closer. "No, you wouldn't. You're a virtuous woman, and I'm grateful."

"Like snow? As in 'pure as the driven'?"

"That pure, but more like sunlight. I think you must be spring or summer because you light up my days and warm my nights."

"Now you're waxing poetic."

He kissed her hair again. "Only you could make me do that, babe."

The jangling of the phone broke the mood, and they looked at each other regretfully.

The bishop went to the extension on his desk in the corner of the dining room.

"Bishop?" The voice was a little quavering; and for a moment he couldn't place it.

"Yes? This is . . . ?"

"It's Lula Rexford, Bishop. I'm so sorry to bother y'all on Christmas, but I'm real worried about T-Rex."

"What's wrong, Lula? Is he sick?"

"He ain't here, is the problem, and he said he'd be back three hours ago! He took his motorcycle out for a spin—got him some new do-dads for it, for Christmas, you know, and wanted to go ride, maybe show it off a little to a couple of friends. I've called all of them, and only one has seen him—and T-Rex left there about six-thirty."

"Well, he's a young man with a lot of friends—he might be anywhere. Maybe he got involved talking to somebody, or something. You know how it goes with guys . . ."

"No, Bishop, I got this creepy feelin', like somethin's wrong with him. I even called the sheriff, but you know you don't get no satisfaction from the law about missin' young'uns. They say they'll keep an eye out, but they don't even take you serious till the kid's been gone at least twenty-four hours."

"What does Tom say?"

"He's worried, too. He went out and rode around a little, but no luck. He don't say much, just sits there and frowns. See, Thomas was gonna come home and watch a movie with us tonight. He was lookin' forward to it. Said he'd be back by seven at the latest. He didn't want to be out ridin' late, 'cause it gits too dang cold. And it is—it's purely howlin' out there. I don't know what to do, Bishop! I want to take off myself and go lookin' for him, but I don't have a clue where . . ."

"What would you like us to do, Lula?"

She was near tears. "I sure don't know. I thought maybe—if there's any menfolks available, they might take a ride—fan out on the different highways, look for any signs of somebody goin' off the road, you know, before the snow covers it up."

"I'll be right over. Just sit tight, and say a prayer."

He reported the news to Trish, and they knelt by the living room sofa and offered a brief but fervent prayer themselves for T-Rex's safety. Then he bundled into a warm jacket, took gloves and a hat with earflaps, and headed out to his truck. So far, no snow had fallen, but the wind came in cold and humid blasts with a sweet smell to it that he associated with the white stuff.

He thought about T-Rex, the Fairhaven Mariners' football hero and object of many a young girl's crush. The boy loved his motorcycle, he knew—loved the feel of its speed and power beneath him and the boost he felt it gave to his image among his peers. The bishop understood, to a point—he had felt somewhat the same about his first truck—the old pickup he had lovingly worked on, souped up, and raced on Saturday mornings during his own teenage days. But, from a grown-up point of view, he worried about T-Rex and his bike. The boy had even ridden it during football season, which was forbidden by the coach. The lure, apparently, was irresistible. He tried to think of all the kids he knew who might have qualified for a visit by T-Rex, to show off his new gadgets, whatever they were. Surely he would be with one of them!

And yet—he couldn't dismiss Lula's fear. He knew that mothers often knew things. A similar fear was nibbling at the edges of his consciousness as well.

He parked in front of the Rexfords' and hurried up onto the porch. Lula had the door open before he knocked.

"Any word?" he asked, and she shook her head. Tom, her husband, sat on the edge of an easy chair, his head down and hands clasped loosely before him.

"Okay—who-all have you called?" the bishop asked.

"Ever'body I could think of, Bishop, from his teammates to the kids at church. Artie Joe Williams was the one said he'd been by to see him, but didn't stay long. And he didn't say where he was headed next. Ever'body else either isn't home, or hatn't seen him."

"Let's get us some help lined up, then," he replied. "Could I use your ward list?"

Tom got it for him and hovered in the background while the bishop punched in numbers on their kitchen phone. "Don't like to bother folks," Tom muttered. "Like to look after my own, you know."

The bishop nodded at him in understanding. He knew very well how independent Tom Rexford was. "But time's passing, Tom—and Lula's right—we need to fan out and see if we can spot him before . . ." He didn't want to say, "Before it's too late," but Tom got the message and subsided to his chair again.

Within ten minutes, men began to arrive at the Rexford home, and several others who lived further out had agreed to search the roads near their homes. The bishop got a map from his glove box and spread it on the kitchen table, and elders and high priests chose routes to follow, in pairs where possible, so that one could drive and the other watch for skid marks or other signs of trouble.

"Brethren, I brought a few bottles of consecrated oil, just in case, if any of y'all would like to take some along," offered Brother Woodrow Likens, the newly-called high priests group leader.

Several pocketed the small bottles. The bishop always kept a tiny vial of oil attached to his key chain. He didn't go anywhere without it. Priesthood blessings, he had learned, were often required or requested at the most unexpected times. Robert Patrenko, his first counselor, offered a prayer, and the men dispersed.

Just as the bishop climbed back into his truck, with his counselor Sam Wright riding shotgun, Rosetta McIntyre, second counselor in the Relief Society presidency, arrived to stay with Lula and help man the phone. The bishop was grateful for Rosetta's calm and steadying influence—and grateful that she was in town, which Ida Lou Reams, the Relief Society president, was not, she and Barker having gone to spend Christmas with their son in Mobile. Rosetta's children were home from college during the holidays and obviously old enough to be left alone, whereas first counselor Frankie Talbot's children were young, and her husband, Gene, was involved in helping search. It was a source of some chagrin to the bishop when Brother Wright suggested that they divide up so that each vehicle had at least one cell phone along, so all could check in and report to home base. He had to admit that though he now owned such a phone, it wasn't ready to use. His wife was wiser than he sometimes gave her credit for, he thought, vowing to get his new phone charged and figured out as soon as possible.

He and Sam headed out along the highway leading toward Anniston, going as slowly as they dared, sometimes pulling off and allowing traffic to pass. They drove about seventeen miles and decided that T-Rex wouldn't have been likely to head out that far from town on that major a road, and turned back.

"I sure hope that boy's holed up somewheres, playin' video games with a buddy and jest forgot to call his folks," Sam said, the strain in his voice belying his confidence that this was the case.

"Buddy!" the bishop said suddenly. "I wonder if Lula called Buddy Osborne? T-Rex knows Buddy hero-worships him. It's a long shot, but he just might've stopped by to see him."

"Where's Buddy, with his dad or mom?" Sam asked.

"He's with his dad, so he's in town. He was over at our place, last night."

Sam punched a number on his phone. "Rosetta? Sam Wright here. Any word? No? Okay, listen. Ask Lula if she happened to check with Buddy Osborne, to see if Thomas went to see him." He waited, faithfully scanning the sides of the road as they crawled along. "She didn't? Okay. Let me know." He gave her his number, and they waited. In less than two minutes, the phone buzzed, and Sam answered. "He did? At seven-fifteen? Great! Thanks."

He flipped the phone closed and put it in his pocket. "Good thinkin', Bishop. Thomas did stop to see Buddy, and his daddy says T-Rex give Buddy a ride back out to his mama's place. They left about seven-fifteen to head out there."

"Oh, man. I hope he's still there, with Buddy! Listen, there's a ward directory in the glove box. Find Twyla Osborne's number—hers and Gerald's are both listed—and call there."

The bishop hardly dared breathe while Sam placed the call. Apparently no one was answering, and Sam looked worriedly at him. Finally he closed his phone.

"No answer," he said. "Maybe they're all asleep. Mercy! I surely do hope it's not *two* boys we're searchin' for."

"Well, I'm heading out there, to see if we can rouse anybody," the bishop replied, trying to keep his hand and voice steady. "We've got to know if Buddy got home all right."

He turned at the first opportunity, onto a connecting road that led to the area where Twyla Osborne lived. Sam called in to let Lula and Rosetta know their plan.

"Brother Patrenko and Brother Nettles are working that area," Sam reported. "She gave me Brother Patrenko's cell number, so we can let them know if we find out anything."

"Good." The bishop concentrated on his driving, no longer crawling, but now pushing the speed limit as much as he dared. A few drops of moisture began to appear on the windshield, and he grimaced. *Not yet*, he thought. *Please, not yet.*

It seemed to take forever, but finally he pulled into the mobile home park and stopped in front of Twyla's unit. All was dark; there was no sign of a motorcycle parked anywhere. The bishop bounded out of his car and knocked loudly on the door. . There was no answer.

He sighed. "Father, if someone's here, please cause them to answer," he prayed softly. Sam was walking around the small yard, peering behind the home. No one came to the door, and the bishop ran around to the back, trying to gauge where Buddy's bedroom window would be. He had visited him there once, when Buddy had shown him his artwork. He should remember—this must be the kitchen, and these the dining area—surely this next one was Buddy's window.

"Buddy!" he called loudly, jumping to knock on the window.

"Here you go, Bishop," said Sam, bending over with laced fingers. The bishop stepped into the makeshift stirrup just long enough to rap sharply three times on Buddy's window.

"Buddy!" he called again.

"What the ever-lovin' hell do y'all think you're doin'?" came a querulous female voice from the mobile home adjacent to Twyla's.

The bishop turned. "It's an emergency," he explained. "Sorry to bother you, but I've got to talk to these folks."

"Wal, Twyla ain't even there, she's off with that guy she goes with—Jeter, or whatever. I don't know 'bout Buddy. He's so quiet, I don't know he's home, 'lessen I see his light on."

"Have you seen it tonight?"

"Seems like it, but I cain't say for sure."

"Bishop!" said Sam, and indicated Buddy's window, where the blind seemed to be pulled back an inch or so.

"Buddy! It's Bishop. I need to talk to you!"

The window inched open. "Bishop? For reals?"

"Yes, Buddy—please open the door, okay?"

"Yes, for mercy's sake, do that, so a body can get some sleep!" The window behind them snapped shut, and they raced around to the front door again. A tousled, sleepy Buddy turned on the porch light and held the door open, blinking.

"What's up, Bishop? Hey, Brother Wright."

"Buddy, bless your heart, I'm so glad to see you!" the bishop said, grabbing the boy's thin shoulders. "Listen, we understand T-Rex gave you a ride home, tonight, on his bike. Is that right?"

"Sure is. Boy, that was cool! Scary, but cool. But why . . . what? Did something happen to him? Did he wreck, or something?"

"We don't know where he is, that's the problem. About what time did he leave here?"

Buddy thought. "It was about—about seven forty or forty-five, I think. He came inside for just a couple of minutes to look at some of my stuff, and then he said he was late and had to get home. He told his folks he was going to watch a video with them—somethin' they'd just got for Christmas."

"So he was in a hurry?"

"Reckon he was, but he didn't seem too worried. Said he knew a shortcut to take."

"Did he say what that was? Or do you know what it might be?"

Buddy thought. "He didn't say. But—reckon it might could be Post Hole Road. I use that sometimes, on my bike. But only in the daytime, and in good weather."

"Could you show us?"

"Sure. I'll just throw on my coat and shoes."

The bishop looked at his counselor with both hope and dread. Sam flipped open his phone and called Robert Patrenko and gave him the news. He listened a minute, then said, "See you along there, somewhere, I expect." He turned back to the bishop. "Brother Nettles knows that road. They'll head in that direction, too."

The three of them, two men and a tousle-haired boy in paja-mas, scoured both sides of the dark roadway the best they could.

The bishop drove slowly down the middle of the two-lane road, so that his headlights could pick up anything suspicious on either side. It ran through a wooded area, and the bishop privately thought it should have been named "Pot Hole Road," in honor of the number of those they had to skirt. What if one of them had caught T-Rex's wheel and thrown his bike out of control? It seemed a likely scenario.

Sam's phone burred in his pocket, and he whipped it out.

"Yes? You did? Tell me." He paused to listen, holding up a cautioning hand to his companions. "We're almost there."

He closed his phone and looked at the bishop. "They found him, a little further down this road. We should see their headlights, any minute. Said he's wrecked his bike, all right, and he's injured. Bob said he's breathing, but doesn't look too good."

The bishop increased his speed.

CHAPTER TWO

" . . . THE SOLEMN FAITH OF PRAYER"

Bishop Shepherd could sense Buddy, huddled between him and Sam Wright in the seat of the truck, shrinking into his coat as they drove down the dark roadway.

"Buddy," the bishop said, "I'm so glad you thought of this shortcut. Who knows when T-Rex would've been found if you hadn't."

"But it's my fault," Buddy said, his voice low and miserable. "If he hadn'ta give me a ride home, he wouldn'ta even been this side of town, let alone needing to take a shortcut home."

"Didn't he offer to bring you? I'll bet he wanted to share the fun of his motorcycle with you."

"Reckon, but he didn't need to. Deddy would've drove me."

"Friend, this isn't your fault, any which way. It's just a result of innocent choices and poor conditions. Don't you go blaming yourself."

"Accidents happen," Sam put in. "Reckon they're just one of the dangers we face in this mortal life, which is uncertain at best. Hopefully, Thomas won't be as bad off as he looks."

"If he was to die, reckon I'd just as leave die, too, as to have ever'body know it happened on account of him givin' me a ride. Ever'body loves T-Rex."

The bishop groaned inwardly. "Let's not even talk about him dying, all right? Let's pray and try to have faith that he's survived this long for a very good reason."

They rounded a curve and there were the headlights of Robert Patrenko's car, which was parked so that they were beaming down into a brushy area off the right side of the road. The bishop pulled his truck into a position that added the benefit of his headlights to the scene.

"Oh, mercy," the bishop breathed, seeing the glint of the light on the shiny cycle that meant so much to its owner, now on its side with one wheel twisted upward. Some distance beyond the cycle, Brothers Patrenko and Nettles were kneeling beside the injured rider. Brother Nettles raised an arm and motioned to them to hurry.

The bishop looked at Buddy. "Maybe you ought not . . ." he began, as they got out of the truck, but Buddy shook his head vehemently.

"Got to, Bishop. Least I can do," he said, his teeth chattering.

"Okay." He put one arm around the boy as they hurried down the embankment, through weeds that were nearly flattened by the gusts of cold wind that whipped through. Pine tops tossed and made a sighing sound, as if they, too, were agitated by the disturbance that had come among them. Robert Patrenko and Bill Nettles were each in their shirtsleeves, their jackets covering the still form on the ground. T-Rex lay on his side, one arm trapped beneath him, and his head twisted backward. His mouth was open, and his breathing raspy and uneven. The bishop gasped, as at first it seemed that the boy's whole head was covered with blood, and cracked open like a pumpkin, but then he realized that T-Rex still wore his helmet, which was a deep, metallic red color, and which, indeed, was split down one side.

"When we heard you were almost here, we waited to give him a blessing," Brother Patrenko said. "The ambulance is on its way. Bishop—who do you want to have anoint?" He held up one of the small bottles of consecrated oil. The bishop considered briefly.

"Would you anoint, Bob? And I'll bless. Buddy, why don't you kneel down here by us and add your faith to our prayers, okay? Brethren, if you'll give me just a minute to prepare . . ." He moved a few feet away from the group, facing the woods, and offered up a quick whispered prayer for guidance and inspiration in that which he was about to do, then turned back and knelt with his brethren as close to the injured boy as they could get. There were rocks in the area, and stumps where someone had partially cleared old trees away.

The bishop felt a measure of comfort as Bob Patrenko placed the drop of oil just above T-Rex's nose, on the only part of his head that they could access, and spoke the familiar words of the anointing. Then he took a deep breath and began the blessing. He heard himself promise the injured boy that if he chose to, he could be healed of the injuries that had occurred this night— that it would require time and courage, but his health would be restored to him through faith and the skills of medicine if that was his desire. He blessed him with strength to withstand the pain, and with patience and endurance and a new understanding of his mission in life, and encouraged him to have an obedient spirit and a willingness to accept the will of the Lord in his future. He blessed his brain and nerves and bones and internal organs—any parts of his body that might be injured or in danger, to be strong and to function properly. He assured T-Rex that the Lord knew and loved him and was aware of his needs at this time, and closed in the name of the Savior.

"That'll help, now," breathed Sam Wright softly. "Thank you, Bishop."

The bishop became aware of Buddy crying quietly nearby, and rose to go to him, but Buddy was already standing and taking off his coat.

"Here, my coat's warmed up—put it over him, and one of y'all take yours back," he said shakily. "Y'all've been standing out here longer." He lifted a jacket from T-Rex's chest and replaced it with his own, tucking it gently around him.

"Good idea, friend," the bishop said, doing the same thing with his jacket, draping it over T-Rex's legs. "Now if you get too cold, Buddy, go jump in the truck, you hear?"

"I'm fine," the boy insisted, but he was already hugging his arms against the cold blasts. The bishop understood that this was part of the penance the younger boy felt he needed to pay for his part, though innocent, in the mishap.

"Lula and Tom been notified?" he asked softly, looking around, and Brother Nettles nodded.

"Bob called and got hold of Sister McIntyre at the house," he said. "Tom's out riding with Brother Likens. Reckon they'll all show up here purty soon."

"I hope the paramedics hurry. I hate that it's so cold, and now the rain's comin', too, feels like," Sam said.

The rain was indeed coming, and now the two coats that had just been put back on were taken off and held as a canopy over T-Rex. Soon everybody was shivering, and they talked little. It was just a matter of gritting their teeth and enduring—and besides, the bishop knew there were four internal conversations with the Lord going on besides his own. He, for one, was fervently thanking the Lord that they had been able to find T-Rex and that something had prompted him to think that Buddy Osborne might be involved. He felt pretty sure that something was the Holy Ghost.

He looked at Buddy, who was hunkered down on his haunches, with his arms thrust between his knees for whatever warmth that could afford and thought how typical that was of the boy—always making himself into as small and inconspicuous a package as possible. He would need to make himself especially available to Buddy through the next weeks, while T-Rex was recovering . . . if he recovered. The bishop had no doubt that he could recover, but he had been as surprised as the others must have been at the indication he'd received that it would be T-Rex's choice whether he chose to live. He fervently hoped, for Tom's and Lula's sake—and for Buddy's, and even his own—that T-Rex would decide to stay around and continue to tease, annoy, and delight those who loved him.

The ambulance could be heard long before it was seen, and the bishop thought he had never heard a more welcome sound than its mournful wail. It screeched to a stop, and the para-medics swarmed down the embankment with a speed that did his heart good. They worked quickly, taking vital signs, examin-ing T-Rex's eyes, assessing potential injuries from his placement and position and that of the cycle and the condition of his hel-met and other considerations that the bishop could only guess at. They called their findings to the hospital and received crackly replies that they apparently were able to interpret. Eventually, they very carefully eased a backboard under the fallen boy, immobilizing his head and neck as best they could, and with a tremendous effort, lifted him and bore him up the hill. They were puffing with exertion as they loaded him into the ambulance.

"He's a big kid," one of them commented, as he closed the doors.

"He's a linebacker," Sam Wright told him. "The Mariners' best. Thomas Rexford."

"This is T-Rex?" asked the young man, frowning. "Shoot, that's too bad. I've seen him play, and he's good. Say—could one of you folks follow along to the hospital and help us get him admitted, until his folks get there? We need a little preliminary information for our records."

"I'll follow you," the bishop offered. "I'll want to stay there with Tom and Lula, anyway. Sam, could you drop Buddy back at home, and—"

"Bishop?" Buddy's voice was small, but urgent. "I gotta come, too."

"Aw, Buddy, there's not a thing you can do there to help T-Rex. You might as well . . ."

Buddy was shaking his head and still shivering all over from cold and nerves, as they all were. "See, the thing is, I just remembered I locked myself out. You know I don't have a key—Mama left the kitchen door unlocked for me earlier, when she left, but I locked it, and when I came with you, I forgot and pulled the front door shut, and now it's locked, too. I'm sorry. But anyway, I just want to be there."

"Right, come along, then. Reckon I don't really want to leave you alone tonight, anyway."

"Thanks. I won't bother nobody."

"You never do," the bishop told him, placing a hand on his thin, wet shoulder as they moved toward the truck.

"I'll take these men home," Robert Patrenko said. "Bishop, you'll call us when you know anything?"

"Me, too, Bishop? Any time of night, dudn' matter at all," Sam added.

The bishop nodded. He was just about to pull away after the ambulance when another car converged on the scene. It contained Lula Rexford and Rosetta McIntyre. He stopped long enough to ask Rosetta if she could bring Lula to the hospital and stay with her there, then drove away. Lula's face was pale and drawn. They passed a truck alongside the road that belonged to Brother Likens. It stopped just long enough to allow the ambulance and two cars to pass, then wheeled around and fell into line behind them. The cars and truck couldn't keep up with the ambulance, but they did their best, arriving at the small hospital's emergency entrance as the patient was being taken in. With Lula and Tom there, the bishop wasn't needed after all to provide information, although the paramedics told him that the police would likely be contacting him to find what he knew about the circumstances of the accident. He and Buddy took seats in the emergency waiting room, where a wall-mounted television was showing some inane infomercial with a tanned, sleek couple flashing unnaturally white smiles at the camera every chance they got. Idly, he wondered what they were selling—but not enough to turn up the volume. A small artificial Christmas tree with winking blue and red lights was decorated with syringes, colored band-aids, and strips of gauze tied into bows. Buddy was gazing at it with distaste.

"Don't much feel like Christmas no more, does it?" he asked morosely.

The bishop shook his head. "Nope," he agreed. "Reckon I'd better call home and tell my wife what's going on," he said, realizing as he stood up how very tired he was, and how wet. He went to a pay phone in the hallway and put in the call. Trish was anxious, and full of questions for which he had no answers. He assured her that when more information became available, he would let her know. He hung up and walked wearily to the admissions station, where he finally got the attention of a clerk and asked if she might be able to snag a couple of blankets for him and Buddy to wrap around themselves.

"Oh, y'all are soaking wet, aren't you?" she said. "We could lend you a couple of hospital gowns, too, if you'd like to get out of your wet clothes."

"Um—no thanks," he said, trying to smile. "Just blankets would be great. Keep us from getting pneumonia and ending up here, ourselves."

She brought them, eventually, and he and Buddy wrapped up in them gratefully.

"T-Rex—he got a new seat for his cycle for Christmas, and new handgrips, and that was his new helmet he was wearing. He sure liked it," Buddy offered after a few minutes of silence. "He'll be mad it got cracked like that."

The bishop nodded. "Better the helmet than the head," he said.

"Reckon so. I heard, though, that sometimes helmets can cause neck injuries in a crash."

"Is that right?" That was not a happy thought, and the bishop hoped it wasn't true. He wondered if T-Rex had been knocked out immediately in the accident, or if he'd had time to feel the pain of his injuries and the fear of not being found before he slipped into unconsciousness. In either case, he wondered if the boy would remember the accident later. He suspected he would not.

Tom, Lula, and Rosetta came to join them. Tom and Lula looked like sleepwalkers, their faces haggard and set with fear. There was no one else in the waiting room at the moment, and the bishop roused himself to lean forward and give them what he hoped was an encouraging smile.

"We gave Thomas a priesthood blessing just before the

paramedics came," he told them. "I was voice, and I felt prompted to tell him that he could be healed." He didn't include the part about "if he chose to." These people needed a stiff dose of hope right now.

"Thank you, Bishop," Lula said. "I believe blessings do help."

"He's young and strong, too—that's definitely in his favor."

Tom nodded. "That's what the feller in yonder said—the paramedic."

"Do they know the extent of any of his injuries, yet?"

"Looks like there's several, they said. Head, neck, plus his arm's broke and shoulder dislocated. Might be some cracked ribs or internal problems, too—they don't know, yet. They're getting him all stabilized now, whatever that means, then they'll do some more X-rays and stuff."

"Would you folks like to have a prayer, while we're alone, here?" the bishop asked.

Lula nodded. "If you'll say it, please," she whispered.

The bishop bowed his head and expressed their sorrow, care, and concern for Thomas and his injuries, as well as his heartfelt thanks that they were led to find him. He acknowledged that they knew that the Lord was mindful of the young man and prayed for comfort and strength for his parents and skill for the doctors and nurses who attended him. He didn't know whether the prayer comforted Tom and Lula, but it made him feel better. He felt the quivering in his midsection begin to settle down.

"How'd you come to find him, exactly?" asked Rosetta. "Did one of you come across him in your search?"

The bishop shook his head. "Buddy, here, had a lot to do with it," he said, and explained the sequence of events. "And, Lula, bless your mother's instinct for knowing that something must have happened and asking us to help. I believe you and Buddy both were inspired tonight."

"Well, and you, Bishop, for even thinking to ask me iffen I'd seen him," Buddy put in.

"Right. That felt kind of like a prompting, too," the bishop agreed. "We had to go rouse Buddy out of a sound sleep, but I knew it was important to do, after we'd learned that T-Rex gave him a ride home."

Tom Rexford spoke. "And that Post Hole Road—whatever the boy was thinkin', to ride that stretch at night, I don't know. How come you to think of that, Buddy?"

"I don't rightly know, except he'd said he knew a shortcut he'd take, so's he could get home sooner to watch the movie y'all got."

"Well, thank you, son, for your part," Lula told him. "We're real grateful. And thanks for that picture you drew of him in his uniform, too. It's hangin' on our livin' room wall. It's just real good. You got a gift."

Buddy looked down. "Welcome," he muttered softly. "T-Rex is a good guy."

The examination seemed to take forever, but finally one of the doctors motioned to Tom and Lula to come with him. The bishop wanted badly to follow, but he kept his seat. Buddy had succumbed to weariness and stress, and slept slumped in his chair, still wrapped in his blanket. Rosetta sat silently, lost in her own thoughts.

Tom came back. "They're gonna take the boy down to Birmingham, to the trauma center at Baptist Princeton," he said. They've just been workin' out whether they ought to fly him down on Life Flight or use an ambulance. Weather's gettin' worse, and I think they don't want to risk a helicopter in the storm, so likely it'll be the ambulance. Lula and me, we're goin' on down there, too. We want to thank y'all—ever'body who helped out—tonight. We'll let you know, Bishop, what happens."

"I could drive you down," Rosetta offered, standing up. "Y'all have enough on your mind without having to drive."

"Thank you, ma'am, but we'll take it from here," Tom replied. "All y'all go on home and get some rest. You deserve it."

He turned and headed back to find Lula, and the bishop looked at Rosetta.

"Rosetta, thanks so much. You've been a real help tonight."

"I wish he'd let me drive them."

The bishop nodded. "I know, but he's pretty independent. Thanks for offering, though. Let's head home now, so if we can be of any help tomorrow, we'll be ready."

She wished him a good night and left. He bent over Buddy and gently shook his shoulder. "Come on, friend—it's time to turn in our blankets and head home. They're going to transport T-Rex to a bigger hospital down in Birmingham, so there's nothing more we can do now. He's in good hands. Let's go home."

The boy nodded, stood, and silently peeled off his damp blanket. The bishop gave them both back to the lady at the desk with his thanks, and they headed out the double doors into a maelstrom of blowing and stinging snow. In the truck, he turned the heater up full blast and drove home. Neither of them spoke.

At the house, he sent Buddy into the downstairs bath with orders to take a good, warm shower and then wrap up in one of his own old bathrobes for the night. He took the boy's wet clothing and put it in the dryer, then stripped his own damp clothes off and got a shower, too, grateful that their water heater had a good capacity. He had planned to offer Buddy a snack, but the boy was curled on a family room couch, almost asleep again, when he came downstairs. He covered him with a comforter and told him to sleep as long as he liked. He considered a snack for himself, but found he had little interest in food, so he went upstairs. The wind still keened around the eaves, and the icy crystals spanged against the windows. Never had his home seemed more welcoming.

Trish roused herself when he slipped into their bed. "What happened?" she asked. "How's T-Rex?"

He told her the latest, then added, "Buddy's asleep in the family room. Locked out, again. Besides, he's real upset about T-Rex, and I think he may need us tomorrow."

"Poor kid," she said. "Well, both kids. I hope they'll both come through this all right."

"So do I. Would you offer a quick prayer to that effect? I expect the Lord's tired of hearing from me tonight."

She did so, and they curled close together. "Hey, babe?" he said, just before sleep claimed him.

"M-hm?"

"About that cell phone? I got the message tonight. That was an inspired gift."

CHAPTER THREE

Y

" . . . TO MAKE OUR HEARTS AS ONE"

The phone rang at six A.M., and the bishop blinked sleepily, struggling for a moment to determine whether he was hearing the phone or the alarm clock. Then the events of the night before crowded back into his mind, and he grabbed the phone.

"Jim Shepherd," he said, leaning up on one elbow.

"Bishop, this is Lula Rexford callin', to let you know about Thomas."

"Yes, Lula. Go ahead."

"Well, they've got him in surgery down here. They figure his brain is bruised, and bleedin', and they're gonna try to get that to stop, and to drain off so's the pressure don't build up too much. He ain't never woke up yet, and they think that's why. He's like, in a coma." Her voice broke, and she was silent for a moment. "I'm purty scared, Bishop. I cain't hardly stand to think of Thomas like this. He's always been such a strong, healthy kid. I don't want him to be . . . any different. And I surely don't want to lose him."

"I know, Lula. Neither do I. I love Thomas, too. What about his neck?"

"They say it ain't broke, but there's a compressed vertebrae. And Tom says he told you last night about his arm and shoulder. His ribs are bruised, too. But right now they don't think there's any internal bleedin', except in his head. Will you keep prayin' for us, Bishop?"

"You'd best believe it. And I'll do even better than that. I'm going to call a ward fast for him. I'll also call his name in to the temple prayer list as soon as the temple opens. We'll bring in all the spiritual power we can muster to help Thomas. You just add your own prayers, you and Tom, and try your best to have faith. I know I can't tell you not to worry, but just keep reminding yourself that you love Thomas and you love the Lord, and the Lord loves all of you, and He's told us that perfect love casts out fear."

"I'll try to keep that in mind," Lula promised. "Thank you so much—and thank ever'body for us, will you, Bishop?"

"I will. Do you want me to come down there? I'll be glad to."

"No, sir, not now, please don't. I reckon the roads are plumb awful. Have you looked outside yet?"

"No. Did we get a lot of snow?"

"There's a ton down here, so I reckon Fairhaven got it, too. And it's slick as—well, it is ice."

"Okay, I'll wait till the roads are better. But call me again, will you, when Thomas is out of surgery? Or as soon as there's anything to report?"

"Yessir, I'll do that."

Trish was awake when he hung up, watching him wide-eyed from her pillow. He eased back down on his own for a minute.

"Tell me," she said softly, and he did.

"So you're going to organize a ward fast?"

"I'll call the priesthood leaders and have them mobilize the home teachers and pass the word that way. It wouldn't hurt to alert the women, too, I suppose, just in case the men don't catch everybody."

"I'll do that."

"Thanks, babe. Lula says there's a ton of snow outside—at least in Birmingham. I'm reluctant to get up and look."

"I'll be brave," Trish said and slipped out of bed to go to the window. "Oh, boy," she said. "I guess there's a ton! It's beautiful, though. And still a few little flakes falling. Our white Christmas was a day late arriving."

"Kids'll be thrilled."

"That they will."

"What time should I start calling, do you think?"

"It's a little early yet. Maybe around sevenish? Start with those you know are early-birds. Which meals shall we fast?"

"I thought dinner tonight and breakfast tomorrow. We should be able to notify everybody in time for that. And I think I'll ask everybody who can to meet at the chapel tomorrow at noon, to close our fast with prayer—and those who can't, to try to pray at the same time."

"Storming the gates of heaven, hmm?"

"Something like that. When it comes to prayer, I believe in strength in numbers as well as in fervency and faith."

"Jim?"

"M-hmm?"

"Do the Rexfords have any health insurance to cover this?"

He sat up, then, frowning. "Wow, I don't know. I hadn't even thought about that. I'm sure as a football player, T-Rex would've had some through the school."

"But the season's over. Does the coverage extend all year?"

"I have no idea. I'll find out. I doubt that Tom or Lula, either one, has any health coverage. Tom's still out of work, and Lula's just part-time. Oh, boy. That's a sobering thought. There didn't seem to be any trouble checking him in, last night, though."

"Injuries like T-Rex's—especially head and neck problems—could require a lot of time and therapy, and run up some big bills."

"I can direct the fast offerings toward their needs for a while. There isn't too much of a drain on the funds otherwise, right now. We've been giving a little help, here and there, but not much."

"That's good. Assuming Tom'll accept it. Maybe they can get some help through the state, too. Once again, assuming Tom—"

"Well, Tom's proud and stubborn, but this just may be more than he can handle on his own. Listen, I think I'll go down and grab a little bite of breakfast before I start calling. You stay in bed, sweetheart—there's no need for you to be up this early. I'm sure Buddy—and our kids—will sleep in for a while yet."

She sighed. "Are you sure? I could make you something . . ."

He leaned over and kissed her. "I'm positive. A little later, maybe you and Rosetta can divvy up the visiting teachers and spread the word. I doubt many folks will be venturing out early today unless they absolutely have to."

"I wish you didn't have to open the store."

"Me, too. But if I don't, and the big guys do, I reckon we'll lose some customers—maybe for good. So goes the grocery business. People expect to be able to buy food whenever they need to."

"We're all spoiled," Trish said sleepily. She was already drifting back into slumber. The bishop went quietly downstairs and spent some time in the living room in prayer, then made himself a couple of pieces of cinnamon toast and a cup of cocoa and sat down at his desk. He began by calling the people who had been involved in the search the night before and letting them know the latest. Then he organized the high priests and elders quorum leaders to get the word out through the home teachers. Finally he sat back, already weary, although the day had barely begun.

"Bishop?" It was Buddy's voice, from the kitchen doorway. "What've you heard about T-Rex?"

"As of about forty-five minutes ago, he was in surgery," the bishop explained and went on to share with the boy what he knew.

"So are you goin' down there, to Birmingham?" Buddy asked.

"Not this morning, that's for sure. Have you looked outside?"

Buddy turned, the bishop's robe wrapped nearly double around his thin body, and went to pull a blind aside. "Oh, my gosh," he breathed. "That's a lot of snow."

The bishop nodded. "Tell me about it."

Buddy turned back to face him. "Bishop, what if . . . I mean, what if we hadn't've found him when we did, last night? He'd be all covered up—T-Rex, he'd be . . ."

"I know. He likely wouldn't have survived, cold as it was. We were greatly blessed."

Buddy perched on the edge of a dining room chair. "Reckon I can see that, all right. That we were blessed, I mean. But—what I cain't get my mind around, is—if the Lord could bless us to find him, why couldn't He bless T-Rex not to get hurt to begin with?"

The bishop sighed. "That's a good question, and sooner or later, we all ask it—or something similar. Like, why do bad things happen to good people? Why did Brother Bainbridge get cancer and die? Why did Rand Rivenbark get burned so badly in that car accident? Why do little children get kidnapped, or killed and injured in wars? Why did people we'd hardly ever heard of fly into the twin towers and the Pentagon and kill so many innocent people? You could go on and on."

"Well, yeah—so what's the reason? I mean, God has the power to stop all that, don't he?"

"He does—but he won't always use it. I know it's a hard thing to come to terms with, but I reckon it has to do with a couple of things we need to understand about Heavenly Father. One is, that he's given us our agency—our free will to make choices about how we'll behave—how we'll treat other people. That seems to be real important. You've heard about that, haven't you?"

"Yessir. How the devil wanted to force us all to act a certain way, and all? But God said no, that wasn't his plan? I learnt about that in Sunday School."

"Right. And he apparently won't infringe on our agency, or else this life wouldn't be a real test, and we wouldn't learn. So some folks are bound to misuse that freedom and choose to hurt other people—or just to make mistakes and do dangerous things that might hurt themselves, like rushing down a dark, chuck-holed road on a fast motorcycle. And it's a fact that a lot of young folks, like T-Rex, feel like they're invincible, that nothing really bad could happen to them."

"Okay, I get that. But what about, like praying for protection and safety? Don't that even work?"

"Well, sometimes we realize that we've been protected from dangers and troubles, that our prayers for safety and protection have been answered. Many times I suspect we simply don't recognize the protection we did receive. Other times, when bad things do happen, we wonder why we apparently weren't protected! I don't know all the answers, Buddy. Sometimes I just think that mortality's a dangerous condition. We're all subject to accidents, all kinds of illnesses, human error, and acts of plain old meanness. But I'll tell you something I do understand—and that is that no matter what happens to us, the Lord's always there, reaching out, ready to comfort us and help us get through it."

"But, how come the Lord created stuff like germs and viruses, to begin with?"

"Gotta wonder sometimes, don't we? I reckon it's probably because we need to experience both health and sickness, good things and bad, so we'll appreciate the good. There's a real good discussion of that in the Book of Mormon, in case you want to look into it. Read the second chapter of Second Nephi, where Lehi's talking to his son Jacob and trying to explain these things to him. He did a way better job than I can do."

"Huh. I will read it. Bishop, you got any clothes I can put on, I'll shovel your driveway for you."

"We'll work on that, together. But clothes? Wow. Let's see— your pajamas and socks and underwear should be dry. I put 'em in the dryer last night. But you can't shovel snow in your pj's! You're too big to wear any of Jamie's stuff, so we'll probably have to cinch up some of my jeans, and you can wear Trish's snow boots and a sweatshirt and one of my jackets. Soon as the roads are clear enough, I'll drive you home. I mean, if your Mom's there."

"She's not. Her and Jeter went to Atlanta till Sunday. So I'm locked out till then. But I've got a few clothes at Deddy's place, and I can go there around six tonight, when he gets home from work. 'Though maybe he cain't work, today, on account of the snow. I'll call and see."

"I expect a lot of folks will have to put work and other things on hold today. Well, let's get you some breakfast, okay? And then I'll tell you what the ward's going to do for Thomas."

Y

The snow reminded Jim of the words from the old carol: it was "deep and crisp and even," and it sparkled as though diamond dust had been sprinkled on the surface. He had found an old pair of sweats for Buddy, which he cinched up with the drawstring at the waist and stuffed into a pair of Trish's boots. The bishop had offered the boy a pair of his daughter Tiffani's jeans, but Buddy had reddened and shaken his head, backing off.

"I 'preciate it, Bishop, but I cain't—I just cain't wear a girl's jeans. No offense."

The bishop grinned. "None taken."

They manned the two snow shovels on his driveway, then moved next door to clear Mrs. Hestelle Pierce's walks.

"You know, if we got this kind of snow very often around here, I'd invest in a good snowblower," the bishop remarked, as they stomped their feet before entering the kitchen door.

"Daddy! It snowed all beautiful!" Mallory exulted, coming forward with Samantha the cat in her arms. "I tried to put Samantha out, but she just poked some holes in the snow and came running back in."

"Well, it's the first snow she's seen in her young life, isn't it? Think how cold it must feel to her paws."

"Maybe I ought to put shoes on her. I could make some."

"Um—no, I think it's better to let her get used to the feel of it. Anybody else up yet?"

"Huh-uh, not yet. Hey, Buddy. How come you're here?"

"Buddy came home with me in the middle of the night," her father explained. "He was helping us search for Thomas Rexford, who got in an accident last night."

"Do you mean T-Rex?"

"I do, sugar."

"Did he get hurt?"

"Yes, he did, and we're all going to pray for him to get better. Will you pray, real hard? I'm sure Heavenly Father listens to your prayers."

"I know," she agreed nonchalantly, then spun off to head upstairs. "I'm gonna tell Jamie!" she said.

Y

The story was told twice more in the Shepherd household, for Jamie's benefit and an hour or so later for Tiffani's—and countless other times throughout the Fairhaven Ward and among others who knew and admired the indomitable Thomas (T-Rex) Rexford. People called in to the bishop for updates, and he finally left the phone duty to Trish and with Buddy in tow, mushed his way to the store, where his right-hand man, Arthur Hackney, had opened the doors and turned on the lights, which the bishop was grateful to have working after such a pounding by Mother Nature. He had already called his office girl, Mary Lynn Connors, and told her to take another day off, that it wasn't necessary for her to try to come in on such a day.

Very few customers appeared, but those who did, most driving four-wheel-drive vehicles, seemed grateful to find the store open for business.

"Hey, Jim," greeted Ronald Westlake, a fellow he'd known since grade school. "How 'bout this snow, eh? I figure we got the whole winter's allowance in one night."

"Boy-howdy, I guess!" agreed the bishop. "Hope we don't have folks dropping in their tracks from too much shoveling."

"Likewise. Hey—tell me I heard wrong about this—but did T-Rex cream his bike last night? He goes to your church, doesn't he? Figured you'd know."

"He does, and he did. He's had emergency surgery for head

trauma and some other injuries, down at Birmingham Princeton Medical Center. We're all just waiting and praying, now, hoping he pulls through in good shape."

"Shoot, that's tough. Sure hope he does okay. He's a heck of a football player."

"He is—and a great kid. He has lots going for him—youth and strength, plenty of support from family and friends. We're all hoping for the best."

"Well, I bet he'll be fine. You take it easy, Jim."

"Thanks."

He'll be fine if he chooses to be, the bishop kept thinking. *Please choose life, Thomas. Please hang on.*

Y

The bishop left the store at four-thirty and drove Buddy to his father's house, promising to let the boy know immediately of any changes in T-Rex's condition. The latest word from Birmingham was that T-Rex had come through the surgery in fair shape but was expected to remain unconscious for some time. The doctors were hoping to keep the swelling down and minimize further damage to his brain.

The late afternoon light cast blue shadows on the snow, giving the town a Christmas card quality that the bishop hadn't seen for many years. Cars crawled along the streets, where the semi-melted slush of mid-afternoon was beginning to ice over again. He fervently hoped there would be no more accidents because of the storm. His mind and heart were already on overload.

"Thanks a bunch, Bishop," Buddy said as he slipped out of the truck. "I'll be fasting for T-Rex too."

"Thanks, Buddy. I know he'll appreciate that. He knows how hard fasting can be."

Buddy nodded. "You want Sister Shepherd's boots back now? I can—"

"No, keep 'em till you see us again. They might still come in handy. She has others."

He watched until the boy was admitted to his father's little house, then drove home in a pensive mood. It had been a strange day.

The evening was a subdued one, for the day after Christmas. With no dinner or snacks to break up the time, it seemed to stretch on and on. They had a kneeling family prayer, after which Mallory, who was too young to fast, had her little dinner—her choice of a peanut butter and jelly sandwich and carrot sticks—but Jamie chose to fast with the rest of the ward.

"It's T-Rex," he explained with a shrug. To the bishop's recollection, it was Jamie's first real effort at fasting. He prayed that the faith and prayers of the young people for their hero might be rewarded, that their faith might grow as a consequence.

He was grateful that no one seemed to want the television on. Jamie and Mallory played quietly with the new toys they had received for Christmas. Tiffani did some reading—her favorite quiet thing to do—and he and Trish sat on opposite ends of the sofa, facing each other with stockinged-feet touching, and worked on catching up in their journals. They took turns answering the phone, as member after concerned member of the Fairhaven Ward called to ask after T-Rex and his parents.

"I asked Lula about insurance," Jim told Trish after fielding one call offering money to help the family. "She said the hospital here thought that Thomas's school insurance was still in force, but they're not sure how much it actually covers. Won't know for a while, I reckon. That was Brother Winslow calling." He lowered his voice. "He offered a thousand dollars to help."

Trish's mouth formed a silent, "Wow."

"Brother Lanier also offered to help, though he didn't specify an amount."

"I'll bet there'll be others, too. People know the Rexfords have been struggling."

He nodded. "I told them to contribute whatever they felt they could to the fast offering fund. Hope Tom can handle all this kindness," he added with a wry smile. "It's not what he does best."

CHAPTER FOUR

" . . . IN FASTING WE
APPROACH THEE"

By noon on Thursday, the sun was out and the snow was receding at a rapid rate. Bishop Shepherd was gratified to see a fair number of cars pulling into the parking lot of the Fairhaven Ward meetinghouse. The members, uncharacteristically subdued and quiet, met together in the chapel, where the bishop updated them on Thomas's condition, which was basically unchanged. He was holding his own, but had not regained consciousness.

"Brother Patrenko and I are driving down to see Thomas and his folks right after lunch," he explained. "Sister McIntyre has been over to their house and gathered up some clean clothing for Tom and Lula. Understandably, they don't want to leave Thomas's side, just yet. We ask that you not try to visit until further notice. He's in intensive care, and only his folks are allowed in to see him for a few minutes each hour. We, as clergy, will be allowed in, as well.

"Tom and Lula are aware of your concern and your prayers and send you their heartfelt thanks for both, and for the several generous contributions that have been turned in, in their behalf." His voice cracked. "For that, I thank you, as well. I'm totally humbled by your kindness and generosity. I want you to know that I have a firm confidence that Heavenly Father is aware of Thomas and his needs and of your love and concern for the Rexfords, and I believe in the effectiveness of fasting and prayer. Now, brothers and sisters, if you would all kneel beside your pews, Brother Sam Wright will offer our prayer."

There was a soft rustle, but no other sound as the congregation slipped to their knees and bowed their heads. The bishop knelt with Trish and the children by the front pew. Sam cleared his throat, then began, "Heavenly Father, we know that thou art the Great Physician, and that thou can do more good for Thomas Rexford than all the doctors put together, though we're thankful for them and their knowledge, too, and we ask thee to bless them as they work to help Thomas. But we've met to combine our faith and prayers, Father, in the spirit of fasting, as thou did command us to do, in behalf of this young man we all love. We pray that the priesthood blessing he already received will be effective to help him. We pray that if it's thy will, that he may be healed in body and mind and return to live amongst us once again. We know he's his parents' only boy, and we know how they dote on him. We know thou sacrificed thy only Son for all of us, and that thou would understand how they feel. Please suit a blessing to their needs, as well as Thomas's, that they may be comforted. Please help us all to have courage and faith and to be blessed in our homes. In the name of Jesus Christ, amen."

The congregation echoed the amen, and again there was a soft rustle as they rose and slowly filed out of the chapel into the foyer, some pausing for handshakes, hugs, or brief conversations with one another. The bishop's eyes met those of his daughter Tiffani, and he thought he saw a gleam of tears there before she ducked her head. Jamie's eyes were round and solemn, and little

Mallory clung to her mother's hand. He watched the retreating membership, pleased to see Melody Padgett there, and the Jernigans. He smiled to see Sister Margaret Tullis, the ward organist, whom Thomas was fond of teasing. He turned off the lights as everyone cleared the chapel and followed his family outside. He caught sight of Buddy, mounting his bike and riding off alone. Barker nodded. The bishop caught Sam and hugged his shoulders.

"A million thanks, good counselor," he told him. "That was a wonderful, sincere prayer, and I'm sure it was heard where it needed to be."

"Well," Sam said softly, and cleared his throat again. "Glad to oblige."

On the drive home, Mallory said, "So, T-Rex'll be okay, now, huh, Daddy?"

"T-Rex is in the best of hands, honey," her father assured her. "You just keep praying for him every day, okay?"

"But what if he dies?" queried Tiffani. Her tone was challenging. "People my age aren't supposed to die!"

Trish turned to smile at her. "You felt the Spirit in there, Tiff—I know you did. You know Heavenly Father's in charge."

"I know, but—"

"He's not gonna die, Tiff!" Jamie told her. "Heavenly Father won't let him."

"People die every day, James," his sister enlightened him.

"Not with that many people prayin' for 'em," Jamie insisted.

"Yeah," Mallory agreed. "Not T-Rex."

"You know," their father began, "when a person's received a priesthood blessing and been prayed for as Thomas has been—if they do die, you can be sure that it was best for them and Heavenly Father's will. Sometimes it might be better, and happier, for a sick or injured person to go on to the hereafter than to stay on earth and have to deal with being handicapped or in pain . . ."

"Not T-Rex," Jamie insisted again. "He's strong. He'll be fine."

"Right," the bishop murmured.

Trish caught his arm as the children preceded them into the house. "Don't you think he'll pull through all right, Jim? What were you trying to prepare the children for, back there?"

He hugged her briefly against him. "Just in case, honey," he told her. "I'm not a hundred percent sure it's been decided, yet, which way things are going to go. I sure hope the kids are right— for their sakes, as well as for the Rexfords'. But I suspect he's not quite out of the woods. Maybe I'll have a better feel for it when I see him."

They enjoyed a simple lunch of soup and sandwiches, and then he hurried off to pick up Bob Patrenko.

"Be safe," Trish admonished him. "Be sure to start back before the roads ice up again."

"We'll be careful," he assured her.

Y

"That was a fine prayer that Sam offered," Bob said as the bishop's pickup splashed through puddles of snow-melt on the highway.

"Sam's a good man," the bishop agreed. "Very spiritual, in spite of his good ol' boy, down-home ways. And close to the Rexfords, which is why I asked him to be voice."

"Good choice. Boy, I wish I knew what to say to Tom and Lula, to bolster them up."

"Me, too. Hopefully, it'll be given to us, as we need it."

Lula greeted them in the waiting room of the intensive care unit, and received the bag of clean clothing and toilet articles gratefully.

"That little Rosetta! It's so dang sweet of her to do this for us—and of y'all to bring it down. Thanks so much. Tom, look! We've got clean clothes!"

"Trish said if you want to clean up and change while we're here, we'll just take the soiled things back and she'll be glad to wash them along with ours," the bishop told her. "I think Rosetta tried to get two clean changes together for you."

She nodded, her eyes watering.

"How's Thomas doing, Lula?" Bob asked.

She shrugged. "It's hard to tell, Brother Patrenko, and that's the truth. I mean, all he can do is just lie there and sleep, and they've got all these tubes and wires hooked up to him, till it's hard to tell it's even him! I'll take you in, next time we get a chance. I already told 'em you was comin'. I said you was preachers from our church. I mean, you know—that's how they think of it."

"Close enough," the bishop said. "Tom, how're you holding up?" he asked, shaking the hand of the man who rose wearily from a sofa to come forward. His eyes were red and bleary, and he needed a shave.

"Reckon I'm doin' a sight better'n my boy, Bishop. Sure do appreciate all y'all are doin' for us."

"Well, let me tell you what the ward's been doing for you folks." He described the fast and the prayer at the meetinghouse and then handed Tom an envelope with the money that had been contributed thus far. "Tom, I want you to know—we didn't ask anybody for a cent. All this is purely freewill offerings of love, some just a few dollars, some much more, according to what people could spare. Everybody knows surgery and hospital care are expensive."

"Now, we don't need no charity," Tom began, but Lula laid a hand on his arm.

"Who was it who was just frettin' to me about how we're gonna handle all this expense?" she asked gently. "We do need it, and we're mighty grateful for it. Open it, Tom. It's from your friends. Best friends you'll ever have."

Tom frowned, but he took the envelope and opened it gingerly, as if something might spring out at him. He riffled through the bills, then turned aside, his shoulders shaking. He found his way back to the sofa, where he sat down, covering his face while he cried.

Bob Patrenko made a move as if to go and comfort him, but Lula stopped him.

"First he's cried, since all this happened," she whispered. "I feel like it's good for him, you know, to let it out." She sniffed, and held a shredded tissue to her own eyes. "You know how it is—reckon sometimes a little kindness is harder on a body's feelin's than bad news. I mean, you kind of steel yourself against bad news, but nothin' prepares you for people bein' sweet." She went and sat beside her husband and took the envelope he had set down on a table. She counted the money inside and shook her head in wonder. "I thank the good Lord," she murmured.

The two men sat on chairs at right angles to the sofa and allowed the Rexfords their feelings. Finally, Tom regained his composure and spoke.

"Brethern, after y'all visit with the boy, I'd like to ask you to go with me down to the finance office and witness that I'm using ever' red cent of this money toward our bill."

"That's not necessary, Tom," the bishop told him. "It's for whatever you need it for. If you need to keep some out for living expenses for you and Lula, that's fine, too."

Tom shook his head. "I'd druther you saw where it went, if it's all the same to you."

"All right. That'll be fine."

Promptly at three-thirty, Lula popped up. "It's time we can go in now. Come on with me. We'll have to wash our hands and put on masks. They don't take no chances."

"That's good," Bob murmured.

They signed in as clergy, then duly washed and masked, were led to Thomas's bedside. The bishop felt his throat tighten. Except for the night of the accident, he had never seen Thomas at rest, his face relaxed in sleep. Always the boy had worn a teasing grin or a fierce or skeptical frown or a look of surprised delight—never this peaceful non-expression. And the tubes and wires and bandages were a bit daunting, he had to admit. Lula, however, had apparently learned to cope. She stepped right up beside her son and spoke in a rather loud voice.

"Thomas? T-Rex, honey—the bishop's here to see you, and Brother Patrenko. They couldn't come till today, on account of all the snow. But it's melting off, now, so they're here, hon. Isn't that nice of them, to come?" She leaned over and whispered to the men, "Go ahead and say something to him. They say it might help to get through to him. Lots of times people in comas can hear what's going on."

The bishop took a deep breath. "Hey, Thomas. You're looking a lot better than you were the other night. I'm glad to see you in such good hands, here. They're doing a mighty fine job. All the kids in the ward are anxious for you to get better and come on home, though. Everybody's praying that you'll be well, soon." He nodded toward his counselor, who leaned forward.

"Hi, Thomas. Good to see you. You just keep resting and getting stronger, all right? I need my home teaching partner back in action. The little Arnaud kids will be real disappointed to see it's just me coming up the walk."

"Bishop, since y'all are here—do you think—I mean, would it be all right if Thomas had another blessin'?"

"If that's what you'd like, sure," Bishop Shepherd said.

"Well, maybe it's as much for me and Tom as for the boy," she admitted. "But I'd feel better, somehow, if I could hear him bein' blessed. I watn't there for the first time, you know."

"That's right. Would Tom like to be in on this?"

"I'll ask the nurse if it's okay."

The nurse agreed, and Tom was ushered into the curtained cubicle.

The bishop asked Tom to anoint, and Brother Patrenko to be voice in the blessing. Tom looked terrified for a moment, then nodded.

"Best tell me what to say, though. I fergit."

The bishop went over the brief anointing prayer with him, and assured him he'd be standing by to coach him, if needed. Tom cleared his throat and took the small vial of oil. He carefully placed a drop on Thomas's head and, voice quavering, made it through the anointing prayer. Then Bob Patrenko took over, and blessed Thomas, encouraging him to rest and recover and respond to treatment, and promising him that there were many important things yet for him to do in his life. He also assured him of the love and prayers of his parents and of all his friends, and included a blessing for his doctors and his parents. Then the bishop patted Thomas's good arm, and the four of them filed out at the behest of the nurse, who moved in to check the boy's vital signs.

"Brethern, we sure do appreciate this," Tom said solemnly. "Now, I was just wonderin' somethin', during your blessin' in there, Brother Bob—how come you can bless somebody who's—you know—unconscious, and yet it's like you're talkin' *to* them, rather than just prayin' *for* them?"

"That's a good question," Bishop Shepherd agreed.

Bob Patrenko smiled. "It sure is. According to my

understanding, when we give a blessing, we speak by the power of the holy priesthood, spirit to spirit. Somehow, that bypasses the need of the conscious mind being awake and aware. Our spirits never tire, you know. Never sleep, never get old, never die. So I figure Thomas's spirit is on duty in there, even while his body and brain are resting. Now, I'm not entirely sure that's Church doctrine—but that's my take on it. Bishop, you know anymore about it?"

"Sounds true to me, my friend."

Tom nodded deeply. "That's real interesting. Makes sense, too. We thank you again, Lula and me—and our thanks to ever'body back home. Lula, honey—you want to go get changed, first? While you're doing that, we'll go pay on the bill, so these men can get on their way home."

"You have any insights now that you didn't, before, about Thomas's condition?" the bishop queried Brother Patrenko on the drive home to Fairhaven.

"I'm just not sure. I'm real glad his dad took part in the blessing. His hands were trembling—did you notice?"

The bishop nodded. "I think that just may have been Tom's first opportunity to take part in an administration. It's valuable experience for him. Tom's a good man. He's coming right along. I hope this trouble doesn't set him back."

"What's your feeling about the boy, at this point?"

"I just keep thinking it'll be a close call—and it'll be Thomas's own decision, in the end, that determines which way he'll go."

"Mmm. You said something like that, I recall, in your blessing at the accident scene."

"Right. The impression came to me then that it would be up

to Thomas. This is confidential, of course. I haven't even felt I should mention it to Tom and Lula, yet."

"Sure, I understand."

Y

The bishop dedicated his evening to making friends with his new cell phone. He programmed it carefully, then practiced making several calls, giving select people his new number. He called those whom he considered "at risk" in his ward—the elderly, the ill, those in financial or emotional difficulty. He was gratified to learn that Sister Bainbridge's walks had been cleared as soon as the snow stopped, that Brother and Sister Mobley's drive had been shoveled as well, and that they were also the recipients of a pot of vegetable soup and a loaf of bread from Frankie Talbot. The Jernigans reported that they were doing as well as usual, and asked for a report on T-Rex; the Birdwhistles said that their road up in the hill country was finally usable, and Melody Padgett said that her home teachers had been Johnny-on-the-spot to clear her drive and to make sure she and Andrea had weathered the storm all right.

He breathed a sigh of relief. It was good to know that people were following through on their responsibilities. He wished Hazel Buzbee had a phone—but she did not—would not, in fact, and who knew whether she would be able to hear sufficiently to use one if she did have it. He would have to drive up soon and check on her.

Y

Trish came to give him a sleepy hug, stifling a yawn as she did so.

"How's it working?" she asked, indicating the new phone.

"Great. I've called several people, and I had Sam Wright call me back, to see if I could push the right button to answer, and I somehow managed to. The only thing that bugs me is that it's so *small*—and my fingers feel like Polish sausages trying to push those little bitty buttons!"

His wife chuckled. "Part of its charm is its size," she told him. "So you won't feel like you have a desk phone stuffed in your pocket. Don't worry—you'll get the hang of it. Speaking of desks, did you see the letters that I put on yours?"

"No—thanks, babe. You heading upstairs?"

"I think so. Can't keep my eyes open."

"I'll just read the mail, then I'll come on up."

He sat at his dining room desk and examined the three envelopes addressed to him. One was from Elder Smedley, another appeared to be a late Christmas card from Elder Rivenbark, and the third was from Elder Rivenbark's mission president. He opened that one first.

Dear Bishop Shepherd,

Enclosed please find a copy of the letter and the doctor's report that I have sent to Stake President James Walker. It is with great regret that we suggest that Elder Rivenbark be honorably released from his mission for medical reasons and allowed to come home. His situation is such that the rigors of proselytizing work in this area create great difficulty for him. We have had him serving in the mission home for the past two weeks, and while he could be of excellent service here, the home is a three-story building with no wheelchair access, and the stairs are just too difficult for him to negotiate. Elder Rivenbark is a fine young man and a dedicated missionary, and all feel, after much prayer and consideration, that he has fulfilled his call to the best of his ability and should receive an honorable release.

The only problem with this decision is that Elder Rivenbark objects to the release and is determined to complete his mission. We have been in touch with the Missionary Department in Salt Lake City, and they have suggested a reassignment to the Alabama Birmingham Mission, with special permission for Elder Rivenbark to live at home and participate as much as he reasonably can, and as circumstances permit, with the elders in that mission. He is reluctantly willing to consider this solution. Do you have any particular feelings on this matter that you would like to have taken into consideration before a final decision is made? In your opinion, would Elder Rivenbark be able to keep the mission rules and spirit while living at home, or would this place an unrealistic burden on him and his family?

Bishop Shepherd leaned back in his desk chair. Did he have feelings on the matter? Did he ever! His throat ached and unshed tears burned behind his eyelids. Not once had Elder Rivenbark complained, in any of his letters, of his pain and difficulty. He had remarked on what a help his companions had been to him and how some meetings with investigators who lived in walk-up apartments had to be held at the chapel, but never with a sense of self-pity or a desire to give up on his mission.

He opened the card from the elder in question. Elder Rivenbark had enclosed a brief note.

Dear Bishop Shepherd,

I hope you and your family and the whole ward, for that matter, have a great and spiritual Christmas season! I am helping out in the mission home for a while, and the Spirit here is really strong. The missionaries are going caroling this evening around our neighborhood and then at a hospital. We have a huge tree in the living room. No snow, of course, but other than that, it's very Christmasy.

President Ruffin is concerned about my strength—or lack of it—but I'm doing okay. I can do this. I really enjoy missionary work. I met an orthopedic surgeon here who is a member of the Church, and he's been really great to me and examined me to see what he thinks might be done to help my situation. He had some interesting suggestions. I'll talk to you about them sometime when I get home. Anyhow—the Church is true! God lives, and sent his Beloved Son to die for us—and that's all that really matters. Have a wonderful Christmas and a Happy New Year!

Sincerely,
Elder Rand Rivenbark

His bishop, having read the other letter first, read between the lines of this message and his heart ached for the dedicated young man. He opened the third letter, from another missionary from the ward, and read:

Hi, Bishop Shepherd,

I wanted to report in and to wish you a happy holiday season. It sure is different here in Brazil, where it's warm at Christmas, but it's also very festive, and the members are being real good to us, feeding us and making goodies for us all the time. The work is still going good. I think I wrote you about Ricardo, the guy who lives in a little shack behind the Rodriguses' family's house? Well, he finally decided he could live without his coffee, and guess what? He's getting baptized on Saturday! We're just real excited, and I'm glad I could stay in this area long enough to see that happen. You know how it goes so much of the time—missionaries work hard teaching somebody and leading them along, and then they get transferred and somebody else gets to baptize the person! But that's okay, and I know it's partly to keep people from getting converted to the missionary, as they say, instead of to the gospel. Well, only a couple more months for me, and I sure have mixed feelings. I love my mission, but I'm real anxious to see my fam, too. Hope everything's okay in the ward!

> Your friend,
> Elder Don D. Smedley

The bishop closed his eyes. It was a time of concern for the young men in his sphere of responsibility—T-Rex and his accident, Elders Smedley and Rivenbark, both dedicated servants, but with very different situations—and then there was VerDan Winslow. He was another story. The bishop slipped out of his chair and propped his elbows on it. It was time for a consultation with the One who knew them all best.

Y

" . . . COURAGE TO ACCEPT THY WILL"

Brothers and sisters, the Rexford family has asked me to thank you for your concern, your prayers, your faith and help—and for the generous contributions to their son Thomas's care. Brother Rexford specifically wanted you to know that every penny given them was paid toward the hospital bill, and he insisted that I witness that payment. The most recent update on Thomas's condition I've heard was last evening, when Lula called and said that his temperature was a bit elevated, but she quoted the doctor as saying that 'wasn't unexpected in cases like this.' Thomas has not yet awakened, and I know that he still needs your faith and prayers in his behalf. And please continue to remember Tom and Lula, that they'll be given the strength and faith to see this through.

"I would also like to ask your faith and prayers in behalf of Elder Rand Rivenbark, who is experiencing some physical difficulties on his mission as a result of his disability. He's a fine, dedicated missionary with a lot of faith and determination, and wants in the worst way to be able to complete his mission. In addition, Elder Don Smedley writes that he's going strong in the homestretch of his mission experience, with just two months to go, and I know we're all looking forward to hearing his report. He has served with distinction. We're also very grateful for the full-time missionaries that serve here in our area—currently elders Tompkins and Bussero."

Bishop Shepherd continued by reminding his congregation of tithing settlement hours, then outlining the sacrament service that was about to take place. He then sat down and watched the congregation with special interest while they sang the opening hymn. It was "Ring Out, Wild Bells," a somewhat unfamiliar hymn that they sang only about once a year—usually on the first Sunday of the new year. He winced during the singing. The tune was hard to pick out, and the tones emanating from the group were rather puny. But he looked around and made mental note of who was at least attempting to sing. He was still searching for the components of a ward—and stake—choir. He observed again during the sacrament hymn—this one perfectly familiar to all—and added a few more names to his list. By the time the closing hymn had been sung, he had a plan.

Y

During the second hour of the block, he supervised the setting apart of new presidencies in the Laurel and Mia Maid classes, then retired to his office for a few minutes' contemplation about his reply to Elder Rivenbark's mission president. He had thought long and hard, and he had conferred with the two missionaries he had mentioned in sacrament meeting—elders Tompkins and Bussero, simply asking them if they thought they could accommodate a handicapped elder and incorporate him into their work. They had looked at each other, shrugged, and said, "Sure. Why not?"

"He's a good man," he had assured them. "Bright and faithful and articulate. He just can't get around very well—and apparently there are a lot of hills and stairs to challenge him in his present mission. It's not settled, yet, but I just wanted to get your feelings about having him in this mission."

"Well, the district leader has a car," said Elder Tompkins, a tall, fair young man from Idaho. "So if he could pair off with him it could work out. We ride bikes, you know, here in town."

"What if he had his own car?" asked Elder Bussero. "Or can he drive? If he does, then whoever's working with him could ride along, or drive him."

"He does drive," the bishop mused. "There should be a way. Well, thank you, brethren. How's the work going this week?"

"Good," answered Elder Bussero, a stocky, swarthy fellow from Detroit. "I think we've about got Billy Newton's folks convinced to let him be baptized. And the Miller family has promised to read the Book of Mormon and pray about it. We've got several discussions set up for this week, and Brother Warshaw just gave us another referral to check into. So, yeah, we're busy!" He grinned.

"Way to go," he encouraged them, shaking their hands. "Let me know of anything we can do to help."

Elder Tompkins grinned, too. "Just be ready to fill the font," he said.

"At the drop of a hat," the bishop promised.

He had a few minutes free. He could execute his plan. He slipped into the Gospel Doctrine class and whispered in Brother Warshaw's ear. That good man nodded, then continued with his lesson as the bishop took a seat and opened his scriptures. It was a pleasure to listen to Brother Warshaw teach—one that he rarely had the opportunity to enjoy. Brother Warshaw closed his lesson a few minutes early, announcing that after their closing prayer the bishop had an announcement.

He stood at the lectern and looked around the faces before him, with their pleasant but curious expressions. He began to read.

"Doctrine and Covenants, section twenty-five, verse twelve: 'For my soul delighteth in the song of the heart; yea, the song of the righteous is a prayer unto me, and it shall be answered with a blessing upon their heads.'" He looked around again, meeting all the eyes he could. "Now, brothers and sisters, you've heard that we've been assigned to form a ward choir, and you saw the results in our Christmas program. Five singers—four of them my own family—and it's obvious that the Osmonds, we're not! President Walker has asked for at least six or seven from each ward to sing in the stake choir next month, and I'm in charge of the ushers, so I won't be that available that morning. Therefore, I'm here to issue a call. You brothers and sisters of the Gospel Doctrine class are hereby called to comprise the Fairhaven Ward choir. Choir practice is in the chapel, and begins five minutes after the third hour ends. Our accompanists, and the only reason the Christmas program was a success musically at all, will be sisters Margaret Tullis and Claire Patrenko. Our director, who is talented and able, is Sister Linda DeNeuve."

"But . . ." spoke several at once, accompanied by, "I can't sing!" and "I don't read music!" and "You wouldn't want me abellerin' up there!" and other related responses. The bishop smiled and held up his hands.

"I'm not calling you for your vocal abilities, although you might find that with a little training, they're better than you thought. I'm calling you because you're good, faithful folks who don't like to turn the Lord down, and I believe this prompting came from Him. Now, I know there may be a *few* genuine exceptions, and good reasons why a *few* of you may not be able to participate. But we'll expect to see as many of you as possible, right after church in the choir seats—and even more of you next week, when you've had a chance to make arrangements to be there. Thank you, brothers and sisters. I know you'll come through on this challenge. The Lord bless you."

He left the room and hightailed it back to his office before any of the astonished class members could buttonhole him. He hated to be high-handed about such things; it wasn't his way. But sometimes you just had to do what was requisite.

Y

The priests were unusually quiet during their third-hour quorum meeting, and had questions that didn't always pertain to the lesson at hand. Bishop Shepherd felt he understood—they were worried about T-Rex. He answered their queries the best he could. He was concerned, too.

Y

As he stood in the hall after the third hour, greeting people and generally making himself available to them, he noted with satisfaction that a number of adults were making their way back into the chapel, some with shaking heads and hangdog expressions, but going, nevertheless. He smiled encouragement and nodded at them. Some of the looks he received in return suggested the term "cruel and unusual punishment," but he didn't waver.

Elaine Forelaw ushered her children toward the door. She wasn't included in the choir calling, since she attended the Gospel Essentials class taught by the missionaries for those who were new in the Church, investigating it, or who simply wanted a review of the basics.

"Bishop, I want to thank you again for them Book of Mormon storybooks you brought the kids. I've been readin' to 'em every night—and I honestly think Sarge is listenin' in. He's still got my Book of Mormon in his truck, and the other day I saw a little New Testament in there, too."

"Really? That's great. You still haven't discussed it with him, though?"

She shook her head. "He's not one to feel comfortable talkin' about deep things, you know? So I'm just lettin' him find his own way, till he's ready to bring it up. But you know what else I've noticed?"

"What's that?"

"Well, his stash of beer in the fridge hatn't needed to be resupplied much, lately."

"Excellent! We'll just keep praying for him. And I'll think and pray about what message to give when I visit. Is Wednesday of next week still a good time?"

"Good as any. Thanks, Bishop!"

"Thanks for telling me, Elaine. Bye, kids!"

The children smiled and waved shyly. He hoped none of them was old enough to report to their dad that their mother had been discussing him with the bishop. This was a delicate matter.

Y

The choir seats were nearly full. A few people were standing in place, singing a warm-up of vowels that went up by a half-step each time it was repeated.

"Okay," Linda DeNeuve said. "All y'all who are left standing—ladies, you're sopranos; men, you're tenors. Those who are seated—ladies, you're altos, men, you're basses. Now let's have all the tenors—all three of you—sit on the left side, here, and the basses sit on the right. Altos, please sit in front of the basses, and sopranos, in front of the tenors. Go ahead and move now."

After the shuffle, Linda began explaining the rudiments of singing parts. "I know some of you have done this before, and it'll come easy to you. I hear alto and bass parts in the congregational singing. For others, this'll be a brand-new experience, and I want you to listen very carefully to those in your part who are strong and follow them—try to hear and sing what they sing. Also, we'll take one part at a time and go over and over it with the piano and organ, so that you'll be learning it like a melody. Then, when we put it together, you'll get to experience the thrill of singing harmony."

"How come us basses cain't just sing the melody we know, only lower?" asked one brother who looked about as intimidated as anyone could. "That's what we're used to doin'."

"And that's fine, for congregational singing," Sister DeNeuve told him. "And sometimes, we do let the basses sing the melody in choir pieces, too. But generally speaking, we're going to sing what's written in the hymns, and I believe you'll grow to love doing that."

"I don't know, sister—I ain't got an ear for this stuff!"

Linda nodded. "I understand. Some people naturally have a good ear, but the rest of us have to develop it. We'll work on that. Now, let's begin with just a line from the hymn we've been asked to learn for stake conference. Please turn to number ninety-nine, 'Nearer, Dear Savior, to Thee.'"

The bishop turned away. Sister DeNeuve would do just fine.

Y

His executive secretary, Dan McMillan, met him in the hall just as he turned the corner toward his office. "Bishop, there's a call for you, from Sister Rexford at the hospital. She sounds upset."

He ran the last few yards and caught up the phone.

"Lula, this is the bishop."

"Oh, Bishop—Thomas is real sick. They say he's got pneumonia, now. His fever's real high—he's purely burnin' up with it. I'm so scared!"

"I'll be down there as soon as I can make it. I just need to run the family home. Is there anything we can bring you?"

"No, sir. Just some strength and courage, I reckon."

"You always have that available to you, just by asking Heavenly Father. Gather up every bit of faith and belief you can and pray really hard. I'll see you very soon, all right?"

"All right. Thank you, Bishop."

He stepped back into the chapel and beckoned to Trish and Tiffani in the choir. They slipped out, gathering up Jamie and Mallory on the way, who were quietly drawing pictures.

He explained the situation to Trish.

"Do you want me to come, too?" she asked. "Rosetta's been a couple of times, and Ida Lou's not back yet from Mobile. Gene Talbot's working this afternoon, so Frankie needs to be with her children. Tiff can supervise and feed ours, so . . ."

"That'd be great," he told her. "I expect Lula'd be glad of another sister there. Let's head out as quickly as possible."

Trish adjusted their dinner plans and told Tiff what to serve the younger ones, then quickly made a couple of sandwiches for them to take along and eat on the way.

"Usual Sunday rules," she told the children. "Mind Tiffani.

No TV. No playing with friends. Just quiet games and reading and puzzles—things like that. You guys know the drill. Be good, okay? We'll be back as soon as we can. And say a little prayer for T-Rex, too, all right?"

"Why isn't he better yet?" asked Mallory. "I already prayed and prayed for him!"

"Some things take a while," her father assured her.

Tiffani followed them outside. "Dad?" she asked, and he knew her unspoken question.

"I don't know, honey. They're doing all they can, but he has pneumonia now and a really high fever. We're going to try to comfort his folks."

Tiffani nodded, and went back inside.

The sky was overcast, but it was a high, pale gray that didn't seem to threaten rain or snow. The grass was brown, the trees bare, and everything seemed colorless as they sped toward the city. They spoke little, each absorbed in thought.

Finally, Trish asked, "Ready for your sandwich yet?"

"You know, I'm really not. Maybe on the way back. You go ahead, though."

"No. I'm not very hungry, either. They'll keep."

They rode in silence for a few more miles.

"Babe, you know how I've had the impression that Thomas will decide his own fate?"

"Right."

"I think it's time to share that with Tom and Lula. I hope I can say it right."

"You will. And I'll pray for you—and for them to understand."

"Thanks." He reached to squeeze her hand. "I'm grateful for you, Trish."

Y

Lula's eyes were red, and she seemed to have aged by ten years, her cheeks gaunt and hollow. Tom also looked miserable, but stoic. He rose wearily to shake their hands, while Lula accepted Trish's hug.

"Y'all are so good to come," Lula said. "I mean, reckon there ain't nothin' you can do, but we sure appreciate havin' you here."

"We couldn't stay away," the bishop assured her. "Not when things are so serious. Let's sit down over there, where it's a little more private, all right? There's something I'd like to discuss with you."

They followed him to a far corner of the waiting room and pulled a couple of chairs around to form a small circle.

"Tom, Lula—when we blessed Thomas the first time, at the scene of the accident, I had a very unusual impression come to me," the bishop began.

"Oh, Bishop—he's gonna die, idn' he? I just cain't bear it!" Lula began to cry.

The bishop reached over to squeeze her clenched hands. "I honestly don't know, Lula," he told her. "But whatever happens, I believe it'll be up to Thomas, himself. He'll make the ultimate decision, whether to stay or go on into eternity. That was the impression I received. And I blessed him to that end, that he can be healed if he chooses to be. Apparently the Lord is letting him choose, in this instance. So, I guess what we need to do is to try to be ready to respect that decision, whichever way it goes."

Tom frowned. "That happen often, Bishop?"

Bishop Shepherd shook his head. "Not that I know of, Tom. I do know that my grandmother once had something similar happen to her. I heard her tell of a time when she was a young mother and terribly sick with typhoid fever. She said she found herself in a bright and beautiful place, with grass and trees and flowers, where two young men came to meet her and told her that she could choose either to go on toward a shining city that she could see some distance away, or she could return and finish bringing up her children. She said it was a really tough decision, as much as she loved her children, because she felt drawn toward that city, and she dreaded going back to her body. But she thought of her husband, trying to take care of the little ones and work on the railroad and take care of his farm all alone, and she decided to come back." He smiled. "She said she never again felt afraid to die, after that experience."

Tom and Lula were silent, contemplating this new concept. Lula stared unseeingly at the orange vinyl chair next to her. Finally she spoke.

"So—do y'all reckon we're bein' selfish, prayin' for Thomas to stay with us?" she asked, her voice quavering. "Should we—should we tell him he can go on, iffen he wants?"

The bishop shook his head. "I don't know," he replied. "But I think it'd be good if, in your own hearts, you could somehow prepare yourselves for the fact that he might not recover. Try to be willing to let him go, if that's the choice he makes."

Tom cleared his throat. "Thought the good Lord was in charge of who dies and who don't," he said. "Didn't never reckon it was up to us."

"I know," the bishop said. "Like I said, I think this may be kind of unusual. Or maybe we just don't know how often it happens. I've also heard of folks being told it's not their time, that they have to come back. I suppose each case is different."

Trish spoke. "Maybe the thing to do would just be to pray that Thomas makes the best and wisest decision, you know? In his best interest," she said.

Lula looked at her and nodded, then bowed her head. "It's

real hard," she said, after a minute. "It's just so hard to even consider Thomas goin' off to heaven. I mean, he's just a boy, Bishop! He needs to finish growin' up, and get married to a nice girl, and have his own young'uns. It's real hard to picture anything else."

"I know," he agreed. "We want a whole, complete life for him, don't we? That's what feels right. It never feels right for children to die before their folks. It goes against nature, and against all our expectations."

Tom looked up from staring at his hands. "And what if he lives, but he cain't play football, or ride his bike, or—you know—be active? He'd hate that, in the worst way. I mean—he's T-Rex, you know?"

Lula began to cry again, silently, the tears just spilling from her eyes and running down her cheeks. "I don't—I don't want him to be different, neither," she said. "But even if he was, I still want him alive!"

"Of course you do," Trish soothed, sitting beside her and putting an arm around her shoulders. "He'd still be himself, and he's your child. Of course you want him to live."

"Well, sure, I do too," Tom put in. "I'm just sayin' how *he'd* feel."

"If he chooses to live, I believe he'll eventually recover to live a normal life," the bishop stated. "He's a strong boy, and even if he did have a few limitations for a while, I think he'd adjust."

"It's about time we can go in, again," Lula said, drying her eyes with a tissue Trish handed her. "Did you want to see him, Bishop? Trish?"

"Just for a second," Trish said. "Then we'll let you be with him, while we head back. Can we do anything for you? Water plants at your house, collect your mail, do some more laundry?

Here—could you use a couple of sandwiches?" She held out the sack lunch she had prepared for herself and her husband.

"Well, thank you, we could—it'll save us goin' down to the snack bar on a Sunday. We sent our soiled things with Rosetta yesterday, and she's taking care of our place, bless her heart. But thank you. Y'all just keep prayin' for all of us."

They moved toward the intensive care unit, donning their masks and washing their hands. In the few days since he had seen Thomas, the bishop thought the boy had lost weight. One side of his head was shaved and swollen, with a line of stitches behind his ear. He lay propped up, pale and shivering, the covers drawn up to his chin. A nurse stood nearby, checking his temperature.

"What is it, now?" asked Lula.

"One-o-three point eight," the nurse replied. "He's in a chill phase right now. His body's trying to fight off the fever and over-reacting to it. You all go ahead and visit for a minute, and then we're going to suction him, and try to clear his lungs."

Tom looked at the bishop. "Reckon it's just as well he's unconscious and cain't feel all his body's goin' through right now, don't you think?"

The bishop nodded. "I've heard that a coma can be a mercy—kind of the body's own defense against too much pain."

"Bishop," said Lula. "Would you give us a little prayer, before you go?"

"Sure." They stood at the foot of Thomas's bed with bowed heads. "Heavenly Father, we ask a blessing of comfort and strength and wisdom for these good people, Tom and Lula Rexford, and for their dear son, Thomas. We pray that the priesthood blessings pronounced upon Thomas may be effective, according to thy will and his best interests, and that those who care for him may be led and guided to do their best, as well. We are aware of thy great love for each of us. We join our prayer with the many others being given in this young man's behalf, and do so in the name of thy Son, Jesus Christ, amen."

The amen was echoed, and hugs were exchanged, then the bishop and his wife slipped out, to give the Rexfords a minute alone with their boy.

In the car, Trish put her head back against the seat. "I feel so drained," she said. "How do they do it, day after day?"

"If it were one of ours, we'd find the strength to do it, too," he reminded her. "But you can see, it's sure taking a toll on them."

"I know. And poor little T-Rex—all those tubes and wires and bandages—he looks awful!"

The bishop smiled sadly to himself. He didn't think the words *poor* and *little* had ever been used in the same sentence with the name "T-Rex" before.

CHAPTER SIX

Y

" . . . RING OUT THE OLD; RING IN THE NEW"

On Monday morning, while Jim Shepherd, proprietor, was working at Shepherd's Quality Food Mart, the cell phone in his pocket burred, making him jump. He snatched it up to his ear, carefully pushing the tiny button with the image of a receiver on it and saying, "Hello?"

It wasn't Lula or Tom Rexford. He exhaled. It was Elder Bussero.

"Bishop? You remember how we said that we might need the font filled soon? Well, how about Saturday morning? Billy Newton's ready to go, and a family that we thought we'd lost called us up last night and asked for baptism, after all! Man, are we stoked!"

"That's great, Elder! Congratulations. And you bet, we'll have the font filled. Ten o'clock a good time?"

"Perfect. Say, could you arrange for somebody to play the piano and lead a couple of songs? We'll take care of the rest. Oh—and maybe invite a few ward members? Somebody from the Relief Society for Sister Kress, and from the Aaronic Priesthood and Young Men for Billy, and so forth?"

"Will do. We'll look forward to it. A couple of good convert baptisms should perk the ward up a bit. We've all been kind of down, with young Thomas Rexford's situation."

"Anything new, there?"

"Not so far, today. Still unconscious, with high fever and pneumonia. All prayers appreciated."

"We're including him in ours—and I can spread the word—ask other elders and sisters in the district to remember him, too."

"Thanks, that'd be great. See you Saturday, if not before. Oh, and Elder? Happy New Year."

Y

"Hey, Jim? How's that football player doin'?" asked his office girl, Mary Lynn Connors.

He sighed. Even if he had been able to put Thomas's situation out of his mind—which he could not—he wouldn't have had a moment's respite. People were constantly asking about him. He felt guilty even thinking that way, realizing what the boy's parents were going through, and Thomas, himself—but the accident had cast a pall over a holiday season that, at best, already wasn't the merriest ever, given the terror situation and the war in Afghanistan.

He updated Mary Lynn, and she twisted her long brown hair thoughtfully. "Reckon you've already done that blessin' thing that y'all do, for him," she commented.

"Twice—and many, many prayers are being said for him. We're all just hoping for the best."

She nodded. "Well. Me, too. And how's that couple doin'—the one where he was hurtful to his wife?"

"They're still separated, and everybody's still in counseling." He smiled wryly. "Hoping for the best there, too."

"Uh-huh. Well. I just wondered."

"How was your Christmas, Mary Lynn?"

"Good. Fine. I was at my brother and sister-in-law's, and it was fun watchin' the young'uns open their Santy Claus."

Not for the first time, he wondered about Mary Lynn's prospects for marriage and motherhood. He knew she loved children; she always fussed over his when they came to the store. But he didn't want to pry. He just smiled and agreed that that was probably the most fun part of the Christmas celebration.

"Dad, you won't believe how many kids from school have called here, asking about T-Rex," Tiffani told him, the moment he walked in the door. "They all want to know every detail, and how he's doing, and I don't know what to tell them!"

"I guess his folks haven't called with an update?"

"Not here. I was hoping maybe they'd called your cell phone. It is on, isn't it?"

"On? I think so. Somebody called me earlier, and it worked."

Tiffani held out her hand, and he meekly placed his phone in it.

"Oh, Dad, look! You've got it turned off. See this little switch? It's s'posed to be this way for the phone to ring."

"Shoot! I'll never get the hang of the dang thing!"

"Yes, you will. It's easy. Let's see if you've got any saved messages." She did mysterious things to his phone and announced, "Yep, you have two messages. Want to listen to them?"

He nodded and put the tiny instrument to his ear. Sure enough, there was Lula's voice.

"Bishop? This here's Lula. Things is pretty serious down here. The doctor sat us down and told us that Thomas is probably about ready to go one way or the other. He figures that if he makes it through the night, he might survive. Y'all don't need to come down, though. My sis from up in West Virginia finally got here, and she's a big strength to me. Just please let ever'body know, and keep prayin'—you know—for the best thing. Thanks. 'Bye."

The other message was from his first counselor, Bob Patrenko—also asking for an update. He carefully deleted the messages, under Tiffani's tutelage, made sure the phone was "on," and went into the kitchen, where Trish was stirring a pot of something savory on the stove.

"That smells wonderful—and so do you," he told her, kissing her cheek. "But would you mind a whole lot if I don't eat with y'all, tonight? I feel like I need to fast, again."

Trish frowned a little. "On New Year's Eve? I've made special treats for family night."

"Oh—right. I almost forgot it's New Year's Eve. Sorry, babe. Let me think about it for a bit, all right? I don't want to be a wet blanket on the fun."

She looked at him. "Why do you want to fast—for Thomas, again? Don't you think the Lord remembers the fasting you've already done for him? I mean, does it wear off this soon, or something?"

His wife's straightforward way of assessing things made him grin a little. "I'm sure the Lord remembers. It's just that it looks like tonight may be a crisis time for Thomas, according to what the doctor told Lula. If he makes it through the night, they think he may recover. I reckon maybe the fasting is for my own benefit—so I'll feel like I've done everything humanly possible to help."

"Ah, Jimmy, I'm sorry. You do whatever you need to. We'll understand. But you are going to be here for games, aren't you? I've told the kids they can stay up as long as they want."

"Yeah," chimed in Jamie, perched at the kitchen table. "Monopoly marathon—woo-hoo!"

"But first, you have to play Candyland and Chutes and Ladders with me," insisted Mallory.

"Right," their father said weakly. "Sounds like fun."

"Dad's not interested in those baby games," Tiffani scorned. "He has more important things on his mind than playing silly games with us, anyway."

He turned to look at his eldest. "Well, now, Tiff, that's not fair. It's true I have worrisome things on my mind, but any time I can grab to relax and play with you guys is mighty welcome. In fact, I expect it's just what I need."

Tiffani shrugged. "Until somebody calls you away," she remarked.

"Well, we'll just hope that doesn't happen tonight," Trish soothed. "You kids sit down at the table; this is almost ready. Dad can eat or not, as he chooses."

"It's tortilla soup, isn't it?" he said wistfully, peering into the pan. "Will you save me some for lunch tomorrow?"

"No," said his wife, with a raised-eyebrow smile. "In case you've forgotten, tomorrow is New Year's Day, and we're having people over for the traditional feast. We've got the Jernigans coming, and Melody and Andrea, and Buddy, and Hestelle."

"Oh, that should be a jolly crowd." Tiffani's tone was wry. "Why didn't we invite somebody fun, like the MacDonalds?"

"Because," her mother said, hugging her daughter's shoulders and speaking in a light but precise voice, "we're not doing this for our own entertainment. We're doing it because all those folks need a little cheer in their lives, right now. Would you like to invite Claire? There's room for her."

"She's at her grandma's. No, I'll just endure as long as I have to."

"It'll be better if you do a little more than endure," her father suggested. "If you help your Mom and be cheerful and kind to all our guests, I guarantee the day'll be happier for you."

"Dad, I don't need a lecture right now," Tiffani said, holding up a warning hand. "I'm not planning to be rude, I promise you. It's just that Mallory'll have Andi to play with, and Jamie'll drag Buddy off to play computer games—which is fine with me, by the way—but there's nobody for me to relate to. So, I'll just be on maid duty, and we'll all be happy. Happy New Year to me!"

Trish ladled the soup into blue crockery bowls. "Would you like to invite Lisa Lou?"

"Mom, will you *please* stop trying to foist Lisa Lou Pope off on me? Besides, I'm sure she'll be with Billy Newton."

"Foist?" the bishop said. "That's an interesting word. Hardly ever hear it. By the way, did you know Billy Newton's being baptized on Saturday?"

"That's nice," Tiffani said. "Now maybe Lisa Lou can marry him, and they can move as far away as possible!"

Trish put the pan of soup back on the stove with emphasis. "Tiffani Shepherd, I don't know exactly what has put you into such a sour mood, but I'm personally not enjoying it one little bit, and I strongly suggest you make an effort to be a little more positive and cheerful, or this won't be a very fun New Year's Eve for any of us!"

"Yeah, Sis—what's the deal?" asked Jamie, frowning.

"It's a girl thing," offered Mallory with an air of nonchalant certainty. "It's 'cause she's sixteen, and she doesn't have a date tonight."

Tiffani burst into tears. "Oh, just hush up, all of you," she said. "You don't know anything!"

Y

For the first time ever, the bishop's eldest daughter boycotted family home evening, secluded in her room with music playing at a louder than usual level, declining any soup or other goodies throughout the evening, and refusing to talk to anyone. The bishop played games with the others, but there was an unaccustomed bleakness to the process, and no one seemed to care much who won. Trish and the children ate popcorn balls and hot mulled apple cider, and then they had family prayer and curled up on the sofas in the family room to watch New Year's Eve celebrations from around the world. Even those were tinged with worry because of the possibility of terror attacks in crowded places. Shortly after eleven, the bishop excused himself and went to his trusty desk phone in the dining room. He punched in the now-familiar numbers of the ICU in Birmingham and waited for Lula or Tom to answer the page.

"Hello?" It was Tom's voice.

"Tom, my friend—it's Bishop. How's our boy doing?"

"Well, Bishop—the news might be good, believe it or not! It looks like his fever's headed down, at last—reckon the medicine finally took hold—and if it stays down, now, they figure maybe he'll make it. Cain't say for sure, of course—but that's the latest. Lula's so relieved, she's sacked out on the sofa, just snorin' away, bless her heart. She ain't slept much, of late."

"And neither have you, I know. It's been a long week. I sure do hope this is a turning point for Thomas. You're all constantly in our prayers, you know that. And lots of Thomas's friends from school and church keep calling to see how he's doing. Hopefully, by tomorrow we'll have good news for the New Year."

"That's what we're a-hopin'. Thanks for callin', Bishop."

Y

He carried a sleeping Mallory up and tucked her in bed, where Samantha the cat was already warming a place for her, then knocked lightly on Tiffani's door.

"What? I'm in bed," came her voice, which sounded as if she had a cold. He knew she did not.

"Tiffi? I love you. Happy New Year, sweetie."

A sniff. "Okay."

Y

Trish was in the kitchen, punching down dough for refrigerator rolls.

"Come to bed, babe—don't knock yourself out, okay?"

"Oh, I'm almost done. Everything's as ready as I can make it. If you'll just steer your son upstairs, I'll be right there, too."

"All right. Honey—I'm sorry if I haven't been spending enough time with you and the kids, lately. I'll try to do better."

She smiled at him wearily. "This has been a rough week for everybody. You're being a wonderful, caring bishop—and that's exactly what I want you to be. We just need to learn to share."

"But if my family's feeling neglected, I'm not quite on the right track. You all come first—you know you do."

"I do know it, Jim. And don't worry about Tiff. She knows it, too. She's just being a teenager."

He sighed. "Why did I think it'd be easier than it is? She's always been such a reasonable kid."

"I wonder if our precocious little Mallory didn't hit the nail on the head? Tiff's sixteen, and she hasn't really been asked out yet. Girls have—you know—certain expectations. Even if they don't always own up to them."

"Well, she wouldn't accept a date on a Monday, anyway, would she? That's always family night. She knows that. It's like a rule in our family. Or at least, a tradition."

Trish smiled. "Maybe she wouldn't go out, but—you can bet your bottom dollar she'd love to be asked."

"Yeah, I reckon that's true."

"Oh—I almost forgot to tell you. Merrie called, to wish us Happy New Year and to tell us that she's starting to feel the baby move. She's so excited. I'm glad for her."

He nodded. "Me, too." He *was* glad; he felt a sort of proprietary interest in this little niece or nephew-to-be, having counseled its mother on how to make clear to its dad that he needed to not only start a family but pay more attention to things at home—specifically his wife, Meredith, Trish's sister.

Y

On New Year's Day—after an early morning call from Lula, informing him that the doctors were now "cautiously optimistic" about Thomas's prognosis, as his temperature was still hovering around the normal range—he found time in the morning to answer the letter from Elder Rand Rivenbark's mission president, affirming that he was certain that the missionary would be able to live mission rules at home, and that the family would honor those rules and not try to distract him. Furthermore, he felt that the terrain would be easier for him—that most dwellings were single-family homes with just a few steps up to the front doors. He hoped this transfer could be worked out. He stamped the letter and set it aside to be mailed the following morning, then went to see if he could do anything to help Trish get ready for the company dinner.

"Everything's under control, I think," she responded to his query. "Just plan on going to pick up Buddy around noon. We'll eat about twelve-thirty."

"Smells wonderful," he told her. "Thanks, hon, for doing this."

"We always do it," she reminded him with a shrug. "Just a few different faces at the table each year."

He looked around the kitchen with satisfaction. A fragrant mince pie and what his mother had called a "Lane cake" sat on the end of the counter. A pot of black-eyed peas bubbled on the stove, and a pan of cornbread was ready to pop into the oven. This meal was a southern tradition in his family on New Year's Day. There would be ham with raisin sauce, fluffy hot biscuits in addition to the cornbread, and cheesy grits, set off by pickled onions, bread-and-butter pickles, and spiced apple slices. He was grateful that his wife had been willing to tackle his mother's old recipes and carry on such traditions—as much for the sentiment of the thing as for the wonderful mix of flavors. He knew that his eldest sister, Paula, would be preparing a similar meal for her family and their mother—but Ann Marie? He chuckled. Not a chance. Middle child, Ann Marie, would likely send out for pizza. The kitchen had never been her domain, and her husband and sons would want to spend the day watching football, game after game, drinking beer and nibbling on whatever snacks were handy. He liked football, too, though not in such quantity. He would sneak a peek every so often to see how certain teams were faring—but he knew there was no chance to devote the whole day to it, even if he'd wanted to. He and Trish would visit with their guests for as long as they cared to stay, and then, once all the food was put away and things cleaned up, the family would relax. Tiffani, whose mood had vastly improved since the night before, would probably call a couple of friends. Jamie and Mallory might watch a video. If the weather stayed nice and there was time before dark, he and Trish might bundle up and go for one of their neighborhood strolls, chatting and informally taking stock of their lives and those of their children to see where improvements or adjustments might be made. It was, he thought, an altogether satisfactory way to begin the year. He bowed his head and sent up a little prayer of thanks, not asking for a single thing. His cup was full.

CHAPTER SEVEN

Y

" . . . STAY THE TIDE OF SIN AND WRONG"

As he struggled through the second day of the year 2002, Bishop James Shepherd became increasingly grateful for the peaceful interlude that had been the first day. His challenges began at seven in the morning, when the phone rang on his desk in the dining room, where he was eating breakfast while perusing the home teaching assignment sheet. Absurdly glad that it was the old-fashioned phone ringing, the one that sat so comfortably in his hand and didn't have mysterious buttons and features, he answered pleasantly.

"Um, Bishop? Uh . . . this is Buddy." Buddy's voice was more hushed and tentative than usual.

"Well, good morning, friend. What's up?"

"Um, well—I hate to bother you and all, but I wondered iffen there'd be any way you might could give me a ride back over to my Mama's place this mornin'."

"Sure, I expect I could. Anything wrong, Buddy?"

"Um—my bike's over there, else I'd just ride it back, see?

And Deddy—well, he ain't feelin' real good, and I think he'd kinda like the place to himself today."

Read between the lines, Bishop, he advised himself. *Read, Deddy's either drunk or has a whopper of a hangover and is in a foul mood, and I don't want to be where I'm not wanted.*

"You bet your boots I can give you a ride. Let me just finish a bite of breakfast, and I'll be right over."

"Cool. Thanks, Bishop."

He told Trish the situation, and she hurried the process of packing him a lunch of leftover tortilla soup, corn chips, an apple, and a wedge of cheddar. He would go straight to work after dropping Buddy off.

Buddy was waiting for him, hunched against the cold on the top step of "Deddy's" small porch, his backpack beside him. He jumped up and started toward the truck, but his father, unshaven and with flyaway hair standing in a tousled halo above his grizzled face, came out the door to say his good-byes.

"You tell that filthy little slut you call your Mama that she ain't gettin' one more penny outa me!" he shouted, waving one hand and then using it to grab for the porch roof-support. "Not as long as she's shackin' up with that no-good . . ."

"Okay, see you later, Deddy," Buddy called, trying to make his voice camouflage his father's as he scrambled into the truck. "He ain't always like that," he added, as the bishop pressed the accelerator.

"I'm sure he's not," the bishop agreed. "Since he is today, though, I'm glad you called me."

"Well. Yessir." Buddy was quiet, and the bishop, sensing his embarrassment, spoke of other things—T-Rex's condition, the basketball chances for the Fairhaven High School Mariners, classes starting again the next day. Buddy answered in monosyllables.

"Had any breakfast?" the bishop asked.

"Oh—no sir, but . . ."

He pulled into a fast-food restaurant and ordered a sausage and egg biscuit and an orange juice, over Buddy's protests that he could get something at his Mama's place. The bishop was glad for the impulse that had turned his truck into that drive-through when he pulled up in front of Twyla Osborne's mobile home and saw both her car and a red pickup there. The drapes and shades were drawn, and all was quiet. He knew, somehow, that Buddy wouldn't knock to be let in.

"You don't have a key, do you, Buddy?"

"No, sir, but I'll be fine. Mama'll be up, soon. Iffen I get cold, I'll just ride my bike around to warm up."

The bishop shook his head. "How'd you like to come help me out at the store for a while? Put your bike in the back of the truck, and when you get bored, you can ride on back out here."

"You don't need to do that, Bishop. I'll be okay."

The bishop pointed. "Get your bike, son."

Y

His second round of challenges came when LaThea Winslow entered Shepherd's Quality Food Mart at approximately ten-thirty. She didn't usually shop at Shepherd's, and he was surprised to see her. He was showing Buddy how to stock canned goods, and he rose and went toward her, holding out his hand.

"Sister Winslow, a happy new year to you. How are you?"

She shook his hand quickly. "Bishop, I'm absolutely beside myself. She's here!"

"Who's here?" He looked around.

"Oh, now, you know who I mean! The *girl!*"

"Ah—the young lady who's taken with VerDan."

"All the way from Utah, Bishop. I knew it'd happen. I told

you she'd hunt him down, if we didn't get him off on his mission! And sure enough, she's here, with her *mother!*"

"Come on in the office, Sister Winslow, where we can sit down and visit," he invited, politely taking her elbow to guide her past the boxes in the aisle. "Carry on, Buddy, you're doing great."

Mary Lynn looked up in surprise as he escorted LaThea Winslow into the office. Her employer gave her a wink and a slight jerk of his head, and she rose from her desk and gathered up a stack of colorful new produce signs that gave nutritional information about various fruits and vegetables. "I'll just put these up, now," she announced as she left the office, glancing back curiously at LaThea from under her long bangs. LaThea didn't appear to notice.

"Okay, now—you sit there, why don't you, in my father's old leather chair. I can guarantee it's comfortable. I'll sit here in Mary Lynn's place. Now, tell me what exactly has happened."

He might have predicted, knowing LaThea, that her next action would be to burst into tears. He offered her Mary Lynn's box of tissues.

"Oh, Bi-bishop, it's so awful," she said, when she could speak. "They're right here in Fairhaven, and they're coming over at one o'clock, and I'm so upset. Harville tells me to be calm, but how can I do that? This girl's determined to get VerDan—she's been after him and after him. I've thrown away her letters and stalled off her telephone calls the best I could, but now she's *here,* and with her *mother,* of all things, to stick up for her, and I just know they're going to railroad VerDan into marrying her, and that's not at all what I want for him! Bishop, you know he's a good boy. Oh, if we could only have gotten him off on his mission when he first came home!"

The bishop looked at her with compassion and something

else—perhaps it was amazement at the rose-colored glasses of motherhood. Or mother-hen-hood.

"Dear Sister Winslow," he said softly. "I can see why you're upset, honestly I can. But let's think for a moment. Why do you suppose this young lady—what's her name, anyway?"

"It's—oh, it's—um—it's Stephanie. No—Bethany. That's it. Bethany Pearson."

"Okay. Now, why do you suppose Bethany and her mother have come?"

"I told you! To try to coerce my VerDan into marrying that little—"

He held up one hand. "And why might they be doing that?" he asked. "Is there a reason, perhaps, why VerDan might want to consider marrying her?"

"Certainly not! She's just determined to have him. I've never seen anything like it. I've been telling you how she's pestered him, for months now."

The bishop knew he needed to tread lightly, and so it was with more than a little hesitation that he said, "LaThea . . . might she be carrying his child? Could that be what she's been trying to tell him in those letters you threw away and those phone calls that you stonewalled?"

LaThea fairly yelped. "Of course not! That would mean— honestly, Bishop! My children have been taught better. We have high standards in our family! VerDan would never—"

"Many a young person with high standards has slipped and given in to temptation. If he has, it needn't reflect on the excellence of your teachings and your home life. Remember when we talked about why I couldn't in good conscience recommend VerDan to serve a mission at that time? You admitted then that you weren't entirely sure whether VerDan and this girl had been intimate."

"But he's never said—never admitted—I really didn't think he would!"

"Maybe he hasn't seen a need to admit to it—especially if he thought nobody would know and he could escape the embarrassment of telling us. But I've never felt that he was being entirely open and honest with me in our interviews. Maybe this is what he's been holding back."

"Oh, Bishop! That's such an awful thought. What'll I say to them, if that's what it is?"

"More to the point, what do you think VerDan will say? What'll he say to Bethany, if she says she's carrying his child? What'll he say to you, when he finds out about the letters and the calls?"

LaThea paled, then gave a little flick of her carefully coiffed head. "Oh, he won't be angry with me. He'll appreciate what I've done—he'll know it was in his best interest. He was glad—relieved—to get away from her. That's why he came home from the U."

"And if you shield him from taking responsibility for this situation, how does that affect his character?"

"I—but Bishop, how can he take responsibility for a wife and child—if that's what this is about? He's just a boy! He hasn't finished school, and he doesn't even have a steady job. He has his mission yet ahead of him, and—"

"No, he doesn't, LaThea. Not if he's had sexual relations with this young lady—or any other. The rules are very strict, now—and very clear."

He watched as the truth was borne in, at last, upon the mind and heart of LaThea Winslow. It was painful to watch; it must have been even more painful for her to bear. All her defenses crumbled—her pride of family, her hopes for her son's mission call, her power and control over circumstances that might bring him shame and discomfort—all fell away into dust, and she looked up, devastated and fearful.

"What'll I do?" she whispered.

"Well, I think the very first thing is to remember that this is not about *you*," he told her. "In all likelihood, this is about VerDan and Bethany—and between them. Her mother may be here for moral support, and that's fine. You can give that to VerDan, too, but not by excusing him or trying to get him out of this. It may be that it's growing-up time for that young man, one way or another. Whether he and Bethany marry is up to them. They're of age. At least, he is—I don't know how old she is."

"But I don't . . . I'm just so scared. I don't know how to act. What to say to them. I . . ."

"Okay, now—this is what you do. First thing, you go home and sit down with both Harville and VerDan and level with them about the calls and letters. And you ask VerDan to level with you, so you'll know the truth. I hope he'll give it to you. And then you and Harville counsel with him about the best options he has, assuming there is a pregnancy—which, I'll admit, we don't know for sure. Then, it'd be wonderful if you could have a prayer together, the three of you, before the girl and her mother arrive. When they do get there—well, you certainly know how to be a gracious hostess and how to make them feel comfortable. Because—keep in mind, LaThea—this just may be your future daughter-in-law, and you'll want to make amends and get off on the best footing possible, if that's the case. Otherwise, if she doesn't like you—you might not see much of your son and grandchildren down the road."

LaThea regarded him with a blank, horrified look. "I've—I've messed up, haven't I?"

"We all mess up, from time to time. Let's just be thankful for the possibilities of repentance and forgiveness. The Lord knows you meant well, and were trying to protect VerDan—and hopefully, VerDan himself will understand that, too. Now, you'd better hurry on home, LaThea—you have a lot to do."

She stood, her fingertips resting on the edge of Mary Lynn's desk. "Yes, I do, don't I? But Bishop—one thing. You'll be there, won't you? At one o'clock, or a little before? Because I'm afraid I'll mess things up even more, if you're not!"

He hesitated. "I don't know. I feel that this should be a private family occasion, don't you? There'll likely be a lot of very sensitive feelings expressed, and I'm not sure that I'd be of any use—"

"Yes, you would. You can make me see things straighter than anyone else—even Harville. He just—you know—keeps a stiff upper lip, and tries not to show emotion. Sometimes I call him my tin soldier! But I'd feel so much calmer if you were there, Bishop. You could—you know—kind of defuse the situation, if it gets too explosive. Please."

He sighed. "All right. But only if Harville wants me there, too. He presides in your home. I'm not going to usurp his place."

"He'll be grateful to have another man there, I'm sure of it."

"Well, one of you be sure to call me if he objects, all right? Otherwise, I'll see you in a little while."

Y

He was still sitting at the desk, gazing unseeingly toward the floor, when Mary Lynn tiptoed back in.

"I saw that lady leave. She looked plumb frazzled. Is ever'thing okay?"

"Oh—sure. More or less. Here you go, Mary Lynn—sorry to kick you out of your place. Thanks for understanding. She just had a family problem she needed to run by me."

"Got a family, got a family problem, is the way I see it."

"They do crop up from time to time," he agreed with a sigh.

"What's with that kid you've got stockin', out there? He a new employee? I hatn't seen any paperwork on him."

"No, I'm just keeping him busy this morning. I'll pay him out of pocket. He's a boy from my ward. Another family problem."

"Well, he looks to be a good little worker."

"I'm not surprised. He's a quality kid, but so quiet he goes unnoticed a lot of the time."

She sighed. "The quiet ones do."

Y

By a quarter to twelve, he still hadn't heard a report from Tom or Lula, and he called home to see if Trish had received any word. She had not, so he checked with Rosetta McIntyre.

"Bishop, I'm glad you called. I was just going to call you. Thomas's temperature is still down—in fact, it's a little lower than normal, which they said was pretty common after a bout with a major infection. He still hasn't woke up, but he's starting to move a little bit, and kind of moan, which might mean he's fixing to come to. The moaning really gets to Lula, but the nurses are tickled about it and see it as progress. I reckon that's about all. Oh, and Lula's sister is there, and she's been a big help, bringing them food and magazines and clean clothes. She's taken over at their house, now, so I don't need to worry about the plants or the mail or anything. She sleeps there, and runs down to the hospital every day."

"Rosetta, thank you so much for all you've done for Lula and Tom. You've been Johnny-on-the-spot ever since the accident, and I'm not sure what any of us would've done without you."

"Well, I'm glad I was available, what with Ida Lou being out of town, and Frankie and Trish busy with young kids. My daughter Kellie rode with me down to the hospital a couple of times, and it was a good chance for us to talk. Not too many of those chances these days, with her away at college."

"Have your kids gone back to school now?"

"Kellie flew out yesterday afternoon, and Kevin goes tomorrow. The nest'll be empty, again."

He hated the idea. "Is that hard to get used to?" he asked.

Rosetta chuckled. "At first. Then you kind of take to the peace and the freedom to go and do whatever you want or need to, and to eat whatever or whenever, or not at all—then all of a sudden, they're back, wanting regular meals and your attention and your car—and their friends are in and out—and you find you're exhausted, even though you love it. So there are pluses and minuses, I s'pose. Anyway, you've got a ways to go before you're there!"

"Right. Although I'm already dreading the time when Tiffani goes off to school."

"Well, maybe she'll do what Kellie did. By the time she actually left, she'd gotten so ornery and out of sorts that I was almost glad to see the back of her. I know now it was just nerves and excitement, but it was a rough patch for both of us."

"You know, maybe Tiffi's working on that angle already," he said. "She can get so emotional and defensive all of a sudden, when I least expect it."

"Trish said pretty much the same thing, the other day. But girls are just that way. Easier, usually, when they're small, than little boys, but harder to deal with in the long run. And way more high-maintenance!"

"Beginning to notice that, too," the bishop agreed. He said goodbye and went to warm up his tortilla soup. It was good, sometimes, to talk to someone who'd been through the parenting mill and survived. And Rosetta had done it on her own, having been a widow since her children were in fourth and sixth grades. Admirable.

Y

He paid Buddy for the hours he'd put in and promised him a summer job if he wanted one. He also made him choose something he'd like to take home to eat, laughing when the boy picked a box of chocolate-flavored cereal.

"It's way good, Bishop, you oughta try it," Buddy advised. "A body gets tired of oatmeal ever' mornin'. That's all Deddy makes. Mama, she don't make breakfast, but she favors granola and gritty bran stuff. This'll be a treat!"

"Happy to oblige."

Y

It was ten to one when he pulled up in front of the Winslow home—a gracious brick and stucco place with a front courtyard effect that reminded him of places he'd seen in Arizona when they had visited Trish's parents. He bowed his head for one more quick prayer before throwing himself to the wolves, emotionally speaking, that he suspected were lying in wait for them all.

He had hoped beyond hope that his phone would ring—that Brother Harville Winslow would feel that the bishop's presence wasn't needed at this confrontation—but that good brother opened the door to him with a look of obvious relief. Harville closed the door, and the two men stood in the entryway.

"Good of you to come, Bishop," he said. "Not quite sure what we're up against here, but we'll hope that cool heads prevail. The womenfolk are likely to be a little . . . you know . . ." He flapped his hands by his face to indicate his meaning. The bishop nodded deeply.

"Have the two of you had a chance to sit down with VerDan and discuss this?" he asked.

Harville closed his eyes briefly. "Oh, yes. It seems LaThea's been trying to protect the boy from being bothered by this girl. Always been a little on the overprotective side, you know, with VerDan especially. Maybe because he's the youngest, I don't know. So we don't really know what's coming down the pike. Says she didn't read any of the letters—just consigned them to the round file, as they say."

"How did VerDan react to that?"

"Didn't say much, actually. To tell the truth, I think the boy's scared spitless. You might say reality reared up and slapped him in the face, just when he thought he was safe."

"Well. Yes, that would be unsettling. What're your feelings on the subject of a possible pregnancy, if that's what this is about?"

"A young man needs to take responsibility, if that's the case. Depends, of course, on what the young lady has in mind, too. Whether she's planning to keep the child, or adopt it out."

"Right. And on how she and VerDan really feel about each other."

Harville shook his head. "So young. What do they know? Hormones going crazy, they think they're in love—and tomorrow it's all different. Don't know about you, Bishop, but I wouldn't want to go through that age again, myself. Well, come on—let's go sit down for a minute's peace before the war breaks out."

CHAPTER EIGHT

" . . . ALL OUR FOLLIES, LORD, FORGIVE"

T he opposing forces arrived as expected. At the sound of two car doors slamming, LaThea pressed her hand against her chest, and VerDan's head, which had been hanging low, jerked up. He sat slumped on a piano bench, knees spread apart and elbows resting on them. Gone was the jaunty confidence he had exhibited in his prior interviews with the bishop.

"Stand up like a man," his father snapped as he went to answer the bell. VerDan dragged himself to his feet with all the enthusiasm of a condemned man bound for the gallows. LaThea cleared her throat and stepped forward, arranging her face in an expression that her bishop assumed was meant to be polite and curious.

There was a murmur from the hallway, and then Harville ushered the two women into the room. The bishop stood back, taking the opportunity to study them. He was especially inter-ested in observing the young woman's attitude toward VerDan. She was a slight figure in a black leather coat over jeans and a turtleneck. Her brown hair was pulled back in a ponytail, and her face, though attractive, was pale. She looked thoroughly miserable.

She flicked her brown gaze quickly toward VerDan. "Hey, Dan," she said softly.

"Beth," he acknowledged, also in a low voice.

The mother was short, like her daughter, but carried considerably more weight. Her cheeks were very pink, and her eyes, also brown, looked around at the collection of people with interest. She appeared, to the bishop, to have the absolutely fearless aspect of a woman who knew she was in the right.

"Nina Pearson," she introduced herself, holding out her hand to LaThea, who pressed the fingers lightly.

"LaThea Winslow," she said, and cleared her throat again. "You met my husband, and this is our bishop, James Shepherd."

Nina Pearson gave his hand a firm shake, and the young lady offered a rather limp one. Her hand was icy.

"Bishop," the mother acknowledged. "Good to meet you. My daughter Bethany. And you're Dan, of course," she said, holding out a hand to VerDan.

"It's VerDan," LaThea corrected almost automatically.

"Mom, it's okay . . ." the boy said half-heartedly, as he responded to Mrs. Pearson's determinedly outstretched hand.

"Won't you please sit down?" LaThea invited, her ingrained manners asserting themselves.

Everyone sat. VerDan went back to studying the weave of the carpet.

Nina Pearson spoke. "I'll come right to the point. My daughter has received no response to her letters or her attempts to contact Dan by phone," she stated flatly. "We felt our only recourse was to fly out here and surprise him, so that he couldn't avoid hearing what she has to say. But I'd be interested to know, first of all, from the young man, himself, why he hasn't responded to Bethany's attempts to contact him." She looked at VerDan expectantly.

The bishop had to give her good marks for her forthrightness and the calmness of her voice. VerDan didn't answer, but flicked a glance at his mother and hung his head, if possible, even lower. LaThea opened her mouth, then closed it again. The bishop and Harville each cleared their throats, looking at her.

She took a deep breath. "All right, I suppose that was my fault," she said quickly. "I thought Bethany's attentions weren't welcome, so I intervened in my son's behalf. I apologize. Perhaps it wasn't the best course to take."

"What do you mean by 'intervened'? You wouldn't let him talk to me?" Bethany asked in a quavery, little girl voice, then turned to VerDan. "But you got my letters, didn't you, Danny?"

VerDan shook his head, but didn't look up.

"Not even one?"

"No, I didn't. I'm sorry, Beth."

"Go ahead and say it, VerDan," LaThea said with a sigh. "Tell her what happened to them, so she won't blame you."

"No, it's okay, Mom. I can take the blame."

"Miss Pearson, I threw your letters away before he could see them. I thought he wouldn't want to hear from you, and I was hoping we could get him out on his mission with no further interference."

The girl gave LaThea a long, level look, said nothing, then turned to VerDan. "I know you came home to get away from me," she said. "But you didn't have to do that. All you had to do was tell me you didn't want me around anymore. I could take it."

"Sorry," VerDan whispered. "No excuse, but I—I guess I got scared. We were getting too close. Going too fast, you know?"

"Well, that's not what you said when we were together. You said you loved me."

"I know. And I meant it, Beth. I did. And that scared the heck outa me. I didn't know what to do about it."

"Well, it didn't scare me." Tears pooled in her eyes and ran unheeded down her cheeks. "I guess maybe it should have, but it didn't. It just made me happy—and stupid. I'm sorry I was so stupid, to believe you. Stupid enough to think that what we shared was different, and special. Stupid enough that I went against everything I'd ever been taught, just to be with you."

He shook his head. "Not stupid. You weren't ever stupid. I was." He lifted his head and looked at her, at last. "I was stupid enough to think that after all that happened, I could run away and act like it was nothing. I even thought maybe I could make myself forget all about you and bluff my way onto a mission—but the bishop, here—he saw through that."

"But I guess you did manage to forget all about me. Right?"

He shook his head. "Wrong. Wrong, because I've thought about you every single day. I mean, I like—tried not to. I tried to be cool, and flirt with other girls, and have fun and all that—but you were always there, in my mind. Only I didn't know what to do about you. I'm nowhere near done with school, and I don't have much of a job. How could I marry you?"

LaThea gave a little gasp, and leaned forward as if she were about to speak, but Harville reached out a restraining hand, and she subsided.

"You don't have to marry me, Dan," Bethany said. "But I did think you deserved to know that I'm carrying our son. And I'm going to keep him. I'm not giving him up, even though in some ways that would be easier. I've prayed about it, and I just don't feel that'd be right for him. So I'll bring him up, with the help of my family. If you'd like to be a part of his life, that'd be great. If you're able to give me anything toward his support, that'd be good, too, but I'm not going to insist on it. I just came to see you, face-to-face, to be sure you know."

"Well, of course we'll contribute to the child's support," LaThea burst out. "Although I think a paternity test is indicated, to be certain—"

VerDan shot to his feet. "Mother," he said firmly, "no offense, but this is between Beth and me. And there's no test needed. Beth's not like that. Beth, will you go for a walk with me?"

She rose, and hugged her coat around her slim figure, which the bishop could now see swelled at the waist, and followed VerDan out into the winter sunshine. The group left in the living room sat in a strained silence.

"So, Sister Pearson, where are you folks from?" the bishop asked conversationally.

"Boise, Idaho."

"Ah. Cold up there, this time of year."

"Yes, sir, it is."

"Never been to Idaho," he replied. "You folks been there, Harville?"

"Um—just skiing once, in Sun Valley, when the kids were all at home."

"Does your family ski?" the bishop asked Sister Pearson.

"No."

"Oh, uh-huh. I see. Well, neither do I, but my wife has done some, when her family lived out west."

Nina Pearson was not interested in small talk. She spoke to LaThea. "How could you keep my daughter's letters from your son?" she asked. "I think there's even some federal law about that. Don't you believe in honesty?"

"Of course I do! Don't you believe in protecting your children?"

"I'm here with my daughter for that very purpose. Her heart's been broken by this boy, thinking that he was ignoring all her pleas, all her efforts to communicate with him. I suppose you read her letters before you chucked them?"

"Certainly not! I wouldn't read someone else's mail."

"No? But you'd throw it away, and never even tell him it came?"

"Um, sisters," began the bishop. "It's certainly true there's been harm done, and I know Sister Winslow's sorry for the part she played. But let's allow the young couple to settle the matter themselves, if they can. I'm not sure, but I suspect they still have feelings for each other. I grant you VerDan's been very immature in his behavior—but then, he's quite young, still—"

"And obviously thoroughly spoiled and overprotected by his mother, and not given to living up to the principles of his Church."

LaThea drew herself up. The bishop was reminded of his cat, Samantha, arching her back against a perceived enemy. "Well, your daughter didn't exactly live up to those principles, either, did she?" she demanded.

"No, ma'am, she did not—and she's paying for it, in a big way. Whereas—"

The bishop intervened again. "Both of them transgressed, and both will need a process of repentance. We don't need to place blame. We just need to be helpful and supportive—and forgiving."

Harville spoke. "Sister Pearson, we're very ashamed of VerDan's behavior toward your daughter—both the . . . er . . . transgression—and his neglect of her these past few months. We apologize to you, on his behalf, and we'll see to it that he apologizes, too, and carries his part of the burden. We're not irresponsible people."

"No," LaThea agreed. "And you have to understand that none of our other children have done anything like this. We have an excellent family heritage, going back to—"

"None of my other children have caused me this kind of grief, either," said Sister Pearson. "Bethany's the youngest of seven, and she's always been such a good girl that I counted myself blessed. The others are all married in the temple and have happy families. I thought Beth would follow suit. Then she met Dan."

"Now, let's not give up on either of them," the bishop said. "True, this is a serious matter, but certainly not one that's unknown in our society—even in our LDS culture, in spite of all our efforts to prevent it. It strikes me that Bethany shows excellence of character in not following the ways of the world and having an abortion, and by praying for wisdom in whether to keep the baby or put it up for adoption. And VerDan—well, we need to realize that he feels kind of blindsided by this. Not to excuse his behavior, but let's see what he does, now that he knows. He's already indicated that he's felt guilty for running away from Bethany, and she's been in his thoughts all this time."

"Hmph," was Nina Pearson's reply.

"Umm—what does your husband do, out there in Boise, Sister Pearson?" inquired Harville.

She fixed him with an unwavering brown stare. "He lies in his grave, and has done for twelve years, now. Otherwise, I'm certain he'd be here beside me, seeing this matter through."

"Oh, I'm very sorry," Harville said, his face reddening. "You've had quite a challenge then, bringing up your family alone."

"A mother does what has to be done. That's why I'm here. But you're right, it's not an easy row to hoe, and that's why I'm not eager to see my daughter embark on single motherhood, although she's adamant about keeping her baby." She allowed a very small smile to touch her lips. "I'm afraid that in some respects, Bethany's as stubborn as her mother."

"That can't be all bad," put in the bishop, answering her smile with an encouraging one of his own. "Seems to me a good dose of determination is needed in today's world, especially if it's directed against all the negative influences around us."

"Yes, and that's what Bethany would normally do," her mother said, frowning slightly.

LaThea took umbrage. "Are you saying our son is a negative influence?"

"Um, well, ma'am—there is a pregnancy." Sister Pearson took a tissue from her purse and pressed it to her nose. "Although, of course, I have to admit they're both culpable. I'll try to be fair toward Dan—especially now that I know he didn't get any of Bethany's messages. That does change my initial assessment of him a little."

LaThea's defensive stance crumbled, and she flicked a miserable glance toward her husband. "But what must you think of me?" she wondered, her voice tinged with tears. The bishop wondered if her query was meant for Harville or for Bethany's mother. Sister Pearson chose to respond.

"I'll admit I don't totally understand you," she said, "but I guess I can see that you had good intentions, of a sort. It's not how I would have handled the situation, but we're all different. In any case, as your son pointed out, this isn't about you—or me, for that matter."

LaThea bowed her head. "That's true."

An uncomfortable silence ensued, with all four persons looking inward. The bishop pondered on the conversation that might be taking place between VerDan and Bethany. Would there be accusations, recriminations, or some kind of conciliation? Would

LaThea's image be forever tarnished in the two young minds? And if the young couple decided to marry, could the union survive the scrutiny of either mother-in-law?

Tension stretched between the adults in the room like a rubber band pulled to capacity. Just when the bishop thought the band would snap, the front door opened and the young couple entered on a waft of cold air. The temperature between the two of them had obviously warmed, however, as VerDan had an arm around Bethany, and she snuggled close to his side. They stood in the entranceway to the living room, and VerDan spoke.

"Mom, Dad—Sister Pearson, Bishop—we're . . . going to be married."

"Now, VerDan, you needn't make any hasty decisions, dear," LaThea began. "You could just wait until the baby comes, and then if you still feel the same, have a nice—"

"No, Mom, we can't. I'm not about to let my son be born out of wedlock. I've been a coward and a schmuck about this whole situation long enough. I do love Beth, and I've missed her—and even though I know I told you she was chasing me, that wasn't really true. I was just trying to run away from feelings I didn't know how to handle. And Bishop—you were right—I would have been going on a mission just to get away. I wouldn't have lasted. I'm glad you could see that."

The bishop nodded. He was glad, too.

"Bethany, are you sure this is what you want?" asked her mother, applying her tissue again.

"It is, Mom. It's all I've wanted, ever since I knew about the baby. In fact, ever since I got to know Danny. We'll be fine. We know it won't be easy, but it'll be so much easier together than apart. And better for the baby."

"But, VerDan, what will you do? Where will you live? How can you support—"

Harville reached a steadying hand to grasp his wife's. "If you'll recall, LaThea, we didn't have a penny when we got married, either, and we survived."

"Yes, but times are different, now. Everything's so expensive! And his schooling—he can't just give that up!"

"Mom, it's time I grew up. I'll get the best job I can find, and go to school part-time. Lots of couples do that. We'll get by. Now, we're going to go apply for a license before the courthouse closes."

All three parents stood up, as if to prevent such a hasty departure. The bishop smiled.

"I think you'll both need some documentation, to do that," he reminded them. "Birth certificates, at least."

"I brought mine—it's in my suitcase at the motel," Bethany stated. "Danny, do you know where yours is?"

"Mom? Where—in the filing cabinet?"

"A pocket in your baby book, on the second shelf of the office closet," LaThea said faintly and sat down as her son left the room, taking Bethany with him. "Oh, my . . ."

Nina Pearson looked at her with more sympathy than she had yet shown. "I know this isn't how either of us wanted things to be," she said. "I pictured a temple wedding and Beth in a lovely white dress, maybe a garden reception in June, with all her friends and family there. But here we are, in January in Alabama—in a town where we don't know a soul—and her six-and-a-half months pregnant. So if you feel a little bit bowled over, please know that I do, too."

"Oh, my," LaThea said again. "How—who—it sounds like they mean to do this right away. Oh, dear. Bishop, would you perform the ceremony?"

"I'd be glad to—if that's what they want."

"Well, of course they will. And let's see. I have my daughter's wedding dress upstairs—it would probably fit, except it'd be a little long. If she wears really high heels, it should—"

"No," said Bethany, who had come back into the room. "I mean, thank you, Sister Winslow, but I refuse to be a pregnant bride in a white dress and veil. I always think that looks absurd—like Barbra Streisand in *Funny Girl*. I'll just wear a nice Sunday dress, and Danny can get me a corsage if he wants. I'll wear white later, when we've taken care of things and can be sealed in the temple."

The bishop nodded silently. He was impressed with the gumption of this girl. She just might be able to survive LaThea— and make something good of VerDan in the process.

CHAPTER NINE

" . . . THE SPIRIT'S BRIGHT ASSURANCE"

Mr. VerDan Compton Winslow and Miss Bethany Kaye Pearson exchanged vows and rings on Friday evening, January 4, 2002, at the home of the groom's parents in Fairhaven. In attendance were the couple's parents and a number of friends. The bride is the daughter of Mrs. Nina Booth Pearson of Boise, Idaho, and the late Geoffrey Pearson, while the groom's parents are Harville and LaThea Perry Winslow of Fairhaven. The ceremony was performed by Bishop James Shepherd of The Church of Jesus Christ of Latter-day Saints, followed by a reception at the same location.

The bride wore a rose-colored, silk shantung sacque dress set off by a corsage of pink rosebuds, white baby's breath, and asparagus fern. The bride's mother was attired in a navy blue suit, accessorized by a corsage of white carnations. The mother of the groom wore a similar corsage against the pale gray suede of her jacket dress. Music was provided at the piano by Miss Claire Patrenko.

The refreshment table, presided over by Mrs. James (Trish) Shepherd and her daughter, Miss Tiffani Shepherd, featured a raspberry-filled, two-layer cake decorated with white roses, as well as mint and nut cups and a pink sparkling punch. The table was covered with an antique rose damask cloth that had belonged to the groom's maternal great-grandmother, Elise Compton Perry of Salt Lake City, Utah. Tall white tapers and two lovely arrangements of roses and carnations flanked the cake, and a matching arrangement graced the smaller table that held the bride's book. After the reception, the couple departed for a honeymoon weekend in Birmingham, after which they will fly to Boise, Idaho, for a reception at the home of the bride's mother. They plan to make their first home in Salt Lake City, Utah, where they will continue their education. (*Fairhaven Lookout*, Monday, January 7, 2002)

Y

"So how do you think it went?" Bishop James Shepherd asked his wife and daughter as they relaxed in their family room later on the evening of the wedding. The bishop had loosened his tie and propped his stockinged feet on a hassock, and his wife leaned back in a rocking chair, her arms draped wearily over the sides.

"Well, given the time constraints and the circumstances, I think things went as well as they possibly could," she replied.

"But I suspect, my not-so-subtle husband, that you're really asking how you did with your part."

He grinned. "Got me. I was fishing, I admit it."

"You did beautifully. No one would know it was your first time to perform a marriage. Your advice was wise, and you seemed completely at ease with the ceremony."

The bishop looked at his daughter. "See? That's why I keep your mom around. She feeds my fragile ego. Well, that and her meatloaf."

"I know, I know. And her lemon icebox pie."

"I'm that obvious, am I?"

Tiffani snorted. "You're that repetitious! But if anybody really wants to know what I think about the whole wedding thing, I'll tell you. I thought it was sick and sad and wrong."

"Oh, come on, Tiff—don't hold back. Tell us what you really think," her father teased.

"Sick, sick, sick. So VerDan got her pregnant. Well, whoop-de-do! How come we all had to get dressed up and celebrate the fact that he had to marry her? If that was me, I'd be so embarrassed I'd sneak off and get married by a judge or something, and never show my face in public again! Especially around my parents' friends and ward members."

"I understand those feelings," Trish said. "It sure isn't the happiest way to do things, is it? It's all backwards. And so many couples are taking that route, these days. Not getting married, I mean, until a baby's on the way . . . or already here. Getting the carriage before the marriage, or something. I mean, even apart from the moral issue, which is huge—it's just a much harder way to get started in marriage and family life."

"You know what? I could hardly stand to look at him," Tiffani said, frowning. "And I used to think he was so cute. Gross!"

"I admit I feel a certain relief that he's married and out of circulation in the ward," Trish agreed. "I never did like the way all you girls fawned on him."

"I never fawned. I do not fawn," Tiffani stated. "Lisa Lou fawns, not me."

"Well, it's true she's a little 'deer,'" her father commented.

"Oh, Dad—that's pure corn," Tiffani objected, but she smiled in spite of herself.

"Sorry—it runs in my family," he told her. "I've gotta say, though—I do think there were some things worth celebrating tonight. Other than the fact that the young ladies of the ward are safe from VerDan, I mean. For one thing, a family was created. True, it had a rocky start, but if those kids truly repent and progress as I hope they will, it has the potential of becoming an eternal unit. And for once, VerDan stepped up and did the right thing. Also, now that perfectly innocent little baby boy will have a mom and a dad, not to mention a chance at life, rather than having been aborted somewhere along the way—which fortunately doesn't seem to have ever been an option with the mother, but still—those are things to celebrate."

"I guess," Tiffani agreed reluctantly. "But I'll tell you what— seeing that girl getting married with her tummy out to here . . ." She demonstrated. "That made me more determined than ever to be married in the temple, and not to do anything stupid along the way to mess up. Oh, well, I'm beat—I'm heading for bed."

They knelt around the hassock for a brief family prayer, the younger two long since having been tucked in by a babysitter, then Tiffani headed upstairs.

"Thanks, honey, for helping with the refreshments, in spite of how you felt," her mother called after her.

"S'okay," Tiffani rejoined. "I did that for you more than for them."

The bishop looked at his wife. "I reckon kids can learn from negative examples, sometimes," he said.

She pushed her dark hair away from her face and stretched. "I hope the lesson lingers."

"Me, too. LaThea seemed to hold up pretty well, didn't she?"

"I think she's still numb, and in shock. This was quite a blow to her pride. But in the end, she put her party face on and braved it through. Harville was just his usual stoic, polite self. VerDan, on the other hand, seemed really happy, didn't he?"

"M-hmm. I think he's euphoric from finally doing the right thing in a situation that's been bothering him for a long time, even though he didn't fully know why. Plus, I think he does care for the girl—and she for him. I just hope they'll let that love grow, and not dwindle, when the tough times come—which they'll start to do by about next Tuesday, with all the challenges those kids'll be facing."

"I think it's good that they don't plan to live with parents, on either side."

"Oh, I do, too. And I hope Sister Pearson and the Winslows all understood my intent in advising the couple to cleave to each other and to turn to the Lord for help, and not rely on their parents to solve all their problems."

"I hope they did, too. Well, at least the kids'll have a nicer wedding memory than they would have had with a judge or a justice of the peace. And LaThea can feel good that she gave them at least a bit of a party."

"I was glad for the way the ward pitched in and helped. Especially you, Sister Bishop."

"My pleasure, Bishop dear. It's sure sweet of Ida Lou to promise to make them a wedding quilt—and to collect for the ward gift, with such short notice. Did you hear how much it came to?"

"About two hundred and twenty-five dollars, I think. And then I'm sure Harville and LaThea will add their bit."

"I'll bet they'll be adding a lot, for a while. LaThea's not one to let her kids struggle too much."

Saturday morning, many of the same people who had helped at the wedding met again at the ward meetinghouse to welcome five new members of the Church on the occasion of their baptisms. The font was filled and the participants, dressed in white, sat on the front row of the chairs set up in front of the font. The bishop had met the baptismal candidates and taken a few minutes to get acquainted with them. The Kress family, youngish parents with a ten-year-old daughter, Abigail, and an eight-year-old son, Josh, seemed nervous but excited at the prospect of their baptism.

The fifth candidate, Billy Newton, was sixteen years old, and a friend of Lisa Lou Pope, who sat beside him, beaming and giving little waves to people as they came in. Billy's parents had declined to attend the service, being somewhat put out that their son had made the decision to join this church rather than the Presbyterian one that they occasionally attended. The bishop was impressed with Billy; for once, he agreed with Lisa Lou's assessment that the boy was "nice enough to be a Mormon already." Who would have thought that flighty, boy-crazy Lisa Lou could serve as a missionary? He hoped the young man was truly converted to the Lord and His gospel rather than to the girl. He supposed time would tell.

As Sister Tullis played soft hymns on the piano, he bowed his head and offered a silent prayer for the five people who would enter the waters of baptism—that they would understand and take seriously the covenant they were entering into, and that they would find fellowship and joy with the Saints and continue to progress in knowledge and faith.

He loved baptismal services, enjoyed the sweet spirit that attended them, and loved to see the Church grow. He only wished there could have been one more little person dressed in white. Tashia Jones wanted so badly to be baptized—but so far, her grandmother, who was her guardian (and the bishop's fifth-grade teacher), hadn't seen fit to give her permission. He included Tashia and Mrs. Martha Ruckman in his silent prayer.

Y

After lunch, the bishop piled the whole family into the car and drove up to visit Sister Hazel Buzbee, to see how she was faring in the winter cold. They took her a roast chicken from the rotisserie at the store and a package of dinner rolls.

"I feel bad I haven't had time to make her anything," Trish fretted. "But maybe it's just as well, considering how she received my first effort!"

Her husband laughed, remembering the sweet-potato pie Trish had so carefully prepared, and its rejection by Sister Buzbee for insufficient nutmeg. "Honey, that was the best sweet-potato pie I ever ate," he told her.

"Good thing you liked it," she replied, grinning. "Else I'm sure her old hound dog would have had a treat."

"She's got a dog?" Jamie asked.

"She does," his dad replied, "and I think it's about as old as she is."

"Does she got a cat?" inquired Mallory.

"Yep. But I don't think it's used to little girls, so don't try to pick it up, okay?"

"How far out does she live?" demanded Tiffani. "We're already past the back of beyond!" The bishop's eldest was predictably annoyed at giving up her Saturday afternoon for a family drive to visit an elderly woman she'd never met.

"So far that she practically never goes anywhere," her dad responded. "When I first came to visit her, she scared me half to death with an old shotgun she carries around."

"No way! Was she gonna shoot you, Dad?" asked Jamie.

"No, the gun wasn't loaded. It's just her way of scaring off insurance salesmen and other strangers. Actually, she used to know your Grandma Shepherd, back when we all first joined the Church. That was when we used to hold our meetings upstairs in the social hall of the Fairhaven BBB, downtown. You know that old brick building, next to Sears?"

"Is BBB anything like KKK?" asked Trish, smiling. "Or is it the Better Business Bureau?"

"Not the first, thankfully, but kind of like the second. It stands for Brotherhood of Business Boosters. Just local business-men who had a kind of 'good old boy' network going. I think my dad belonged, for a while. Maybe that's why they let the Church use their hall on Sundays. Not that Dad ever attended our meet-ings, himself. It was amazing, when you think about it, how strongly we could feel the Spirit under those circumstances. I used to go early with the missionaries sometimes, and we'd sweep up the cigarette butts and ashes and throw away the beer bottles so we could set up for church."

"That's gross," Tiffani said. "Why didn't they clean up after themselves?"

"Oh, they had a janitor, but he didn't work on Sunday. He came in on Monday. I expect he was grateful for our help."

"But didn't it stink?" Tiffani pursued.

"First thing we did was throw open the windows—even in winter," her dad replied. "Sometimes we froze through Sunday school, until the building could warm up again." He chuckled.

"I think we must've had a special bunch of extra-bold mission-aries to be brave enough to invite investigators to a place like that. And there were so few of us—sometimes only ten or fifteen, at first."

"Yuck. I don't think I could've felt the Spirit there."

"You know, there's a scripture that applies, Tiffi," Trish said.

"There always is," agreed Tiffani in an exaggeratedly patient voice.

"Well, this one's in Matthew, as I recall, and it's Jesus speak-ing, saying, 'where two or three are gathered together in my name, there am I in the midst of them.' So I think we don't have to have a big congregation or a nice chapel. The Spirit can be present in a tiny hut in Guatemala or a hogan in New Mexico or in the social hall of the BBB, or wherever—as long as the people gathered there are sincere and want to worship the Lord."

"Oh, yeah, I remember—we read that one in seminary," Tiffani agreed. "But I'm still glad we have a nice chapel, with no cigarette butts to sweep out."

"Me, too, Tiff. Me, too," agreed her father. "Although I've gotta say, those were sweet days."

Y

Hazel Buzbee was delighted with their visit and passed a package of Fig Newtons around to the children, bending to peer into each face to see them better.

"Well, this here's a fine crop of young'uns, Bishop," she pro-nounced loudly. "Now, y'all have another cookie, all right? I can have my neighbor get me some more. These here are real good to keep a body reg'lar, now that I don't have my fresh collard greens to do the job. I do hate to be bound up."

The bishop didn't dare look at any of his family. "Are you

keeping warm this winter, Sister Buzbee? How'd you fare during that big snow? I worried about you."

"Oh, I was fine and dandy. My good neighbor come down with that blade-thing on the front of his truck and plowed a path to the house, and made sure my chimbley flue was open—and his little wife cleared off the porch steps for me, but I didn't hardly poke my nose out for a day or so. I brung my critters inside, and my kitty slept against my back, and ol' Buster here, he kept my feet warm for about half the night, then went to stretch out by the door with his nose to the crack. Liked the fresh air, I reckon."

"What's your kitty's name?" asked Mallory.

"What's that, honey? I don't hear good."

Mallory repeated her question, and then Trish did too, with added volume.

"Oh, she's just kitty. I didn't never give her a name. Would you like to give her one, sweetheart?"

"My kitty's named Samantha. I'll think of a good name for yours, okay?"

"All right, baby. I swanny, y'all are good to me, to drive clear out here and bring me this chicken! You'll purely spoil me, 'tween you and that Miss Ida Lou. She shore is a nice woman."

"She sure is," Trish agreed warmly. "She's a wonderful Relief Society president."

"Relief Society, you say?" shouted Hazel. "I 'member I used to like that meetin'." Didn't always understand the lessons, 'specially them culture 'finement ones, but I liked bein' with other women. All of us believers, you know."

"I don't even remember those lessons, but my mom used to talk about them," Trish told her. "Now we have lessons from a different Church president each year." She looked around. "Do you have a tape recorder?"

"A what, honey?"

"A tape recorder."

"No, no, all I've got's a radio. Wouldn't know what to do with one of them gadgets."

"It's real easy to work. We could send you tapes of the Relief Society lessons to listen to, if you wanted."

"Oh, I 'spect I'm too old and ornery to learn how to use it. Likely I'd break it or something."

"You know, a tape recorder's a real good idea," the bishop said. "Maybe we could even tape some sacrament meeting talks for you, too. Bring a little church to you, since you can't get in, that often."

"Wal—reckon I could try. Think I could hear it?"

"Sure, you could turn it up real loud, like your radio. It wouldn't bother anybody out here."

Hazel Buzbee cackled. "Reckon not," she agreed. "'Ceptin' old Buster and kitty. How 'bout it, baby doll—you got a name for kitty, yet?"

"I think her name should be Stormcloud, 'cause that's what color she is."

"Say what, honey? You got you such a little bitty voice."

Mallory stepped close to Hazel and shouted in her ear. "Stormcloud! Maybe Stormy, for short."

Hazel hugged the little girl and kissed her forehead. "Stormy it is!" She looked at Trish, her eyes growing misty. "Been such a long time sinc't I held a little one," she said. "A body fergits how soft and sweet they be."

Trish nodded.

"Dad, can I ask her about—you know?" Jamie asked softly, nodding toward the back door. His father nodded, and Jamie stood up and leaned over to say loudly, "Sister Buzbee, can I see your shotgun?"

She laughed again. "My old blunderbuss? Shore. It was my daddy's, and I don't reckon it'd even shoot anymore, but it's scared off more than one troublesome sort." She stood up and took the old gun from its place by the back door. "Serves me as a walkin' stick and a snake-discourager sometimes, too." She offered the butt end to Jamie, who sagged under the weight of the weapon.

"Whoa, it's heavy!"

"Yessir, it's made for a man. Here, looky." She broke the action open and showed the boy where the shells should go and how to look down the barrel. "You just remember that guns ain't toys, sonny. All right? They're meant to discourage varmints, two-legged or four-legged."

Jamie nodded. "Yes, ma'am." He handed the gun back to her. "That's cool."

"Been a good friend to me. Didn't scare off your daddy, though, not that I'm callin' him a varmint. He kept comin' back, even though I told him I drink coffee. I still do," she said in the bishop's direction.

"All right," he said mildly. "Could I read you a scripture or two before we go, Sister Buzbee?"

"Land, ain't nobody called me Sister Buzbee for so long! It sounds right sweet to me. Yessir, please read me a scripture—only not that one about no hot drinks."

The bishop grinned. He read a passage or two about love from the New Testament, including John 14:15: " . . . if ye love me, keep my commandments." Then he turned to Moroni, chapter ten, and read, "And again I would exhort you that ye would come unto Christ, and lay hold upon every good gift, and touch not the evil gift, nor the unclean thing. . . . Yea, come unto Christ, and be perfected in him, and deny yourselves of all ungodliness . . . and love God with all your might, mind and strength, then is his grace sufficient for you, that by his grace ye may be perfect in Christ; and if by the grace of God ye are perfect in Christ, ye can in nowise deny the power of God."

He paused and took a deep breath. It was tiring and went against his grain to read the word of God at such a decibel level. Then he asked if they could have a prayer and who she would like to give it.

"Wal, I'd like that young lady, thar—ain't heard a peep outa her the whole time you been here," Hazel said, pointing to Tiffani.

"Me?" asked Tiffani, looking dumbfounded.

"Sure," encouraged her father in a whisper. "Just bless Sister Buzbee to be safe and well and so forth, and do it loud."

"Okay," she said doubtfully, and stood with her arms folded. "Heavenly Father, we're thankful for this day, and the chance to come see Sister Buzbee. We ask thee to please bless her to be safe and well and protected from harm and evil of all kinds. We pray she'll be able to use the tape recorder, if she gets one, and to learn more about the gospel. Please help her to feel thy love for her. In the name of Jesus Christ, amen."

"Amen," they all echoed, including Hazel, who stood and enfolded Tiffani in a warm embrace.

"That's the sweetest prayer I ever heard said, especial for this old sinner," she said, her voice quavery. "Thank you, darlin'."

"You're welcome," said Tiffani, whose voice was quavery, too. "Heavenly Father does love you, Sister Buzbee. He let me feel that while I was praying."

"Well." Hazel wiped her eyes with the tail of the flannel shirt she wore over her housedress. "Reckon I love Him back."

Trish Shepherd looked at her husband and exchanged a small smile with him. "Two or three gathered together," she whispered, and he nodded.

CHAPTER TEN

" . . . AS TESTIMONY FILLS MY HEART"

His stomach growled as he reviewed the agenda for the nine o'clock ward council meeting. He had thought he was getting pretty good at this fasting business, and he was dismayed to find distinct hunger pangs already making themselves felt so early in the day. If this kept up, he'd be ready to gnaw the desk by four or five o'clock!

"Hush up," he told his complaining gut. "You'll get fed when I say so, and not before. I'm in charge, here. After all, one of the things we're here to do is to learn to control our appetites and passions."

The door to the clerk's office opened, then swiftly closed again, as Brother MacMillan heard the bishop's voice.

"Hey, Dan," he called. "It's okay. Come on in."

"Sorry, sir. Were you praying? I didn't mean to interrupt."

The bishop felt his neck reddening. "No, I wasn't praying. I was just talking to myself—or at least, to a part of myself. Telling my stomach to stop growling."

Dan smiled politely. "Does it do any good to issue an order? I might try that."

"I'll let you know. What's up?"

"Just wondered if the agenda covers everything, or if there's something you'd like to add."

"It looks pretty comprehensive. I think I'll give Lula a call and see what the latest is on Thomas." He looked longingly at his desk phone, then reached for his cell phone. On his wireless plan, Birmingham wasn't long-distance.

Lula, when she came on the line, sounded more cheerful than he'd heard her for what seemed a long time.

"Bishop? Guess what—my boy squoze my hand today when I asked him to! He hatn't opened his eyes yet, but ever'body here says he's close to it. And it makes me feel bad, but they had to restrain his good arm 'cause he was tryin' to pull at his ventilator and his IV tube. So I know he's feelin' somethin', and I know he can understand us. We're doin' a lot of talkin' to him now, real positive, encouragin' things, so he'll know it's safe to wake up."

"You've been doing that all along," he reminded her. "It'd be interesting to know how much he's been aware of, on some level. Maybe he'll tell you, one of these days."

"Oh, Bishop, I sure hope so. It's lookin' to me like maybe he's made his choice to stay here and live, don't you think?"

"It looks more and more like that every day," he agreed, hoping he was speaking the truth. It would be cruel for Lula and Tom to get their hopes so high, only to have them shattered.

"I'll come down and visit again real soon. And we're all still praying for Thomas, and I know many of us are fasting again for him, today."

"Oh, that's right, it's Fast Sunday, idn' it? I plumb forgot, what with ever'thing here. The days just sort of run together. But did you know I slept home, last night? My sis talked me into it, and she stayed there with me so if Tom called we could jump up and head right back down here. I didn't think I would sleep, but I tell you what, I was out like a light."

"I'm glad. You needed that. Well, I've got a meeting in just a minute, but I wanted to be able to report on Thomas, and I'm so grateful the news is positive."

Y

After the opening prayer, the Kress family and Billy Newton were confirmed members of the Church, and the bishop warmly welcomed them into the ward family. The Kresses went to sit on the third row, and Billy went to sit with Lisa Lou Pope and her family. Lisa Lou smiled radiantly at him, and he blushed.

About a third of the way through the testimony-bearing, much to the bishop's surprise, LaThea Winslow stood and approached the stand. He couldn't recall that LaThea had voluntarily done this in the months he had known her. Her voice, when she spoke, was rather more subdued than usual, and he noticed her hands were trembling.

"Brothers and sisters," she began, "I need to express my gratitude both to you and to our good bishop and to my Heavenly Father today. I appreciate so much all the generous help and encouragement we've received with our son's rather sudden decision to marry. You know I like things to be nice and done right, and you all helped to make his wedding a memorable and pleasant occasion, and I'm grateful for that.

"You know, I've discovered something in myself during this last week that I didn't know was there, and that's a wide streak of pride. Not the good kind of pride that we sometimes call self-respect, but the kind that makes us think we know best in a lot of things, and that we have the right to control matters—or people—any way we can. I need to confess that sin to you, today, and ask your forgiveness—and yours, Bishop—and my Father in Heaven's, especially. I . . ." She paused for a moment, helped herself to a tissue from the box under the podium, and blew her nose delicately.

"This is really hard for me to say. Sometimes I've felt, since we moved here, that I was misplaced. That because I grew up in Salt Lake City, in the shadow of Church headquarters, so to speak, that I knew more about how things should be run than most people here ever could know. I felt that my pioneer heritage set me apart from those who were new in the Church and just beginning to understand the gospel and the history we have. I even thought that because my older children grew up and served missions and married well, in the temple, that it should follow as a matter of course that my youngest son would do the same thing. When it didn't look like he was headed along that path, I tried to force things.

"My good husband, to give him credit, tried to stop me from making a fool of myself, but I was determined to push VerDan out on a mission even though he wasn't worthy or ready or even much inclined to go. Thankfully . . ." She turned to glance at Bishop Shepherd, seated behind her, and pressed the tissue to her nose again. "Thankfully, we have an inspired bishop who had the discernment to know VerDan wasn't ready to serve, and to stand up to me in my demands, which isn't always easy."

There was a small chuckle from a few people, but most were raptly attentive, knowing that LaThea was baring her soul, probably for the first time ever. The bishop glanced at his wife, who was giving LaThea a small, encouraging smile and also plying a hanky. He looked at Harville, who sat ramrod straight, gazing at his wife with what the bishop suspected was a new respect.

"When this ward was formed," LaThea continued, "I even

had the nerve to approach Bishop Shepherd and let him know that I thought I'd make a good Relief Society president." She smiled tearfully at Ida Lou Reams. "Sisters, aren't you grateful that he didn't believe me—that he relied on inspiration in that calling? I mean, could we have a sweeter, humbler, harder-working president than Ida Lou? So I need to ask everyone's forgiveness for my pride and stubborn bullheadedness because I can see now that's what it is. I'm going to try hard to be different from now on, but I've had fifty-five years of prideful living, and I know I'll slip, so please just whisper to me, 'LaThea, your pride's showing,' or 'you're doing it again,' and I promise I'll try to change. I'm afraid I've been one of those 'Utah Mormons' you hear about that give those folks a bad name in some places, and that's not fair, because Utah has lots of good, humble Church members who don't behave the way I've been doing. I do love my Heavenly Father, and I do know that Jesus is our Savior. I've been humbled by the realization of how quickly and unexpectedly our lives can change."

She closed her testimony and returned to her seat. Harville didn't look at her but reached an arm around her shoulders and pulled her close. For a few minutes, no one stood to speak, as if they were all assimilating what they had just heard. Then Ida Lou made her way to the stand.

"Now, brothers and sisters, you all know my weaknesses, on account of they're plenty plain to see," she said. "But dear Sister Winslow, you need to know how much I admire you for your talents and your education. It's just a wonder, the parties and programs you put on for the ward, and you can take real satisfaction in that. And don't you worry about your boy—he stepped up and done the right thing by that nice young lady, and I reckon you're gonna have a little family there that you can be proud of.

"Or . . . " She stopped in confusion. "Y'all know what I mean. Not proud, like—I reckon 'grateful for' is better. You know, we don't all grow up the same, at the same speed, I mean—and it just takes longer for some young'uns to take hold of the gospel and learn to live by it. We're all still tryin' to do that, if you think about it. Main thing is, I think, that we love the Lord and know Jesus is our Savior, and I want to bear testimony that I do that, and that I'm so very thankful that I can go to the temple, now, and take part in what happens there. It's such a sweet blessing, and I hope I'll always be grateful for it. I hope and pray that someday my good husband, Barker, will take hold and see what the gospel could do for him, but for now I'm just glad to be a-goin', even if I'm by my lonesome. Now, Lord bless each and every one of you, and I say these things in the name of the Lord Jesus Christ, amen."

Little Tashia Jones, who had been teetering on the front row, scooted up to the stand and leaned over to whisper to the bishop, "Is it okay for me to bear my testimony, even though I'm not baptized?"

"It sure is," he told her with a smile.

She stepped up and pulled the microphone down to her level. Her many braids, with their vari-colored elastics, bobbed with her excitement.

"Hey, brothers and sisters. The bishop says I can bear my testimony to y'all, even though I haven't been baptized, yet— 'cause my grandma hasn't given permission. But I've wanted to join the Church for a long time, and I'm real glad she lets me come, instead of going to her church where the minister is real educated and real long-winded when he preaches, and I don't get more'n half of what he says. But I like how things are done here, better, and I have a testimony that this is Jesus's true church, brought back to earth through Joseph Smith. I know that because when I read the little book the missionaries left at our house a couple of years ago, I did what it said, and prayed to know if it was true, and I got a real strong, warm, good feeling all over me, like nothing I'd ever felt before. I told Grandma, and she said I could come to visit one of your meetings if I wanted to, and see what I thought. She said I might not be welcome, 'cause there aren't very many black Mormons around here, but I always felt welcome.

"So I came in and sat down, and people were nice to me. Somebody handed me a hymn book, and somebody else asked me my name, and showed me where to go to Primary. My teacher there was Sister Spendlove, and she was so sweet to me, and taught me so much about the scriptures that I'd never known. I hated when she had to move away. Then I had Sister Padgett the next year, and she's been real nice, too. I love Jesus—I always did, even before I came here, 'cause my grandma's a good Christian lady, and she taught me about Him. And I feel close to Him, here, and that's why I come. Um . . . thank you. In the name of Jesus Christ, amen."

"Amen!" echoed the bishop and reached to shake Tashia's hand as she passed by to return to her seat. His heart swelled with affection for the little girl, and again, he sent up a prayer to know what might be done to persuade Mrs. Martha Ruckman to allow Tashia to be baptized. There was another quiet spell, and then Doctor Scott Lanier suddenly stood and hurried to the front, as though he might think better of it if he delayed. He cleared his throat and ran one hand over his thinning but impeccably groomed hair.

"I would like to bear my testimony of the truthfulness and efficacy of the restored gospel of Jesus Christ. I'm grateful for the knowledge and the testimony I have, and I pray it can always remain strong. That it will, is something I used to take for granted, but because of events in my own household this last year, I no longer do. I understand now that testimonies, like love, need to be nurtured along the way and expressed.

"Most of you are aware, I know, that this last year has not been a very happy one for me. My wife, Marybeth, has chosen to have her name removed from the rolls of the Church, and in fact, informs me that she no longer even believes in a Supreme Being. She has decided that all religions are manmade, and that people of strong mind and will have no need to rely on such superstition. She regards herself as enlightened and freed from pressure to conform, and she fully expects that in process of time I'll mature to the point that I'll follow suit."

He bowed his head in an effort to control his emotions. "I fervently hope and pray that I will never 'mature' in that direction. I love my wife, and it breaks my heart to see her take this stance, and throw away all that I cherish and hold dear with regard to the Savior and our hope for eternal families. I can't even begin to comprehend her thinking process, and I feel that I've aged ten years in the last ten or so months. I wasn't anymore dismayed by the collapse of the towers in New York and the Pentagon than I've been by this collapse of all I've hoped for. But I'm so very grateful to our good bishopric and stake presidency and my priesthood leaders, and all of you good people for the support and encouragement you've given me.

"I don't know what the end of all this will be, but I hope for the best, and I know the Lord is aware of me and my situation. I feel His love and His comfort extended to me daily, and without that, I can't imagine what life would be. I bear testimony that He lives, that He hears our prayers and answers them—though not always when and how we think is best, but according to His own infinite wisdom and understanding."

After Brother Lanier sat down, Sam Wright stood to

announce the closing hymn and prayer. Bishop Shepherd found he had a hard time singing, so he just mouthed the words. He thought how, a year ago, he would have listened to the testimonies of ward members with a degree of sympathy and understanding, but what a change had been wrought in him since that time! He now felt intimately involved with each one, and attuned to their needs and their situations as never before. He felt a love and responsibility for them that was superseded only by the love and responsibility he had toward his own family. *No wonder,* he thought, *the bishop is often referred to as the father of the ward.*

Y

He peeked into the chapel a few minutes after the third hour and was relieved to see a fair number of people occupying the choir seats. Sister DeNeuve was passing around hymnals, and Sisters Tullis and Patrenko were settling themselves at the organ and piano respectively. He would have joined them, but he had several settings apart and one interview to take care of.

Y

At dinner late that afternoon, he rejoiced in the opportunity to relax and be with his family while they enjoyed Trish's baked beef stew and homemade rolls. Her willingness to cook good meals for the family was a trait he appreciated, and his comments to the children about having married her for her meatloaf and lemon icebox pie, while teasing, had a basis in truth. As she reminded him, he had never tasted her cooking before they were married, but he had been pleasantly surprised at the quality of it. Her mother was a good cook and had taught her daughters well. On days such as this, having been fasting for more than twenty-four hours, his hunger-sharpened appreciation was greater than ever.

"Oh, I had a call from Miz Hestelle when I got home from church," Trish remarked. "She seems to think we're getting new neighbors next door."

"Is that right?" Hestelle Pierce lived west of them, but the house on the east side had been vacant for a couple of years. It belonged to an elderly man who had gone to live with his daughter in hopes of being able to recuperate from a kidney disease and come back to his home. "So it's not Mr. Jenkins coming back? Or some of his family?"

"I guess not. Renters, Miz Hestelle said. I didn't even know the place was up for rent. She said Margery Roane talked to Mr. Jenkins's daughter last week when she was over there cleaning out his personal effects. The daughter said he's doing pretty well, for his age, but can't live on his own anymore, so he's just going to stay on with her, and they'll rent the place furnished. I guess they must have advertised the place in the paper or something because I sure haven't seen a sign up."

"Neither have I. The only people I've seen there are the usual crew they hired to come in and keep the place up. Well, that's too bad, about Mr. Jenkins. Nice old fellow—I was hoping maybe he'd get to come back for a while."

"I don't know him," said Mallory. "Do I?"

"Sure you do," replied Jamie. "Remember? He used to give you peaches from his tree, 'cause he said you had a peaches-and-cream complexion."

Mallory shook her head. "What does that mean?"

Her mother smiled at her. "Means you have pretty skin and rosy cheeks. You were probably too young to remember."

"He didn't give me peaches," Tiffani said darkly. "He gave

me what-for when my friends and I played our music, out in our own backyard."

"Well, he probably wasn't feeling well, and needed to rest," soothed her mother. "Anyway, it looks like we'll be having neighbors on that side, again, so let's all be sure to be nice and make them feel welcome."

Y

Jamie was laboring through a lesson on choosing to act as Jesus would at their Monday family home evening when the phone rang.

"Excuse me," his dad whispered, removing Mallory from his lap and setting her in his vacant chair. He thought the call might be from the Rexfords, or someone else who needed his attention, and he answered it at his desk. It was a youthful male voice, asking for Tiffani.

"Tiffani's busy with a family activity right now," he replied. "Can she call you back, or would you like to try again in about an hour?"

"I'll call back," the voice promised.

"And your name is . . . ?" prompted the bishop, knowing Tiffani would ask.

"Oh . . . this is Pete MacDonald."

"Well, hey, Petey. How's your family?"

"Good," Pete said cautiously. "I'll call back, okay?"

"Okay. See ya'. Oh, and say hey to your dad."

"I will. Bye."

He returned to Jamie's lesson and found Trish's and Tiffani's eyes fixed inquiringly upon him. He nodded toward his daughter. "Petey MacDonald. He'll call back," he whispered.

He wasn't prepared for her reaction. Her eyes widened, and a wave of color rushed up her cheeks. She drew a deep breath and glanced at her mother, who gave her a small, raised-eyebrow smile.

He settled Mallory on his lap again and tried to give his attention to Jamie's presentation, but he was concerned about Tiffani's response. Trish had always assured him that Tiff was level-headed with regard to boys and that she would never behave like Lisa Lou—or even openly acknowledge or display her feelings in front of her parents. But a call from Petey MacDonald was obviously an event in her life, and he wasn't sure how he felt about that.

"So, like, if somebody says something to you that hurts your feelings, how can you do what Jesus would do? Uh—Tiff."

"What? Oh. Um—well, you could just ignore it, and not act ugly back, I guess."

"Okay. Good. Anybody else . . . Mom?"

"Well, Jesus said we should go even further than that and try to return good for evil. Try to do something nice for that person, or be especially kind to them."

"And pray for them," added the bishop. "It's not always easy. Well, maybe not ever easy—but it helps you feel better, and might even do the other person some good, too."

"I can't do that!" Tiffani objected. "I mean, like at school— kids are mean and sarcastic to each other all the time, and I'd feel like a total idiot being nice to some girl who had just dissed me!"

"As I said, it's not easy," her father said. "But if you could just keep from reacting in the same nasty spirit, and then try later to remember to pray for that person, it'd be worth the experiment."

"I'd feel like a hypocrite, praying for them. I'd feel, like, 'please bless Suzette to fall and break a leg in her next cheer routine.' You know? How could I be sincere?"

"It takes practice, and maybe a certain amount of maturity,"

Trish said. "Maybe you could start out by reminding yourself that Suzette is also a daughter of Heavenly Father, just as you are, and that maybe she doesn't know that, yet. Maybe she's feeling insecure inside and lashes out at other girls to try to make herself feel better. Who's Suzette, anyway?"

"Oh, she's just an example. There are tons of snotty girls at school. I get called 'metal-mouth' and 'thunder thighs' and 'goody-goody' and 'ice queen,' just because I won't do some of the stuff they do."

Thunder thighs? the bishop mused. His slender little Tiffi? Ridiculous! He remembered "metal-mouth" and "four-eyes" from his school days. In fact, he remembered Sally Lovelace, a pretty girl who sat on the front row and squinted at the chalkboard in English class, ashamed to wear her glasses because of the "four-eyes" taunt from a particular classmate.

"High school can be a tough place," Trish was sympathizing. "Things'll be better in college, I hope. They were for me, anyway. Just hold to your standards and remember that even those girls who tease you about them will respect you for them—later, if not now."

"Okay, so . . ." Jamie began, trying to regain control of his class.

"Dad, did Pete say what he wanted?" Tiffani interrupted.

Her father shook his head.

"Probably just something for geometry or Spanish," she murmured.

"Okay, so, Dad? What if a kid comes in and steals stuff from the store?" Jamie pursued.

"Depends how old he is, and what he takes," his father responded. "I'd need to talk to him and make him understand that stealing is wrong and can get him in big trouble. Then I'd try to find a way for him to earn whatever it was he wanted."

"Why wouldn't you just call the police?"

"If he were an older kid, I might need to do that. But I'd rather take care of it myself—if it's a younger person. I wouldn't let him get away with it, however. Jesus didn't let the money-changers get away with what they were doing in the temple. But I'd try to be kind and forgiving."

"Did he say what time he'd call back?" his daughter inquired.

Oh, boy, the bishop thought. *I do believe we've got something new here.*

CHAPTER ELEVEN

Y

" . . . DEAR ARE THE NINETY AND NINE"

It was Trish's turn to supply dinner for the bishopric's Tuesday night meeting, so after work, the bishop swung by the house to pick up her offering, which consisted of a thick, creamy version of chicken noodle soup, green salad, whole wheat bread, and apple pie. He kissed her gratefully.

"Any more words from Tiff?" he asked quietly.

Trish wrinkled her nose and shook her head. "I think she really wants to go. Should we let her? On a single date?"

He shrugged. "How can we not? I mean, it's Mac's boy—and he just wants to take her to a movie. He's probably a great kid. His dad was."

"Well, I hope Petey's taken after his dad, but that's hard to know. I was kind of hoping she'd just date LDS boys. Not that that's any guarantee, but most of the guys in our ward seem like good kids."

"I know. I was hoping the same thing. I reckon they don't seem all that exciting—just the same old boys she's grown up with. And Petey is good-looking. I expect it's considered an honor at school to be asked out by him. Still . . ."

"I know. Still."

"Well, I'll leave it in your hands. Whatever you think best."

"Thanks a lot!"

He winked at her. "I trust your judgment, babe. Thanks again for dinner."

Y

He lingered over his pie, having taken it to his office to eat while he prepared for the evening's interviews, particularly one with Melody Padgett. He also had a couple of youth interviews—one with Lisa Lou Pope and one with Ricky Smedley.

Ricky arrived first, with a cheerful smile and cheeks red from the cold.

"Hey, Bishop," he greeted.

"Good to see you, Ricky. Come and sit down. Hey, I've been wanting to tell you that I sure do appreciate the fine way you priests take care of blessing the sacrament. I notice you dress appropriately, speak clearly, and always have someone assigned to do it. Knowing that it's going to be taken care of makes my job easier."·

"Well, we have a good bunch of guys. Most ever'body's willing to help."

"That's what it takes. That and organization. So how are things going for you, Rick, in your personal life? School, church, friends, personal study and prayer, plans for the future—start anywhere."

"Um—school's going okay, church is fine. Reckon I oughta study the scriptures more, on my own, but what with homework and having to get up early for seminary, I guess I just hope that studying 'em there is good enough for a while. I do say my prayers, night and morning, even if they're real short, sometimes."

The bishop nodded. "Sometimes mine are real short, too. Like, 'I thank Thee for today and all it's blessings. Please continue to be with all of us, according to our needs.' That short?"

Ricky grinned. "Yessir. 'Bout that."

"You just wouldn't want all of 'em—or even most of 'em—to be that short. We need to get real specific, a lot of times, and report in to the Lord about all we're doing, what we're trying to work on, what we're happy about, and what bothers us. Heavenly Father is interested, and he wants to hear from us. Imagine being a parent with a kid away at school, and the kid calls and leaves a message on your answering machine that says, 'Hi, Dad. Thanks for the money. Send more when I need it. Bye.'"

"Yeah. I mean, yessir. I get your point. I'll work on that."

"You dating anybody, Ricky?"

"Well, I don't date a whole lot. It costs money, you know? Movies and stuff aren't cheap, and food, neither. So I just go out once in a while, like to a special dance or something."

"Anybody in particular that you like?"

Ricky blushed. "Oh, I don't know—I took Claire out, a time or two."

"Claire Patrenko's a sharp young lady. Nice-looking, smart, talented."

"Yessir. But I mean, it's not like—I wouldn't want it to get back to her that I—you know . . ."

"Oh, I know. What's said here, stays here. Still, I expect she'd be flattered. Everything okay with you morally, Ricky?"

"Yessir. I'm real careful that way. I don't want to mess up my chances for a mission, like some . . . well, you know."

"I do, indeed. Continue to be careful. Avoid R-rated films?"

"I've seen one or two, but I don't usually go past PG."

"That's good. I've noticed that even a lot of the PG-13s are getting pretty bad."

"I know. Mom checks them out on the Internet before we go see anything."

"That's good. No dealings with any kind of porn, I hope?"

"Oh, no way."

"Excellent. Anything I should know, as your bishop?"

"Um—no, sir, I don't reckon so. Donnie's a real good example to us younger kids. He's always writing us about how important it is to keep the commandments and not do anything stupid."

"He's serving a good mission—almost ready to come home, isn't he?"

Ricky grinned. "Mom's countin' the days."

"You bet she is. And she'll count 'em when you're serving, too."

"Yessir, I expect so."

The bishop thought about Twyla Osborne. If Buddy were to serve a mission, would she count the days? More to the point, would she notice he was gone? His conscience smote him. He probably wasn't being fair to Twyla.

He smiled at Ricky. "Be grateful for a mom like that," he advised, shaking the young man's hand and ushering him out. And, he wanted to call after him, you may take my daughter Tiffani out, any time you want!

Y

Lisa Lou Pope entered his office with a little less flounce than usual. He approved the change. A little more decorum, a little less flounce would be an improvement in Lisa Lou.

"Hey, Bishop," she said tiredly. He wondered if her weariness was due to the dedication with which she was chewing what had to be an extra-large wad of gum.

"How are you doing, Lisa Lou? You seem tired tonight."

"Oh, it's just that I've been working every night for the last week, and up early for seminary every morning, and doing homework in between. And of course, Billy wants me to spend time with him, whenever I can."

"Billy Newton seems to be a fine young man."

"He is. I'm real glad he got baptized. It made me feel like a regular missionary, you know?"

"Yes, I do, and you can be grateful for the part you played in introducing him to the Church."

"Well, like I said before, he was so nice it just seemed like he ought to be a Mormon. But he hatn't ever heard of the Church! Isn't that weird? I thought ever'body had, by now. Anyway, I told him some stuff about it, and he wanted to find out more, so I got hold of the missionaries for him—and here he is, all baptized and ever'thing."

"That must be very satisfying for you."

"Well, sure, but you know what? Now I don't know what to do, 'cause Billy acts like we're going steady and practically engaged, and I didn't ever agree to that! Well, I mean, I reckon I was interested in him, romantically, you know, for a while. But now I'm real interested in another boy, but I never get to talk to him at school, on account of Billy! He's just always there, all happy and glad to see me, and I feel real mean that I get annoyed with him for it. What should I do, Bishop? I don't want to run him away from church!"

"Hmm. Do you feel that Billy's truly converted to the gospel of Christ, and not just converted to you?"

"Oh, you bet I do! He just keeps reading ever'thing he can

get his hands on, and he talks to his friends about it, and he wants to go on a mission and all. It's just that he thinks I go along with it, you know? Like I'm part of the package. It just plumb worries me sick!"

"Well, I think you should be honest with him. Tell him that you think he's a wonderful guy, and you're really glad he was baptized, and you always want to be his friend, but that you should probably not get too serious right now, and should both date other people. Something like that. Feel free even to tell him that the bishop suggested to you that it'd be a good idea."

"Bishop, would you . . ."

He shook his head. "You go first. I'll be talking to him soon, anyway, and I'll back you up. I'll explain that a young lady your age is too young to consider a true, committed relationship and should get to know a lot of people. It's Church policy. Isn't there something about that in the 'Strength of Youth' pamphlet?"

"You're right! I b'lieve there is. Oh, good. I can use that. Thank you, Bishop!"

"And don't wear yourself completely out, Lisa Lou. If you're going to do well in school and make good choices and be strong against temptation, you need proper rest. Don't try to burn the candle at both ends."

She blinked. "Come again?"

"That means you can't try to do too much, or you'll burn out."

"Oh. Okay. I'll try to cut back my hours at work."

They chatted a while longer, and then it was nearly the hour for Melody Padgett to arrive, and he wanted time to say a brief prayer before he met with Melody. He walked to the door of the building with Lisa Lou and saw her into her car. He took several deep, bracing breaths of the cold air before returning to his heated office.

When Melody arrived, Dan McMillan showed her in, then withdrew to the clerk's office, leaving the adjoining door ajar. Melody slipped out of her coat and let it fall over the back of her chair.

"Melody, we haven't spoken for a while. How are things going for you? Where's little Andi?"

"She's tucked in bed, and my neighbor is sitting with her, reading her stories. It being a school night, I thought that'd be better, plus we can talk freely without her fretting or hearing things that might worry her."

"That's probably a good idea. How's she doing?"

"She still doesn't want to let me out of her sight—but she's starting to believe, I think, that she won't be stolen away from me again. It's tough for me, to tell you the truth, to leave her. I even get emotional dropping her off at school in the morning."

"That's understandable. So you've decided not to home-school her, as you once talked about when Jack was here?"

"That was Jack's idea—it was just another way to control us and keep anyone else from knowing it. I would've been happy enough to do it, too—just to have the time alone with her—although I'm sure Jack would've been popping in at odd times just to make sure we were still there."

"Has Jack seen Andi yet?"

Melody shook her head. "They're not going to allow supervised visits for another couple of months—and then only if his therapist thinks he's ready. You know, I kinda feel sorry for him on that count, because I think he really does love Andi, and he's probably missing her a lot. He was allowed to send her a Christmas present, though, and she got real excited."

"Do you think she wants him to come home?"

Melody paused, considering the question. "If things could be different, I think she'd like that. But it scared her, too, when he would yell and slap me around. She's only six, but I think she feels protective of me. She'll say, like, 'Mommy, it's just me and you going to the store, right?' Or, 'We'll have fun playing with my toys, won't we? Just you and me. No Daddy.' But then one day when it was cold and stormy, she said, 'Mommy, do you think Daddy's cold? Should we call him and let him come get warm?'"

"Mixed feelings, then," the bishop agreed. "Understandable. How about you, Melody? Are your feelings mixed, too?"

She made a wry little face. "Not so much, to tell you the truth. I've learned to appreciate the peace, and the knowledge that I'm not going to get punished if something isn't exactly right. I can come and go as I please, and take Andi with me, and it's like being let out of jail! If I want to go to Enrichment meeting, I can—and if I want to take Andi to see a movie, we go and I can wear what I choose and buy what I want to eat. Maybe all that sounds shallow, Bishop—and I suppose it is—but when you've been so totally controlled, it feels like heaven! Down the road a ways I might feel differently—I don't know. Sometimes I miss Jack, in a way, but mostly the Jack I thought I married. He wasn't quite so bad at first, you know. It just kind of developed, over time. I thought it was my fault, that I'd done something to make him think he couldn't trust me, and that I was a terrible housekeeper and mother. Now I know that's just not so."

"It's not so, indeed. I'm glad you're feeling freer. You know, Jack has confided in me some things about his childhood that helped me understand why he has these tendencies to be controlling and abusive."

Melody held up one hand. "Don't tell me, please, Bishop. I mean, I know there have to be reasons why he's like he is, and I know sooner or later I'm going to have to forgive him, but I'm not ready, yet. Does that sound selfish and awful?"

He smiled at her. "Believe it or not, I wasn't going to share the things he told me with you. That's for him to do, if and when he has the opportunity. Maybe it'll need to be done in a therapy session, for that matter. We'll let the professionals handle that. I mainly wanted you to know that his abusive behavior didn't just erupt out of left field. There are reasons for it. Not excuses, I might hasten to add, but reasons. As for forgiving him—I expect the good Lord will have to make you equal to that. And forgiving him doesn't mean having to take him back into your lives, if you can't bring yourself to do that. One step at a time, okay?"

"Sounds good to me. Right now, I'm just enjoying finding out who I am, again. And mothering Andi the way I've always longed to."

"Sounds good. And how do you feel about staying in Primary? Jack can't tell you what calling you're allowed to accept, anymore."

"You know, I still love my little class. I'm probably better off there than in Relief Society, right now, because all those wonderful lessons about eternal marriage and families and the temple really make me hurt inside. I'd have to pick and choose which ones I went to according to what I thought I could stand. I s'pose I'm not very brave. I'm sorry."

"That's understandable. We'll leave you where you are, then. How are you doing financially?"

"Well, Jack's been coming through with the house payments and child support, so at least he's reliable that way. And I have my little part-time job. Sometimes I'd like to move to a smaller place, but I know I shouldn't do anything hasty or stupid, financially. I mean, nothing's decided, yet, about our marriage, so I'll just stay put, even though the memories there are not the best."

"Sister Padgett, I happen to think you're very brave—and it sounds as though you're being very cautious and thoughtful about your decisions. Please know that the Lord is mindful of you, and that we are, too—and that we stand ready to help you, any way we can."

"Thank you," she whispered. "You've already helped me more than I deserved, the way I treated you when I thought you were the one responsible for Andi being taken from me. I won't forget how kind and patient you were."

He shrugged. "The fact is, things might've come to the point that I would have had to report Jack's behavior, and the same thing might have resulted. Your day-care lady just beat me to it. And if not one of us, eventually someone else would have done the same. It was becoming apparent that you and Andi needed help. We might not totally agree with the way the family services folks went about it, but at least they're interested in Andi's welfare."

She nodded. "I know. But that sure was a bitter pill to swallow."

"For me, too. But that part's behind you, now, and it sounds like Andi's responding to your love and understanding. I'll let you get back to her. But, Melody—never, ever hesitate to call us, any time, if you need anything at all, including a blessing. All right?"

She stood, and the bishop helped her put on her coat. "Don't worry, Bishop," she said with a small smile. "I doubt you've seen the last of us, yet."

As she left the office, he thought about that small smile, very different from the one that used to be plastered across Melody's attractive face so continually. At least, this one was genuine.

Y

Tiffani was seated at the kitchen table frowning at her calculator when he let himself in. Samantha the cat lay sprawled across Tiffani's math book, taking her usual interest in whatever was going on.

"Evening, Tiff. Oh, hey—let's not allow the cat on the table. You know how Mom feels about that."

Tiffani frowned harder and punched a few more buttons. Finally she sighed and wrote down an answer on her paper. "It's not so much a matter of letting her on the table. It's a matter of finding a way to keep her down. I've taken her off about a dozen times, and she, like, thinks it's a game and jumps back up and tries to scatter my homework every which way at the same time."

"Put her outside."

"No, it's way too cold! Cats hate to be cold."

"Well, here—let's put her in the laundry room, in timeout."

He scooped up the Siamese, who suddenly developed awkward angles and unexpected twists that made her difficult to hold on to, and deposited her in the laundry room off the kitchen and closed the door. It wasn't heated, but it had been open to the warmth of the kitchen and was comfortable enough for a furry creature.

"She won't like that, either," Tiffani predicted. "She hates to be alone."

Samantha proved Tiffani right by yowling in a deep, offended tone and throwing her body against the door.

"She'll settle down and go to sleep pretty soon," the bishop said, hoping he was right. "She's just spoiled."

"Sure she is," Tiffani said lightly. "What's a kitty for?" She pulled her math book closer to examine her next problem, then looked up. "By the way, thanks for letting me go out with Pete."

"Oh—is that what your mom said?"

"Well, she said you'd talked it over, and that it was okay. But why wouldn't it be? It's just Pete. His dad's, like, your best friend from forever ago. I mean, it's not like we don't know them or something."

"That's true. And if Petey's anything like his dad, we don't have anything to worry about. Mac was always a gentleman around girls. His mom wouldn't have stood for anything else."

"Pete's nice, too. All the girls like him."

"How about the boys? Has he made some guy friends, too?"

Tiffani shrugged. "Most of them are just jealous, 'cause he's a new guy, and cute, and the girls don't give them all the attention anymore."

"Mmm. Does he do any sports?"

"Pete? I don't know. He's tall enough to play basketball, but of course the team was already chosen, last spring. Maybe he'll go out for that next year."

"What's he interested in?"

Tiffani looked up. "I don't know! I haven't talked to him like that, about his interests. Just about—you know—school and movies and music and stuff. We have two classes together— that's probably why he talks to me at all. That and the family friend thing."

"So what are you planning to see?"

"I don't know. He'll pick something."

"Well, I hope . . ."

"Oh, Dad! I know what you hope, of course. Something decent, not R-rated, with no swearing or sex or too much violence or—"

"I was going to say, Tiff, that I hope you have a good time on your first date."

She threw him a glance that plainly said, "Right. Of course you were."

Samantha threw herself at the door again and yowled.

He sighed. He had thought of having a small bowl of bread and milk, but he decided he was too tired.

"Night, honey," he said mildly and picked up his briefcase to haul it over to the desk in the corner of the dining room.

"Besides," Tiffani said, apropos of nothing, as he passed her chair, "it seems to me that if I'm old enough to date, I'm old enough to decide who to say yes or no to, without having to say, 'Just a minute, let me run ask my mommy and daddy!' That's beyond embarrassing."

The briefcase went down with a thump. "Actually, Tiff, sixteen is a good age for group dates, and at the most, double-dates. Single dating is best left for eighteen and older. Check your 'Strength of Youth' pamphlet on that point. We're letting you go with Petey, this once, because we trust you to be mature enough to uphold your standards and because we're pretty sure Petey's been taught similar standards, even though he's not LDS. Frankly, we were hoping that you would choose to date LDS boys, to avoid conflicting standards and expectations."

"Like who? Ricky Smedley? All he can see is Claire. Or maybe T-Rex? Oh, wait—he's unconscious, still. And even if he weren't, I'm not his type. Or maybe you'd like me to date Buddy? Oh, no—he isn't old enough—thank goodness! And the Birdwhistles live too far away. Or, let's see—the new boy, Billy Newton? Whoops, nope, he's in love with Lisa Lou, poor guy. Or maybe I should have a crush on one of the missionaries. Elder Bussero's pretty cute. Oh, that's right. Arm's length, girls, from the missionaries. So, just who should I go out with that's LDS and my age? There isn't anybody!"

"I'm not exactly clear what you're so upset about, Tiff. We are letting you go, Friday night, even if it's a little bit iffy in our book—and it's certainly not our fault that there aren't more fellows your age in the ward to choose from. As for not having to ask—I'd say that while age sixteen has its privileges, it's not quite like eighteen or twenty-one—and you do still fall under our parental care and supervision. So I'm not quite sure what you're unhappy about."

"Oh, just forget it, Dad. I need to finish my math, or I'll be dead meat tomorrow."

"Good night, Tiff. I love you."

"Mmm."

He trudged up the stairs and encountered his wife, all warm and fragrant from her bath, in the hall.

"Hi, babe," he said wearily.

"Hi, honey. What's the cat yelling about?"

"She was on the kitchen table, and I banished her to the laundry room."

"Thanks. Is Tiff still doing homework?"

"Yep. And maybe you should ask what she was yelling about. Only, I wouldn't know how to answer that. Maybe she needs a little timeout, too."

"She's so moody these days."

"It's like beyond moody,'" he said, imitating their daughter's voice. "It's, like—Dad can't say the right thing—ever!"

"I know. I don't do so well, either. Come talk to me," she invited. "*I* like what you say and how you say it."

He slipped an arm around her waist. Home at last.

CHAPTER TWELVE

Y

"... THROUGH CLOUD AND SUNSHINE"

Bishop Shepherd and Trish arrived early Wednesday evening at the Forelaw home, armed with a flannel-board Book of Mormon story for the children. He was warmed by the way they sat forward on the edge of the sofa, following the narrative and solemnly advising Trish which figure to move where as the story progressed. Sarge Forelaw hovered in the doorway to the kitchen, munching a sandwich and observing the activity. The bishop pretended he didn't see him, and Elaine didn't say anything, either, just watched her children and smiled. Once the story was done, she told the little ones to scamper off to bed, and Trish packed up the flannel board.

"You know," the bishop said, "I think we can all understand what Lehi was experiencing at the Tree of Life in his vision. I know that as soon as I find out any good news or learn something important or helpful, the first thing I want to do is to share it with Trish and the kids. I want them to know what I know and feel what I feel about the Lord and his gospel."

"And you just gotta hope they'll understand you're sharing something good," Elaine agreed, nodding.

"Right. And what we have to realize, and what Lehi had to come to grips with, too, is that each person receives what's offered to him in his own way, and of course everybody's free to accept and believe good, true doctrine if they choose to, or to reject it and turn away from it. That's part of Heavenly Father's plan for us, from the beginning. We hope and pray that those we love and care about will be like Nephi and Sam, rather than Laman and Lemuel, and accept and partake of the fruit of eternal life, but it's ultimately up to them. Laman and Lemuel in this vision chose not to partake of the fruit that Lehi had found, and that was prophetic of their later lives, when they turned totally away from the truth and from their parents' wishes."

Elaine nodded. "Reckon that's how it has to be, else it wouldn't be fair. But it's hard, idn' it?"

"It sure can be. Heavenly Father guarantees us our moral agency in this life, to choose good and happiness or to choose evil and reap the results of that choice, which is misery. He absolutely will not force us to do good. That'd be Satan's way. However, as the hymn says, 'He'll call, persuade, direct aright, and bless with wisdom, love and light. In nameless ways be good and kind, but never force the human mind.'"

He paused and grinned at Trish. "Of course, when our kids are small we're pretty much in control of everything they do. Then suddenly, they're teenagers, and lots of times we wish we could continue to be in control or force them to be good. But that's when we have to learn to follow Heavenly Father's pattern, and 'call, persuade, direct aright.' Sometimes it's tough. Trish and I are just beginning to learn."

"We sure are," Trish agreed. "But when you think about it, being good, or doing good, wouldn't mean a thing if we were forced to do it. We wouldn't even appreciate the blessings that we'd get because we wouldn't have known anything else. We wouldn't know that it hurts to touch the stove and burn your finger or that it makes you feel sick and sad inside when you've broken a commandment, if nobody was ever allowed to touch a stove or commit a sin."

"Reckon that's true," Elaine said. "Only, it seems like some folks just keep goin' back to touch that stove, even after they know it hurts."

"That happens, all right," the bishop said. "Especially with things like addictions—whether it's to alcohol, drugs, gambling, pornography, or whatever. But even those cycles can be broken, with the help of the Lord. It's hard, but it can be done, with the proper kind of counseling and determination and constant prayer. I often think about one fellow I know who stopped smoking after twenty-six years by, first of all, getting rid of all his cigarettes, and by avoiding stores where they were sold and by praying each morning as soon as he woke up, asking the Lord to remove the craving for tobacco from him for that day. It worked. I remember him saying how good his food tasted, after just a week or so of not smoking. He'd forgotten how much flavor an orange had, and he was thrilled to death with the taste of it, like it was the first one he'd ever had! He hadn't realized how smoking had dulled his sense of taste and smell."

"Heavenly Father doesn't want us to be addicted to anything," Trish added. "He wants us to be free and healthy and to enjoy life. Anytime we're addicted to something, we're not free. We're slaves to that thing or that activity. We're controlled by it. And like we just said, control and force are Satan's way. Jesus said, 'ye shall know the truth, and the truth shall make you free.' I suppose that has a lot of meanings, on several levels, but I sure do think freedom from addictions is part of it."

"You know," her husband added, "some folks think the gospel is restrictive and binding, but it's been my experience that it's liberating. Repentance and the atonement of Christ free us from the effects of sin, so that we can move forward again and not be bound by guilt or addiction or spiritual blindness. Repentance is a great blessing—don't you think so, Sarge?" He turned toward the kitchen doorway.

"Hmm? Oh. Hatn't never quite thought of it thataway, but reckon it makes sense," said the man of the house. "Always thought more about bein' punished for sin than about repenting and gettin' free of it. Where do y'all reckon punishment comes in? My old preacher used to be real big on punishment and hellfire."

The bishop's heart sang. Sarge was listening; he was thinking!

"There is a place for punishment," he agreed. "That's what happens to those who refuse to believe and repent and follow the Savior and who turn down or ignore what He did for us in the garden of Gethsemane and on the cross. See, our sins have to be paid for—either by the Savior, who suffered and died for us for that purpose—or by us, if we're so stubborn that we refuse to go through the repentance process and accept the Savior's offering."

"Huh," said Sarge. "Hatn't never thought of it just that-away," he repeated. "Y'all excuse me, now," he added, and took himself away from the doorway. Elaine looked at the bishop, smiling broadly, her eyebrows raised. He winked at her, and the three of them had a prayer before the bishop and his wife left the Forelaw home.

Y

"The new neighbors are moving in," Jamie informed them importantly when they returned home. "But I ain't seen any kids yet."

"I *haven't* seen any kids," Trish corrected him absently, peering out the kitchen window.

"You, neither? Shoot."

Trish exchanged a suppressed smile with her husband. "It does appear there are lights on over there, all right. I suppose we should take something over and say hello and see if they need any help."

"You made bread today, didn't you?" he asked.

"I have a loaf of wheat bread, but you never know if folks like that. Maybe if I included a jar of peach jam . . ."

"Bound to please. Do we all go, or just the two of us?"

"I want to go," offered Mallory.

"Me, too," said Jamie.

"Count me out," said Tiffani. "I'm swamped with homework."

The house to the east of them was a two-story structure of about the same vintage as their own, but it seemed much older, not having undergone the updating and renovation theirs had enjoyed. The porch was sound, but the floor boards were warped and uneven, and the doorbell sounded with a wheezy buzz. A thin wedge of light spilled out upon them as the door was opened to the extent that a chain lock would allow, and part of a woman's face appeared.

"Yes?" she said guardedly.

"Good evening," said the bishop cheerfully. "We're the Shepherds, your next-door neighbors, and we've just come to say welcome to the neighborhood."

"Oh. Well, step in a minute. We're in a mess, here, since we just started moving in, so I'm sorry I can't offer you a chair."

"We won't stay. We know how busy you must be," Trish said, ushering the children forward into a small front hallway paneled in dark wood and stacked with cardboard boxes marked "Kitchen" or "M's room" or "Bathroom."

"We thought you might enjoy a fresh loaf of bread and some jam," Trish continued, holding out her offerings to the woman, who took them with no change in her sober expression. She was probably in her sixties, with a narrow face, and dark, gray-streaked hair pulled back into a bun.

"Thank you very much, but you needn't have bothered," she said.

"It's no bother," Trish told her with a smile. "I'm Trish Shepherd, this is my husband Jim, and our two youngest children, Jamie and Mallory. We have a sixteen-year-old daughter, Tiffani, as well."

"I see. Well, I'm pleased to meet you all. I understand from Mrs. Pierce that y'all are good, Christian people. If you hadn't been, we wouldn't have taken the house."

"Well, it's nice of Hestelle to give us a good recommendation," the bishop remarked. "We'll surely try to live up to it. She's a fine neighbor, herself. Now, what can we do to help you folks get settled? Jamie and I could carry some boxes to the proper rooms, if you'll direct us."

"Oh, no, I couldn't impose. Marguerite and I will just take care of everything, a little bit at a time. We had help getting the heavy things in, today, and we can handle the rest."

"Is Marguerite your daughter?" queried Trish.

"She's our youngest."

"I see. And where did you folks move from?"

"We came up from Dothan, to be near Henry's mother,

who's ninety-three and isn't well. There wasn't a place right in her neighborhood, so we took this."

"Well, we're glad you found this one. It'll be good to have neighbors here again," said the bishop.

"How old's Marg . . . Margreet?" asked Mallory.

"Thirty-four," responded the woman.

"Do you got a kitty, or a dog?"

"Certainly not. They make work. I have all I care to take care of with Henry."

"Henry's your husband?" asked Trish. "Is he not well, either?"

"He's feeling his age, is all. As am I."

"I understand. I didn't catch your name," Trish pursued.

"I didn't give it. I'm Maxine Lowell."

The bishop gestured toward the stacked boxes. "Mrs. Lowell, are you sure we can't help you with these? Jamie and I are quick. It wouldn't take us but a minute to get them distributed, and then you could unpack at leisure."

"No. But I do thank you—and thank you for the bread and jam. Marguerite will enjoy it. Henry and I don't eat sugar, of course."

"Oh—I'm sorry," Trish said. "I didn't think of that. Why don't I bring you over a pot of homemade soup, tomorrow?"

"No, please don't. We have very strict eating patterns, which I couldn't expect you to know."

There was little more to say. The bishop cleared his throat. "Well, we won't keep you from your work any longer, but please let us know if there's anything at all we can do to help. If it snows again, don't worry about your drive and walk. We'll take care of it."

"That won't be necessary. Marguerite is young and strong, and she enjoys getting out in the snow."

"Well, goodnight, then," Trish said, turning to herd the children outside again. "And welcome to the neighborhood."

"Thank you. Goodnight."

The door closed behind them with a decisive click, and the Shepherds were silent as they crossed the crunchy, frosted grass and the driveway.

"Okay, that lady's *weird*," Jamie declared, as soon as they were back in the lighted warmth of their own home. "You shoulda come, Tiff! It was creepy. She didn't crack a smile, not once."

"Well," his dad said, "maybe she just doesn't feel she has much to smile about. Maybe she has lots of problems or burdens."

"Dad, you always make excuses for people when they're rude or ignorant," Tiff said, lifting her head from her book.

He shrugged. "Well, you know—I try to give 'em the benefit of the doubt," he told her. "Lots of times, we just have no idea what folks are going through." He smiled at his son. "I do understand what Jamie meant, though."

"I got the feeling we weren't entirely welcome," Trish said dryly. "Certainly the bread and jam weren't a big hit."

"Does she have any kids?" asked Tiffani.

"She has a little girl named Mar-greet," offered Mallory.

"How old is she?"

"Thirty-four," answered Jamie. "She's the youngest, and she likes to shovel snow."

"We only met the mother, Maxine," Trish added. "Henry Lowell is the dad, and I guess the other children are gone from home."

"Well, I'd hope so!" said Tiffani, rolling her eyes. "I'm certainly not planning to be living at home when I'm thirty-four—

or older. And that's not a 'little girl,' Mal—that's almost as old as Mom."

"Maybe there's some special circumstance," Trish replied. "As I said, we haven't met Marguerite yet."

"And she doesn't have a kitty or a doggy, because she says they make work," Mallory reported. "Samantha doesn't make work, does she, Mommy?"

"Well, not for you, my sweetie. But who do you think usually feeds her and cleans her litter box and picks up all the strange stuff she chooses to drag around the house and play with?"

"You," admitted Mallory with a giggle.

When the children were in bed and Trish was finishing up in the kitchen, the bishop sat at the kitchen table enjoying a bowl of bread and milk. Trish glanced out the window at the house next door, where the lights were on in several rooms.

"Well, we tried," she said with a sigh.

"Sometimes that's all that's required," her husband responded. "Kind of interesting, though, that she quizzed Hestelle about the neighbors' religious preferences, before moving in."

"It is. Maybe they've had a bad experience somewhere, with somebody of another faith."

"Could be. Maybe we'll find out about it. And then again, maybe we won't, given her preference for privacy. Well, we'll do the best we can to be good neighbors and hope things work out. But between you and me—she was a little weird, wasn't she?"

Trish raised her eyebrows. "Way weird," she agreed.

The phone on the desk rang at eight-thirty Thursday evening. The bishop was seated there, poring over three bids from food services to set up a salad and sandwich deli in his store, and he picked up the phone ready to be diverted for a while. A young man's voice spoke in his ear.

"Bishop Shepherd? This is Elder Rivenbark. I'm calling to let you know I'm back in Fairhaven, and I've been reassigned to work with the full-time elders here."

"Elder! It's great to hear from you. Welcome back—and I don't know how you feel about this, but I'm grateful you can continue your mission with this assignment."

"Frankly, I'm not sure how I feel about it. I mean, I'm grateful, too, that I wasn't just flat-out released, but it feels really strange to be back with my family and still on my mission! I guess I'll get used to it. And I wouldn't want to slow down the elders in my mission in Cali—I guess that's what I was doing, though."

"I think the concern was for your health and comfort, not for your companions' convenience. That was the understanding I had, from the letter I received."

"I didn't complain, Bishop."

"Well, you wouldn't. I know that much about you. You're a valiant missionary—and you'll be just as valiant and valuable here as you were there. It's just a change of scenery."

"That's pretty much what President Butler told me. And I'll do my best to stay upbeat and not get discouraged. But I can't help feeling like I failed, to some extent."

"You absolutely did no such thing! Every report I've heard or read has been glowing with praise. The mission here is glad to get you—and so are the elders. You'll be a great asset."

"Well, I'll try. Thanks for the vote of confidence, Bishop. And my first assignment is here in the Fairhaven Ward with Elder Bussero, so I guess I'll see you Sunday, if not before. I'm supposed to get up every morning and do my personal study at the same time as usual, and then meet with the other elders for companion study before we go out and work. It'll just seem strange to come home and sleep in my own room instead of with my comp. And I'm supposed to rest for an hour every day after lunch." The wry tone of his voice told what he thought of that.

"You know what? I'll bet the elders'll be at your house as much as possible. Your mom'll probably feed 'em every chance she gets."

"Apparently she already has been," Elder Rivenbark said. "Elder Bussero keeps raving about her cherry-apple pie." He chuckled.

"Well—sounds like a man of good taste." The bishop was glad to have heard at least a small improvement in the missionary's spirits. "We'll continue to pray for your success, Elder—and thanks so much for calling. Who knows but what there's somebody here whose life you can touch in a way that the others can't."

"I s'pose that's possible. Thank you, Bishop. And thanks for all your letters and prayers while I was in California. I'll be in touch."

He talked over the deli proposals with his produce manager and his office girl, Mary Lynn Connors, who had suggested the idea in the first place. They debated whether to go with a supplier that would bring all the food in each day, prepared and ready to sell, or whether they wanted to hire cooks to prepare the food on-site, which would include constructing a health-department-approved kitchen behind the scenes. They also talked about the advisability of setting up a few tables and chairs, so that people could eat their selections on the spot.

"I don't know, Jim," said Art Hackney, his forehead wrinkled in concentration. "It'll take a chunk away from our produce stands as it is, just to put in the new counter and deli case. I'm not sure we could keep up all the varieties of produce we sell now if we was to cut back too much on the space."

"Personally, I don't reckon I'd sit and eat my food right out in plain sight in the grocery store," commented Mary Lynn. "I mean, it's not like we're a diner or somethin'. We're just tryin' to save folks a little time with some prepared salads and meats and stuff."

"Well, I feel pretty much the same, on both counts," agreed their employer. "And, frankly, this bid from the Southern Belles' Caterers is just too steep, and the foods they offer seem a tad too exotic for our customer base. So I think we can eliminate that one. I also think the expense of putting in a kitchen and keeping it up to standard, and hiring cooks whose food we're not familiar with is a bit beyond what I'm bargaining for. So my feeling is that we go with Libby's Catering Service. They've got a pretty good-sounding menu that we can choose from, and we can vary what we offer from time to time and see what folks will buy. They also include a couple of soups every day, which the other caterer does not. What do y'all think?"

"I'm with you on that one," agreed Mary Lynn. "That other outfit, I didn't even recognize half the stuff on their menu by name! I'd be scared to eat it, and I reckon at least some of the folks who shop with us would feel the same."

Art nodded deeply. "Most of our customers ain't the high-falutin' society types that'd run in to pick up a pint of pickled mushrooms or some anchovy and artichoke pasta salad. I think if we offer 'em a real good potato salad, and a macaroni, and some fresh green stuff, maybe Caesar's salad on some days and somethin' else on others, and have some sandwiches and all the ham and turkey and beef and cheeses and stuff available, and the soups you're talkin' about, why, I reckon we could do right well. We've already got the chicken rotisserie, and it's been popular."

"Sounds right to me. I'll start the ball rolling, then. I thank y'all for your input."

"We're protectin' our own interests, too," Mary Lynn reminded him. "We don't want you to go belly-up on account of investin' in somethin that ain't gonna work."

Her employer grinned as he turned away to make some phone calls to set things in motion. He intended to use the desk phone in his office, but the cell phone in his pocket played the little melody that Tiffani had programmed into it for him.

"Hello!" he answered, sounding gruff and hurried after fumbling with the buttons.

"Bishop? Is this Bishop Shepherd?" The tearful voice of Lula Rexford sent chills through him. He reached for the back of his grandfather's desk chair and pulled it toward him.

"Yes, Lula? What is it? How's Thomas?"

"Oh, bishop! He—he . . ." She broke off into gasping sobs.

"Take it easy, Lula. Take your time. What's going on?"

"He—Tommy—he opened his eyes! He looked right at me, and he wiggled a finger at me, I know he did! He's—he's wakin' up, Bishop, and I confess all this time I wadn' too sure he ever would." She began to sob again.

"Lula! Lula, that's wonderful," he said, flopping back against the chair in relief. He had been so afraid—but no time to think of that, now. "Lula, I'm so thrilled," he told her. "I'm going to come down there as soon as I can, in hopes he'll wake up again while I'm there. You and Tom just hang in there and say your prayers to let the Lord know how grateful you are for this moment. Hopefully, it'll be steady improvement from now on, but you know it'll still take a while."

"I know. I'm just so happy. I'm so relieved. I cain't stop cryin'! Ain't that the dumbest thing?"

"No," he told her gently, past the lump in his own throat. "Not dumb at all."

CHAPTER THIRTEEN

" . . . THE STRANGER WE HAVE WELCOMED IN"

Bishop Jim Shepherd, proprietor of Shepherd's Quality Food Mart, quickly related the news about T-Rex to Mary Lynn, whose eyes lit up with delight even though she had never met that young man. He forced himself to make the requisite call to the caterers chosen to supply the proposed deli counter before he called Trish and gave her the news and got on the road to Birmingham. The day was sunny and brisk, and the traffic wasn't too onerous, so he made good time, arriving at the now-familiar hospital by one P.M.

"Tell me all about it," he encouraged Lula, who by this time had stopped crying and was smiling tremulously, as though a more confident expression of her joy might cause a relapse in her son's condition. She gripped his hand in both of hers, while Tom stood by, nodding, a gleam of hope in his eyes that the bishop hadn't seen for some time.

"He knew me, Bishop," Lula said. "I could tell. He cain't say nothin' yet, of course, with that breathin' tube still in him, but I could tell by his eyes and by the way he moved his finger. Like this." She demonstrated a little forefinger wave. "And then, he did this." She moved the same finger sharply sideways three times. "I says, 'Tommy, you want the breathin' tube took out, don't you, hon,' and he blinked his eyes at me and tried to nod his head. I told him I was sure they'd be doin' that pretty soon, and for him not to worry about anything, and just relax. Then it was like he drifted off to sleep again. We'll go in again in a few minutes, and I'll try to rouse him. They say all his signs are real good, right now. We're just so relieved, I cain't even tell you!"

"Now, it ain't all over, hon," Tom cautioned. "Boy's got a lotta ground to cover to get well, yet."

"Oh, I know that," she replied. "But you wasn't in the room! Just wait till you look in his eyes and actually see he's awake, in there!"

Y

"So, like, what'd you say to him?" Jamie questioned at the dinner table that evening.

"I said something like, 'Welcome back, Thomas! We're mighty glad to see you improving. You had quite a spill on your motorcycle, and we've all been concerned about you.'"

"And what'd he do?" Jamie pursued.

His elder sister gave him a scornful glance. "What d'you think he did, James—jump up and hug everybody? He's just waking up from a coma!"

"I know, but—"

"Actually, what he did was wiggle a couple of fingers at me, like this." The bishop demonstrated, as Lula had done. "They've still got him restrained, so he won't yank out important tubes and things, and he can't talk yet because of them, but it was so good to know he was aware."

"That's such a blessing," Trish concurred, coming to the

table with a bowl of mixed vegetables. "Let's remember to thank Heavenly Father for that in our prayer."

Y

The news of Thomas's improvement spread like floodwater through the Fairhaven Ward, as well as to his many fans and friends in school and in the town. The bishop took calls on his cell phone and his home phone and talked to people on the street and in the store who were interested in the boy's progress. Most were delighted with the news; a few pessimistically opined that he would probably never "be the same." The bishop didn't know how Thomas would eventually be, but given the assurance he had received in blessing the young man, he was optimistic.

Doctor Scott Lanier stopped in at the store late Friday afternoon to pick up a few items, and ran into the bishop just as he was preparing to go home for the day. He was one of the optimistic ones.

"The human body has wonderful capabilities to heal itself, given the proper treatment and nutrition, and considering T-Rex's condition going into this accident, I'd say he should be fine. Of course, brain injuries are tricky and often take a long time to heal, but from what I've heard, I think he has a great chance at full recovery."

"I think he does, too," the bishop agreed. "Thanks again, Scott, for your prayers and support—especially for the financial boost you gave the family. Tom and Lula were bowled over."

"I was happy to do that," Scott said. "You know how it is when something major happens to people you care about. You cast around for something—anything—you can do to help, and in this case, there was a little something I could do."

"More than a little, my friend. And how are your spirits, these days?"

Scott frowned slightly. "Christmas was tough," he admitted. "Marybeth decided not to put up any decorations—no tree or anything—because she said they were the trappings of outmoded superstitions. So it was just another day. She spent most of it helping out at a soup kitchen down in Birmingham—and asked what I had done to help humanity's situation when she got home. I mean, she said it in a teasing way, but there was a definite barb, there." He smiled sadly. "And after all, what had I done? Moped around the house, read, called John and Meg, watched a couple of Christmas concerts on TV. Nothing, really."

The bishop thought of his own Christmas day—of how fun and fulfilling it had been, spent with his family.

"I'm sorry, Scott, I truly am," he said. "If I'd had any idea, you'd have been at our house, celebrating with us. We'd have been glad to have you."

"No, no—that's okay. I wouldn't have been great company. I survived, anyway."

"Has Marybeth said anymore about the Church, of late?"

Scott shook his head. "She just spends more and more time in her various charitable efforts. I guess she finds that satisfying."

"Well—I s'pose she could do worse."

"That's certainly true. I should be grateful, shouldn't I?"

The bishop reached out and squeezed his shoulder, giving it a little shake. "Sometimes small favors are all we have to be grateful for," he acknowledged.

Y

Friday evening, shortly before seven, Tiffani appeared in the family room dressed for her movie date with Peter MacDonald. The bishop looked up from his reading, a mixture of emotions welling up in him. She wore the requisite jeans, with a red turtleneck sweater that brought out the color in her cheeks, and her hair was styled with the front part pulled back in a complicated pattern of little twisty things, the back a tangle of dark gold curls. She looked older, suddenly—almost like a college girl, he thought.

"You look nice, sweetie," Trish said casually.

"Thanks," Tiffani replied, with an equally casual air, although her hands seemed to have a mind of their own, finding little meaningless things to do, fiddling with a pencil from the table, patting restlessly against her jeans-clad thighs, smoothing her eyebrows, and fingering the little dangly gold things in her ears.

"So!" her father said heartily. "All ready for your first date! Let's get a picture of you before he comes."

"Oh, Dad! Honestly, what's the big deal? It's just Pete."

"Just Pete?"

"Well, you know what I mean. You guys are friends with his folks. Probably his dad told him to ask me out, or something."

"Oh, I doubt that was necessary. Come on, Tiffi, stand by the fireplace."

Tiffani let out an exasperated sigh but stood obediently, her head cocked to one side, while her dad snapped her picture.

"There," he said. "Thanks for indulging your sentimental old dad."

"Okay," she said in a voice of strained tolerance, but there was the quirk of a smile at the corners of her mouth. "Now, Dad—you don't need to give Pete the third degree, all right? And I'm perfectly capable of telling him what time I need to be home, so don't worry about that—or anything, okay?"

"I'll try to be good," he promised. "But I reserve the right to worry about anything and everything I choose."

Y

He worried about the content of the movie they would see; he worried about whether Pete was a safe driver; he worried about whether Pete's standards were anywhere close to Tiffani's; he worried about whether they would each have a good time and what they would each report to their friends about the date. He worried . . .

"You're worried, aren't you?" Trish asked, when he had sighed deeply for about the fourth time and had drunk several small glasses of water at the kitchen sink. "Either that, or dinner was way too salty."

He looked at her miserably. "I can't seem to find the off button," he confessed. "Is it going to be this bad every time she goes out?"

"I hope not. I can't seem to settle down to anything, either. We're probably being silly. Pete seemed very nice when he came to get her, didn't he? Very polite and respectful and all that."

"He has nice manners," the bishop allowed. "Around us, at least," he added in a low growl.

"Jim! Do you have any reason to believe he's different, away from adults?"

"Just the fact that they all are," he said.

"Were you?"

"Me?"

"Yes, you. You acted scared to death around my folks!"

"I still do."

"Oh, not so much now. Our last visit was pretty relaxed, I thought. But when we were first getting together, and you came to visit in Arizona—I thought you'd have a stroke every time my dad asked you a simple question. Your face would turn so red!"

"Well, that was different. I was just a rube from the boonies, and he was a scholar and a gentleman—in every sense of the word. I respected him a lot—still do—and I was just afraid he was going to see me for the nervy little upstart that I was, daring to court his beautiful daughter when I had no credentials and little schooling and nothing—"

Trish interrupted him. "You had the credentials of being a fine member of the Church, with a strong testimony and a natural kindness and concern for other people. That's what my dad saw—and that's why he didn't run you off. Plus, I think he suspected that if he had, I'd have gone, too."

"Would you?"

"I'd have put up a major fuss, that's for sure. I saw your good points, too—always had—and I wanted to be with you more than with any other guy I ever dated."

"I didn't even date anybody else."

"Well, you were shy. I suppose I should be grateful for that— you might have discovered you liked somebody else better."

"Not a chance. I looked them over; I wasn't that shy. But I never saw anybody who compared."

"Do you think the kids today have that kind of steadfastness?"

"Not most of the ones I know well," he replied. "Although, to be fair, some of them might. I mean, I didn't exactly tell everyone I knew how I felt about you."

"You told Mac."

"Right. And how was I to guess that Mac would go and father a kid who wants to take our little girl out? Life's so unpredictable."

"Meant to be, I guess."

They tucked Mallory into bed, kissed Jamie goodnight, and watched the late news.

"Well, okay, it's time, isn't it?" he said, glancing at the clock on the mantel.

"If they made it into the early movie and then got something to nibble on after, it's just about time—depending on how long they take to eat. They might be talking—to each other, or to other kids they know. That can go on indefinitely."

"No it can't, because her curfew isn't indefinite!"

"She's a sensible girl, Jim. She'll be home, soon."

"You guarantee that?"

"She has twenty-five more minutes."

"That wasn't a guarantee."

Tiffani let herself in the front door just as they were turning out the lights in the kitchen and family room and feeding Samantha her bedtime snack.

"Well, hey there," her dad boomed. "How was your evening, sweetheart?"

"Fine," Tiffani said, turning to lock the door behind her.

"Did you have fun?" asked Trish.

"Uh-huh," Tiffani said.

"Did you like the movie?" pursued her mother.

"It was okay."

"Did you like Pete?" inquired her father.

"He's okay." She drifted toward the stairs. "I'm tired—I'm going to bed now."

"Okay. Thanks for getting home on time," Trish said.

"I said I would."

"Right. Well, we appreciate it. Goodnight, sweetie."

"'Night."

They stood together and watched her climb the stairs. The bishop turned to his wife in frustration.

"Uh-huh? Fine? Okay? That's all? What kind of communication is that?" he demanded.

His wife wrinkled her pert little nose at him. "Sixteen-year-old kind," she explained. "Maybe we'll get more tomorrow."

"We'd better," he grumbled. "I didn't spend my entire evening worrying, only to be repaid with uh-huh's and fine's!"

Y

They were enjoying one of Trish's Saturday morning breakfast extravaganzas when a knock sounded at the kitchen door. Trish answered.

"Come in," she invited. "You must be Marguerite Lowell! I'm Trish Shepherd. We're just having a late breakfast—won't you join us? We have way too much food."

"Oh, no, I couldn't do that," stated the woman who stepped just inside the doorway. She held out Trish's jam jar and a small envelope. "Mother sent me over to say thank you for the bread and jam. The jam's real good—I like it. Here's the jar, all washed."

"Oh, you didn't need to return the jar," Trish told her. "But thank you. Marguerite, this is our family. My husband Jim and our children—Tiffani, Jamie, and Mallory."

The bishop smiled and nodded at her, taking the opportunity to take stock of the daughter who liked to shovel snow. She was slender except for a little weight through her hips, and her coloring reflected her mother's—pale skin and dark hair—the hair, in Marguerite's case, braided into thick plaits that were pinned on top of her head. She wore no makeup, and she had a faint, dark mustache on her upper lip. She looked back at his family, almost eagerly, he thought.

"Hello," she said in their direction. "Well, I have to go back. Mother said not to stay too long. Thanks again."

"You're very welcome," Trish replied. "Come again, when you can visit," she added, closing the door behind the visitor.

"Okay, so she's weird, too," pronounced Jamie, reaching for another pancake.

"Now, Jamie, let's not judge the lady, on first meeting. We may get to be real fond of her, who knows?"

"Dad, she was weird," Tiffani confirmed. "She acted like she was scared not to do everything just like her mother said. When you're thirty-four—that's weird."

"Maybe she's just a little slow or backward," Trish said. "Let's not worry about it. Maybe we'll have a chance to get better acquainted and find she's not weird at all."

"Maybe she'd like to play with Samantha, since her mommy doesn't let her have a kitty," suggested Mallory. "Only, she'd have to play with her here. Samantha can't go over there."

"That's sweet of you, Mal," her dad told her. "But she may not like kitties, either."

Mallory's expression showed what she thought of anyone who might not like her beloved pet. "That *would* be weird," she echoed her older siblings.

The bishop sighed. They had some work to do regarding tolerance of differences.

Y

Trish read the thank-you note that Marguerite Lowell had brought and handed it silently to her husband. He read:

> Dear Neighbors,
> Thank you so much for your welcome to the neighborhood and for the gift of bread and jam. Our

Marguerite is enjoying it very much. She likes sweets, and she doesn't get very many. It's good to know we have Christians next door.

Thanks again.

The Lowells

"Nice enough note," the bishop commented. "Sounds just like the lady."

"Very correct," agreed Trish. "Do you suppose when she finds out we're LDS, she'll still think we're Christians?"

"Well—we are."

"Of course. But you know how some folks think."

"Sure I do. I reckon we'll just have to make sure we act like Christians. Remind the kids, will you, to cut back on the heathen rituals and sun-worshiping?"

"Oh, you joke, Jimmy—but you and I both know that in some circles, Mormons are considered anything but Christian! And it makes me wonder, because she's already made such a point of mentioning it, and asking Hestelle about us in advance, whether she might not belong to one of those groups."

He shrugged. "She might—but let's try real hard not to borrow trouble in advance. Let's just be good neighbors and the best examples we can of what we know and believe. By the way, Tiff didn't volunteer much more about her date, yet."

"I know. But maybe there simply isn't much to tell."

He wished he were certain that was the case.

Y

"Bishop Shepherd? Elder Bussero here. Got a problem, Bishop, and we're not sure what to do about it."

"A problem? What's that?" *Not a problem working with Elder Rivenbark,* he hoped.

"Well, it's with the Kress family. They think maybe they've made a mistake, being baptized."

"That was only a week ago! Why would they change their minds already?"

"See, it was something that came up in a discussion in the Gospel Essentials class. You remember we sang 'O My Father' in sacrament meeting? And you remember how it talks about having a 'mother there'? Well, somebody asked if that meant our earthly mothers who had died, and were waiting for us in heaven, and somebody else answered and said no, that it meant God's wife, our Heavenly Mother. Well, the Kresses freaked out, and said they didn't believe God would have a wife. I guess they've been stewing about it, and they just called and want us to come back over and talk to them about it."

"Okay. And that would be you and Elder Rivenbark, right?"

"Yessir. Only I hate to bother him with too much stressful stuff right off, you know? So I wondered if you might meet us there and help explain things to the Kresses. Since, actually, you know, our work is technically done when the folks are baptized, and then the ward takes over fellowshipping and teaching and all . . ."

"I know how it works, Elder. But just a word of advice about Elder Rivenbark—don't baby him, okay? He'd resent that, and he's used to working hard. In fact, why don't you ask him to spearhead this discussion with the Kresses? But give him a little time to prepare. And I'll be glad to be there, too. I need to visit the family, anyway. What time?"

"Seven, this evening."

"See you there." He hung up and consulted the calendar in

his briefcase, certain that there wasn't any conflicting meeting this Saturday evening, but double-checking to be sure. He was right—there was no conflicting *meeting*. However, he had penciled in, "Date w/Trish—dinner, movie."

Oh, boy, he said to himself. He had forgotten. He had planned to take her to a nice, quiet place for dinner, where they wouldn't be likely to be interrupted or distracted. It had been a while since they had been out on a date, just the two of them. The holidays had been busy, and then there'd been Thomas's accident. He'd been so tired, so worried of late. He knew Trish was looking forward to this evening out. She deserved it—and far more. He sighed and headed upstairs, where she was vacuuming their bedroom carpet. He motioned to her to turn it off.

"Babe," he began, in the sudden silence, "about tonight . . ."

He hated the stricken look in her eyes. "Something's come up, right?"

He told her. "I'm so sorry, sweetheart. I was looking forward to it, too. But I'll take a rain check for the first available evening, okay?"

She shrugged. "Sure. Another month or two—whenever you can fit it in."

"No, no, babe—I'm talking next week!"

She ticked the days off on her fingers. "Monday's family night, Tuesday, you're in meetings, Wednesday, you're going home teaching again, Thursday, I'm giving a presentation at the PTA meeting, and then it's Friday, when you told Jamie you'd take him and Buddy to the basketball game. Saturday's the Ward Game Night, and then it's Sunday, Monday, and Tuesday again. I understand how it is, Jim. You have to prioritize. Don't worry about it."

She switched the vacuum back on. Her cheeks were pink, and he suspected there were tears forming in her eyes, but she turned the machine away from him so that he couldn't see. He wanted to go to her and hold her, but he was afraid she would shake him away. He had been dismissed.

CHAPTER FOURTEEN

" . . . O'ER-RULE MINE ACTS TO SERVE THINE ENDS"

He knew he had a problem. If there was anything that distressed him more than having disappointed his wife, it would only be having disappointed his Father in Heaven. Now, he suspected that having done the first, he had done the second, as well. Something, obviously, had to be done. What was not so obvious, at least to him, was exactly what that something should be. He went downstairs, pulled on a warm jacket, and got into his truck. A thin, cold drizzle was falling, distorting the view through his windshield. He didn't have anywhere particular to go, but he wanted to be alone and unobserved for a time of pondering and prayer. If he felt he could have spared the time, and if the weather were more clement, he would have driven to Shepherd's Pass, his ancestral home and favorite thinking place. As it was, he started the truck, turned on the wipers, and almost automatically headed toward another home—the ward meetinghouse. Nothing was going on; the parking lot was deserted, and that was just how he wanted it.

He let himself into the building, locking the door behind

him, and made his way into his unheated office, where he knelt, bowed his head, and presented his problem to the Lord, asking forgiveness and direction. He knew it was Church policy for husbands and wives to set aside time each week for each other, and he had heard it said somewhere, by somebody he respected—he couldn't remember exactly who—that during the judgment process, men would be asked what they had done to make their wives happy.

He thought back over the last several months. He and Trish had gone to visit T-Rex in the hospital; they had, of course, both been involved in VerDan's wedding; they had attended the temple together, once with another couple and once with a ward group; and of course they had been together for Christmas and New Year's festivities in their home. None of these, however, had been a real date—the pair of them alone with time to talk and relax and enjoy being together.

Even their traditional Sunday afternoon walks had gone by the board more often than not, either because of other pressures or due to miserable weather. Frequently they went to bed at different hours—one being asleep before the other made it upstairs. No wonder Trish was feeling neglected! He needed to repent. She, after all, was his first priority, his companion, helpmeet, and love—without her, nothing else would matter quite as much.

On the other hand, he really did want to help the missionaries, and he was concerned about the Kress family and their confusion. He knew how much a newly baptized family had to learn and become accustomed to, and he knew he played a part in making them welcome and keeping them happily involved in Church activity. However, it occurred to him, nowhere was it written that this was his total responsibility. Others needed to be involved, too—home teachers, visiting teachers, the Gospel Essentials teacher, priesthood leaders, Relief Society presidency,

Primary presidency, and teachers for the children. In addition, the DeNeuves had been assigned as a special friendshipping family to the Kresses, having children of about the same age and interests. Any of them might help. But this was a delicate matter of doctrine, as well—and one that perhaps not everyone might be equipped to handle successfully. Again the bishop bowed his head.

Some minutes later, he arose and reached for his phone and his ward directory. He made a couple of calls, and then, feeling confirmed in his decision, called Trish.

"Jim? Where are you?" she queried. "You left without saying anything."

"I know, sweetheart, and I'm sorry. I should've at least left a note—but I didn't know exactly where I was going. I ended up at my office at church, and I'm calling to tell you that it's all set for us to have our evening out, after all."

"No, no—that's not necessary. You need to take care of whoever needs you. I'm just being spoiled and selfish, and I'm sorry. Honestly, I don't know why I acted that way!"

"Honey, you reacted that way because you were hurt and disappointed, and I don't blame you a bit. I was the one in the wrong on this, but I've got it covered, now—so let's plan on leaving about six-thirty, okay?"

"Jimmy, what are you bypassing, to keep our date?"

"Nothing that can't be handled as well or better by somebody else, so don't even worry. I'll tell you about it later. I want to be with you tonight, babe—not anybody else. They can have me tomorrow—all day, if need be. I'll be home within an hour."

"If you're sure . . ."

"Never been more sure of anything in my life. See you soon."

Y

He rang the bell at the home of the Kress family, trying to brush the icy rain from his clothing.

"Come in," invited Deborah Kress with a curious look. "I thought you were coming tonight, with the elders," she added. "I was surprised when you called."

"I apologize about that. You see, what happened was that I had agreed to come with them without checking my calendar first. I forgot that my wife and I had plans to go out this evening, and I think it's important for a husband and wife to have time together."

"Well, I can understand that," she agreed. "May I take your jacket?"

"Thank you. Sorry it's so wet. Is Jacob here?"

"He is, I'll get him. Please, sit down." She gestured into a nicely furnished living room, where he gingerly sat on the edge of a chair, afraid that his jeans would soak the upholstery. He looked around at the family portrait over the piano, the order, cleanliness, and good taste of the furnishings. He could hear happy sounds of children playing somewhere else in the house. These, he felt, were quality people. They mustn't be lost to the Church because of some misunderstanding of a doctrinal point that is new to them.

"Hello, sir," said Jacob Kress, a balding young fellow with fine dark eyes. "To what do we owe the honor of this visit?"

The bishop stood and shook his hand heartily. "To my desire to visit you folks in your home and offer my personal welcome to the Lord's Church. I was all set to accompany the elders tonight, but I'd forgotten that my wife and I have plans, and I don't want to disappoint her."

"That's commendable. Please—sit down. If you were coming

with the elders, I suppose they've mentioned to you that we're not at all sure that we've done the right thing by joining your Church, I'm sorry to say. Perhaps we were too hasty in our decision."

The bishop nodded. "They did mention that. I believe your concerns can be put to rest, though—and I've taken the liberty of asking one of our finest scriptorians and doctrinal scholars to come in my place tonight, and answer any questions you may have that might stump the missionary elders. That's Brother Levi John Warshaw, who usually goes by John. Have you met him, yet?"

"I don't think so," replied Jacob, looking at his wife, who shook her head.

"He's an interesting fellow. He and his wife were originally from Poland, but they were Jewish and were hidden and passed around as children because of all the persecution in Europe. Amazingly, they both ended up in Germany, years after the war, where they met and married—and where they eventually joined the Church. Theirs is quite a story."

Jacob and Deborah looked at each other. "Did you know that we're of Jewish ancestry?" Deborah asked slowly.

"No, I had no idea," the bishop replied. "Where were your folks from?"

"My grandparents were lucky enough to leave Germany and migrate to America a few years before the war," Jacob said. "My parents converted to Christianity in Cincinnati. Deborah's people were from Holland, and she's a first-generation Christian."

"Well, that's interesting! You and the Warshaws will have that in common. They're wonderful people."

"Um—sir—Bishop," Jacob began. "If you don't mind, we'd like to hear your take on this idea of a mother in heaven. It distresses us to think of God as a married man. It seems rather sacrilegious. Absurd, in fact! And we can find nothing in the Bible to support it."

The bishop nodded, and sent a silent prayer heavenward. "I understand your feeling. It's a radically different concept from any you might find in Judaism or mainstream Christianity, isn't it?"

They nodded in turn.

"I'm a convert, myself, so I understand a bit about what it takes to grapple with new and unfamiliar concepts and put them all together to make a cohesive picture. Frankly, I'd rather leave the deep, doctrinal explanations to the elders and Brother Warshaw. All I'd like to do is ask you a simple question or two. All right? Just to give you some food for thought."

"Go ahead," invited Jacob.

"What does a puppy grow up to be?"

They looked at each other. "A dog," replied Deborah.

"What does a tadpole become?"

"A frog," said Jacob, frowning.

"And a boy?"

"A man, of course," said Deborah.

"Then what may a child of God eventually become?"

"A . . . a god, perhaps," ventured Deborah. "But that doesn't mean that God Himself has a wife! He's the Almighty Creator, all by Himself! He wouldn't need a—a goddess—to create man, would he?"

"What have the elders taught you about eternal families?" the bishop asked quietly. "Did they explain that you and your children have the potential to become an eternal family unit?"

"They did," Jacob said. "It was one of the doctrines that seemed to ring true with us. Something that we'd dearly love to hope is possible."

"So if that is possible, and you achieved it, you would be married throughout the eternities. Does our Father in Heaven ask us to do anything that he hasn't done, or isn't willing to do?"

They were silent, obviously preoccupied with the concepts that were new to their thinking.

"But the Bible . . ." Deborah began.

The bishop smiled and held up his hand. "I know. This isn't something that's specifically taught in any of our scriptures, ancient or modern. Rather, it's implied. However, I'll save that for Brother Warshaw and the elders," he said gently. "Except that I would encourage you both to pray sincerely about this, just like I'm sure you did about the other concepts the missionaries taught you. Remember what we're told in Moroni, chapter ten, verse five: 'And by the power of the Holy Ghost, ye may know the truth of all things.'"

The Kresses looked at each other. "Fair enough," Jacob said.

Y

"Whoa, Jimmy—you didn't have to spring for the most expensive place in town, just to say you're sorry about forgetting," Trish whispered as they were ushered into a dimly lighted and posh restaurant where soft music obscured even the distant clatter of dishware. A subdued fire flickered in a three-sided fireplace, giving off a cozy warmth against the wintry rain that persisted outside. When they were seated, with menus placed before them, he replied.

"Once in a while we can afford this sort of thing. But the real reason I wanted to come here is because it's about the only place in town where we can have a conversation over dinner without having to shout over noisy music or noisy kids. In fact, it's surprising, when you think about it, that Fairhaven has such a place. I bet they don't even serve hamburgers or meatloaf!"

They opened their menus, declined the offered wine list, and thanked the hostess who lit two slender candles on their table.

"Nope, no meatloaf," the bishop confirmed. "Not that I would order it here, anyway, when I live with the best meatloaf cook in the world. Since I can't have that tonight, let's see— what looks good?"

They ended up with an appetizer of barbecued prawns—over which Trish made happy little moaning sounds—to be followed by salad, prime rib, roasted potatoes, and a medley of steamed vegetables.

"These prawns are fantastic! I've got to learn to season them like this."

"They are good, though I'd have called them shrimp. And it feels good to be here with you. Much as I love our kids, there are times when I like it to be just us."

She reached for her purse. "Speaking of our kids—look what I found when I was vacuuming Tiff's room today. It was wadded up by her wastepaper basket, so I figured it was meant to be inside. I don't know what made me look at it."

He took the half-sheet of crumpled paper and smoothed it on the table. It was covered with variations of the name of Peter MacDonald—Pete, Petey, and even a couple of Mrs. Peter MacDonald and Tiffani S. MacDonalds. He stared at it in horror and looked at Trish openmouthed. She was smiling at his reaction.

"You wanted some indication from Tiffi how her date went— how she felt about Petey. So—here you go. Offhand, I'd call it a major crush."

"But Tiff's always been so sensible! Look how she's always made fun of Lisa Lou. And even you said you didn't think she'd ever behave like that . . ."

"Keep in mind that we're viewing something meant to be

private. Even something she probably meant to throw away. I think she's just kind of trying on roles, you know? She's obviously attracted to Pete—he is a good-looking kid, and bright and personable—and she's sure to be flattered that he's showing some interest. I don't even know whether she's ever had a big crush before. Unlike Lisa Lou, she doesn't advertise her feelings to one and all—but it doesn't mean she has none."

"Sure, but this . . . this is kinda scary."

Trish shrugged. "I don't know—I used to do that with your name. Wrote it all over the inside covers of my school notebooks—and even with the 'Mrs.' attached, like this."

"You did? When was that?"

"Even before we moved away from here. And afterwards, when we were corresponding. Actually, I guess I never quit! And then one day, we went to the temple—and after that, I could write it legally, for all the world to see. You were my big crush, Jim. Thankfully, it worked out. Most of them don't."

"Yeah. Thankfully, indeed, ours did. But Tiffani and Pete . . ."

"Probably won't amount to a hill of beans."

"You think?"

"I really do. She might pine and wish and hope, for a while, but she's pretty firm in her feelings about a temple marriage, and Pete just doesn't fit in with that. I think once she realizes that, and reality sets in, it'll all just dissipate."

"But what about Pete's feelings? What if he really likes her, the way I liked you?"

"But I think your personalities are way different. You were capable of long-term patience and shy around other girls, so it was maybe a little easier for you to maintain a long-distance relationship. I doubt Pete would even consider such a thing, in the same circumstance. Nor should he—he should date lots of nice young women and find a girl who's on the same page he is. He's just a kid, and likely won't be ready for a committed relationship for a long time. Boys, after all, usually mature a little later than girls—which is why most husbands are a little older than their wives. At least, that's my theory."

"Oh, really?" He passed his skewer, one prawn remaining, across to her. "So we're a slow bunch, are we?"

"Thanks, honey." She accepted the skewer. "You catch up nicely, however. Most of you, anyway. Some never seem to."

"Yeah. Such as Dugie Winston, Jack Padgett—"

"To name a couple."

"How's Muzzie doing, anyway?" Muzzie Winston, Trish's old and dear friend, had parted ways with her husband after his lifestyle had grown too wild for her and their children to tolerate.

"She's okay. She's working full-time and studying for her real estate license. She filed for divorce, and that was hard, but I think, overall, she's feeling a little more upbeat. And, Jim—she told me she prays everyday, by herself and with the children. And she attributes that to you and the good counsel you gave her. I thank you again for that, too."

He lifted both hands, a self-deprecating gesture. "I'm just grateful the Lord gave me something to say to her, 'cause I sure didn't know what it should be!"

"Well, it helped her. Dugie's being a rat, fighting her and contesting everything she wants to do, trying to get custody of the kids—but he doesn't have a prayer, according to her lawyer."

"Will he get visitation rights?"

"Probably, supervised. After the way he snatched Brad from his boarding school and took off with him, that's about the most he can expect. How's Jack Padgett doing? Have you talked to him, lately?"

"I haven't. I need to do that. Last couple of times we talked, he was still pretty bummed about the whole thing and missing his wife and daughter."

"Does he seem to be changing his attitudes, at all?"

He considered. "I think I see a little change. He kicks and complains about his counseling sessions, but I think he's figured out that he had unreasonable expectations and that they were born out of the fear of losing Mel and Andi. Boy, I'll tell you—his childhood, his whole background, was such a mess, and it seems like he's starting to realize what an effect that had on him, too. I don't know—I have hope for Jack. I don't know whether Melody will ever want to take him back, though. That's still an unknown factor."

"I don't think she has a clue yet, herself. It's good they have time apart, for each to find out who they are, before they try to be a family again."

He sighed. "Man, I hope we're not doing anything awful to our kids, messing them up for the future! Do you think it's okay for Tiffani to not share her feelings and her crushes with us?"

"I do. I think she just has a private personality. Plus, she probably has figured out that there's not a young man out there who'll ever be good enough for her, in your eyes. Also, on some level, she probably knows she's going to have several crushes or little romances before she settles down, and she doesn't want to be like Lisa Lou, who thinks each one is 'it!'"

"Ah. I hope you're right. It's funny how, as a dad, I'm almost more anxious for my children to avoid any major mistakes than I ever was for myself."

"Mmm. Maybe it's like driving a car. When you're in the driver's seat, you feel more confident in scary situations than you do watching somebody else at the wheel."

He nodded. "Could be."

Their prime rib arrived, looking succulent and delectable.

They ate quietly for a few minutes, and then Trish said, "So, Jimmy—what is it you gave up for me tonight? You said you'd tell me."

He described the situation, while she listened intently.

"And you didn't know the Kresses were Jewish, when you invited Brother Warshaw to stand in for you?"

"No idea. Hadn't entered my mind."

"I think that was inspiration. Not that being Jewish has anything to do with the question that's bothering them, but it gives them something in common anyway. Plus, Brother Warshaw knows practically everything there is to know about the scriptures and Church doctrine."

"Right—and that's why I thought of him. At least, I think that was the reason," he added with a smile.

The restaurant wasn't crowded, and they decided to skip the movie, preferring instead to linger over their dinner, sharing a piece of Key lime pie for dessert and continuing their chat. The bishop felt himself unwinding, when he hadn't even realized he'd been uptight. It was a much-needed treat, to talk at length, uninterrupted, with Trish. He promised himself (and her, in an unspoken vow) that it would happen more often. She wasn't the only one who needed it.

CHAPTER FIFTEEN

" . . . TO MINGLE WITH MY FELLOWMEN"

Bishop Shepherd was in his office early on Sunday morning, pondering some needed changes in the Sunday School faculty, when an energetic knock sounded on the door. He opened it to see two beaming young men with shiny missionary tags on their lapels. One of them leaned on a pair of crutches.

"Elders! Elder Rivenbark, good to see you—welcome to your new mission field!" he said, shaking that young man's hand and then giving him a hug. He was glad he had caught himself. He had almost said, "Welcome home," and that would never have done.

"Thanks, Bishop—good to see you, too," responded Elder Rivenbark.

"And Elder Bussero, how're you?" the bishop continued, ushering them into his office.

"I'm good. Wow, Bishop—this one's somethin' else," said Elder Bussero, gesturing toward his new companion. "You shoulda heard him last night at the Kress's! He laid it all out on the line, point by point."

"I'm not surprised. And how did Jacob and Deborah react to that?"

Elder Bussero shrugged and grinned. "Wasn't much they could say to refute it, the way he put things. And Brother Warshaw was awesome, too. I think they were real impressed with him."

"We explained to them that all the fine points of doctrine can't possibly be covered in the missionary discussions," Elder Rivenbark said. "They promised that when anything comes up again that they don't understand or agree with, they'll study about it, make it a matter of prayer, and also ask for help from somebody knowledgeable. And like Elder Bussero said, that somebody will likely be Brother Warshaw."

The bishop drew a long breath of relief. "Good, good! Couldn't be better. Thank you both for responding to that need. The Kresses are a fine family, and they'll be almost as much of an asset to the Church as it will be to them. Now, Elder Rivenbark, how are you settling in?"

Elder Rivenbark shook his head ruefully but smiled. "Frankly, it feels really weird, but it was good to get my feet wet last night. Now I'm stoked about getting back to work! And I guess it is true that there aren't as many walk-up apartment complexes and houses with lots of front steps here as there were in my area of Cali. It's probably better for all concerned, I guess."

"I know you'll do a lot of good here. Already have, for that matter."

Elder Bussero nodded. "He sure has. He handled that question way better'n I would have. Well, Bishop, we just wanted to stop by and say hi and let you know how things went. Now we're off to pick up a couple of new investigators for sacrament meeting."

"Way to go! Thanks again."

Y

As was his custom, he looked out over the congregation during sacrament meeting with a prayer in his heart that he might be led to know if there was anyone in particular who needed him. He reminded himself that Pratt Birdwhistle was about to turn nineteen and needed an initial mission interview. Probably Dan McMillan was already on top of that, but he would check. Little Tashia Jones came in, smiling as always, and cute as a button in her yellow sweater and skirt. She slid in beside her friends, the Arnaud girls. Their mother, Camelia, leaned around her daughters to give her a welcoming smile and hug. Elders Bussero and Rivenbark accompanied a tall young black couple, pausing at the row where Scott Lanier sat alone, asking if they could sit there. Scott scooted toward the wall, then reached over to shake hands with the four. The bishop saw Elder Rivenbark's little sister, Rosalin, watching her brother with pride.

Buddy Osborne came in, sat by himself as usual, and tried to appear engrossed in the Sunday bulletin. The bishop was pleased when Jamie turned around, got Buddy's attention, and beckoned to him to come and sit with the family. Buddy declined with a shake of his head, but he smiled. Melody and Andi Padgett slipped in and sat toward the rear of the chapel, beside Frankie Talbot and her brood. He saw Brother Warshaw greet the Kress family and take them over to meet Magda. He watched for the Jernigans, but they never appeared.

Ida Lou Reams entered, with Hilda Bainbridge leaning on her arm, the two of them moving slowly to a seat toward the middle of the chapel. Dear Hilda, the bishop realized, was getting older and less well. He knew she sorely missed her husband, Roscoe, and had no living children or grandchildren to fill her hours. Her vision was too bad to allow her to read or do needlework, and even seeing the television was a strain. He blessed Ida Lou for her friendship and care of Hilda. Ida Lou helped her shop and clean, took her to the temple, and invited her over often for meals.

He smiled to see the Parsons, Lori and Joe, taking a seat close to the exit with their beautiful miracle baby, Alyssa, whose total deafness had been cured—at least in one ear—in a way the doctors had yet to explain. Alyssa now reacted to sound as any baby would and fussed up a storm during meetings. Don and Connie Wheeler were also experiencing the joys of parenting for the first time, with their little adopted baby boy, Collin. The Lord was blessing the Fairhaven Ward, and for each instance of that, the bishop was grateful. For once, he wasn't aware of anyone he should invite into his office for a talk.

Y

After Sunday dinner that afternoon, Brother Sam Wright stopped by to pick him up, and they headed to Birmingham to visit T-Rex, who, with his breathing apparatus removed, was able to speak a little and had been moved from Intensive Care into a regular room.

With a sense of anticipation, the two men knocked on the door of the room assigned to Thomas Rexford, and heard the voice of Tom Sr., inviting them in. Tom shook their hands. A reclining chair made up with a blanket and pillow crowded one corner of the small room. In his bed, T-Rex lay propped in a semi-sitting position, looking, the bishop thought, somehow diminished—smaller than he should be. The bone-structure of his face was more visible, and showed his distinct resemblance to his mother.

"Hey, son—you got you some comp'ny," Tom said, rubbing his son's arm. The young man's eyes opened sleepily, and he looked from one to the other of his visitors.

"A-ay, Bish," he whispered hoarsely. "Brother Wright."

"Hey, Thomas," the bishop said, his own voice a bit hoarse with emotion. "It's great to see you awake and talking."

"Sure is, T-Rex," agreed Sam. "Gave us all a good scare, son. How're you feelin'?"

"Weak. Like a little bitty kitty-cat."

"That'll improve," the bishop told him. "You'll regain strength now—more every day."

"Hope so. See . . ." He gestured toward the shelf that was intended for flowers and cards. "My helmet? Shoulda been—my head."

They glanced at the metallic red helmet, split down one side and dull with dried mud, but still in one piece.

"I'm sure grateful you were wearing that," the bishop told him, gripping the boy's fingers.

"Yeah, the police come and told us it looks like his head caught the edge of a tree stump," put in Tom. "That helmet may have caused some injury to his neck, but it also saved his life."

"Do you remember the accident at all, Thomas?" the bishop asked.

"No sir. Last thing—openin' presents."

"Reckon that's pretty common when you've hit your head," Sam said.

"Heard y'all was out lookin' for me."

"We split up into pairs and fanned out all over town," the bishop told him. "But it was Buddy Osborne who clued us in as to what shortcut you might have taken on your way home. And he came with us to look for you. Put his coat over you, to keep you warm, and went with us to the hospital."

"Huh. Lil' ol' Buddy. Saw him—no, hadda been—a dream."

"He's anxious to come see you. We'll give it a couple of days, though, before we bring him down."

"Yeah, the docs don't want the boy overwhelmed with visitors right off," Tom agreed. "They say he needs to gain some strength and try to process ever'thing that's happened."

"Sure," the bishop agreed. "Understood."

"Mom go home?" Thomas asked, looking toward his father.

"Gone home for a shower and a nap," his father told him. "She'll be back in a couple of hours." He looked at Bishop Shepherd and Sam. "She's so relieved the boy's woke up, she hates to leave his side. But she needs a break. We been takin' turns sleepin' here, nights, since they moved him in this room."

The bishop nodded. "Looks a little more comfy than the ICU waiting room."

"And a little darker, late at night. And, o'course, closer to the boy."

"The boy" in question seemed to have drifted back into a peaceful slumber. It was good to see his chest rising and falling in a regular, natural rhythm. The bishop gripped Tom's hand again.

"We'll be going, now. It sure is good to see this improvement. The Lord continue to bless you all."

"He has been, Bishop. He shore has been."

Y

Monday was a sunny day—a January thaw in the best sense of the word, with birds venturing out and twittering in their search for food, kids at recess shedding jackets and sweaters— and in many cases, leaving them strewn around the playground—and shoppers taking advantage of the good weather to get out and stock up on groceries and other needs. There were lines at Fairhaven's one automatic carwash and lines at the checkout counters of Shepherd's Quality Food Mart. Proprietor Jim Shepherd was pleased to see them and manned one of the cash registers to relieve the other two checkers.

"I can take you over here, folks," he called to a couple who were approaching one of the other lines with a laden cart, their backs turned toward him as they conferred over an item.

"Oh," said the woman. "All right." As she turned toward him, Jim was startled to see that it was Marybeth Lanier. The man with her was not Scott. He was Dugie Winslow, Muzzie's soon-to-be-ex. The bishop struggled to maintain a friendly, casual professionalism as he began to ring up their purchases.

"Hi, Marybeth. Dugie. How's it going?"

Marybeth smiled broadly, her very attitude challenging him to say anything. "I'm doing wonderfully, Mr. Shepherd. How're you?"

"Doing great, thanks."

Dugie didn't say anything. He looked distinctly uncomfortable.

Bet you wish you'd gone to Albertson's, the bishop thought. *I kinda wish you had, too.*

"Looks like you're getting ready for quite some event," he said aloud, noting the paper plates, cups, and plastic flatware that they were buying in large quantities, and breaking his own rule, which he carefully instilled in all his checkers, about not commenting on customers' purchases.

Dugie cleared his throat. "We happen to be in charge of a luncheon tomorrow of the Fairhaven Youth Sports Association," he said. "It's a fundraiser. Mrs. Lanier, here, has been good enough to volunteer to help with arrangements."

"It's a good cause," the bishop said mildly. "Believe I received an invitation to that, come to think of it. I can't make the luncheon, but I'll send a check."

"All help greatly appreciated," Marybeth all but sang. "It's a wonderful feeling to be involved with an organization that does so much to help our youth."

"It's important, all right," he agreed.

"We need lots more volunteers, both in this organization and in the Red Cross. Maybe, if the time ever comes when you aren't so involved in your *religion,* you'll find time to be of help to your community." Her smile continued to be bland, but her emphasis on the word *religion* dripped with vinegar. He chose not to rise to the bait. He chose not to say, "Maybe, if you weren't so involved with other causes, you'd find time to know and serve the God who made you and to respect the husband who loves and agonizes over you." He didn't say that. That would be petty. He said it later, however, to Trish.

She looked at him, appalled. "You don't think—surely Dugie and Marybeth aren't . . ."

"I'm trying real hard not to think the worst of either of them. I mean, you can't complain about community service, and of course, plenty of men and women work together on projects like that without anything shady going on. But, yes, sure, I wondered. They seemed pretty chummy. And Marybeth has become so—I don't know—so 'in your face' about her stance. I don't know how Scott tolerates it."

Trish looked pensive. "I wonder how long he will."

Y

In the backyard, in the waning sunlight of this gift of a day, her father watched as Mallory played with Samantha, trailing a twisted piece of paper on a long string around the brown grass for the Siamese to chase and pounce upon. Something caught Mallory's attention, then, and he saw her gather Samantha up in her arms and carry her behind the garage. Curiosity got the better of him, and he slipped out into the rapidly cooling air to stroll into the yard where he could see what was going on.

Marguerite Lowell stood pressed against the fence, reaching to receive the cat from Mallory, cradling it gently against her like a baby. Samantha pulled her head back indignantly to gaze into the stranger's face, her front paws pushing against Marguerite's chest, her position clearly communicating the thought, *Excuse me, but do I know you?* Marguerite turned the cat around, stroking her back and kissing the top of its head.

"Marguerite? Where in the world are you? I need you in here."

Her mother's strident tone broke the spell, and Marguerite thrust the cat toward Mallory and turned to hurry back to her house as if guilty of an evil deed.

"Hey, Mal," said the bishop, strolling forward. "Playing with Samantha, I see."

"Yep. And Mar-greet really likes her, too. I wish she could come over and play."

"I bet she wishes she could, too."

And why can't she? He wondered.

Y

By Tuesday morning, the sunshine had disappeared, replaced by unseasonably mild breezes and high-flying clouds that spoke of March rather than January and which—the bishop knew from long experience—heralded the approach of a moisture-laden storm. *Ah, well,* he thought, philosophically, *Monday had been lovely, while it lasted.*

The appointment during his lunch hour, which prevented his

attending the Fairhaven Youth Sports Association luncheon, was with the Jernigans. He had called Ralph and Linda on Sunday evening, having noted their absence from sacrament meeting, and Ralph had said that Linda wasn't feeling well. The bishop felt they needed a visit—and Ralph had learned that when the bishop wanted to visit them, he didn't take no for an answer, even if Ralph was worried about danger from the ubiquitous, unnamed "enemy" that haunted the periphery of his thinking. Most recently, of course, with the 9/11 attacks and the war in Afghanistan, the enemy's faces were bearded and their heads wrapped in turbans. Ralph had a way of personalizing general-ized threats; the bishop knew that the man wouldn't have been at all surprised to find Osama bin Laden himself, scaling the barbed-wire-topped, chain-link fence that surrounded his home.

The gates to that formidable fence rolled back, and the three guard dogs swarmed out to inspect the bishop's vehicle for explo-sives or for whatever it was that Ralph had trained them to detect. Satisfied, they returned to sit beside the steps to the house, waiting for Ralph to emerge and toss them a treat. Having thus done their duty, two of the dogs subsided into ordinary doggy behavior, one crunching his biscuit and the other rolling around in the grass in an effort to scratch his back. The third dog, a German Shepherd mix that bore a distinct resem-blance to a wolf and whose eyes revealed a near-human intelli-gence, had for some reason unknown to the bishop taken a liking to him, and now cavorted about him like a puppy, thrusting his head into the man's hand for a caress. The bishop, strangely flattered, complied.

"Corporal! At ease," Ralph commanded, and Corporal sat in place, though his eyes beseeched the visitor for another morsel of affection.

"Good boy," the bishop said. "Ralph, how're you? And how's Linda feeling? Any better?"

"Come in, Bishop. No sir, I wouldn't say she's improved. We don't know what the trouble is. Can't help wondering if she ate something from the grocery that had been tampered with. Not to cast blame on your store, you know—everybody's subject to it."

The bishop walked into the Jernigans' living room, where Linda lay on the sofa, covered with a quilt. Her face was paler than usual and beads of sweat stood on her brow and upper lip.

"Hey, Linda," he said, pulling a chair closer. "Not feeling so great, huh? What seems to be the trouble?"

"S—sorry, Bishop. I don't dare sit up. I get all woozy and nauseous. And seems like my back hurts worse when I move around, too."

"Sounds to me like you should probably see a doctor," he suggested.

"Don't trust the medical establishment," Ralph said, his own forehead wrinkled in worry. "Hard to know what to do. Maybe a blessing, Bishop? If it's not too much trouble?"

"That's never too much trouble, my friend. That's what the priesthood is for—to bless mankind—which of course, includes women," he added in Linda's direction. "I have some oil here, on my key chain. You want to anoint, Ralph, or bless? Your home, your call." He pulled out his key chain and unscrewed the cap on the tiny vial of consecrated oil.

"You bless, please, Bishop. Trust your judgment, and all."

Ralph performed the anointing, and in the blessing that followed, the bishop felt prompted to encourage the Jernigans to seek medical attention, promising that if they did so with full faith, Linda would be healed.

"I know that wasn't exactly what you wanted to hear, Ralph,

but that was what came to me," the bishop explained afterward. "And I've learned to listen to what the Spirit says at such times."

"Thought somehow the blessing would take care of things by itself," Ralph said, his brow furrowed in deep concern.

"I know. And sometimes they do. But I also think the Lord has blessed the world with lots of medical knowledge and advances and expects us to make use of what he's already given us. Now, who's your family doctor?"

"We don't have one," Linda said weakly. "Neither of us ever been to a doctor, whole time we've lived here. No clue who to call."

Ralph lifted his head. "What about that Dr. Lanier? At least he's in the Church."

The bishop considered. "Well, he's a foot specialist—but he might know who to recommend."

"Didn't he have to study general medicine before he specialized in feet?" Linda asked.

"I believe that's true, all right."

"Know him pretty well, Bishop?" Ralph inquired. "Would you call him for us? Not sure he'd know who we are. Never spoke to the man. Just heard his testimony. Seemed a good sort."

"He is a good sort. Sure, I'll call him."

He took out his cell phone, ignoring Ralph's start of alarm, and contacted Scott Lanier's office, giving his own name and explaining to the clinic's receptionist that this was something of an emergency, so that she would contact Dr. Lanier during his lunch break. Scott's voice came on the line almost immediately.

"Bishop? Scott Lanier here. What can I do for you?"

The bishop explained the situation, then handed the phone to Linda. "He wants to ask you a couple of questions," he told her. She raised up on one elbow but looked ready to collapse.

"Yessir," she said into the tiny phone. "About three days,

now. A lot of pain, yessir, clear through my body on the right side, under the ribs. No sir, it never seems to let up for long. Oh, yessir, I can't seem to stop, though there's nothing in me. I can't even keep a swallow of water down. Yessir. Okay, I guess so. Well, thank you."

She sank back against her pillow. "He says it sounds like my gall bladder. And I'm likely dehydrated. Wants us to go to the emergency room and says he'll meet us there, see that we're taken care of right. He says . . ." She paused, grimacing while a spasm of pain gripped her. "Says they can give me something to settle my stomach. That'd sure be good."

Ralph looked conflicted.

"I'll go with you," the bishop promised. "I know it's way outside your comfort zone, folks, but I think it's necessary. Let's get you up, Sister Jernigan, shall we? Where's her coat, Ralph? Or would it be easier to just stay wrapped in the quilt?"

"Coat," decided Linda, pushing herself to an upright position. "Oh, mercy, here I go again," she added, grabbing for a small, plastic-lined wastepaper basket. The bishop turned away, both for his own comfort and to save Linda embarrassment as she suffered a session of dry heaves, bringing up only a little bile.

"Sorry, Bishop," she apologized, wiping her trembling mouth with a tissue.

"No apology needed," he told her. "Here's Ralph with your coat. Your truck or mine?"

"Both, if it's all the same to you," Ralph decided. "Then you won't be stuck there, in case we have to stay."

The bishop was proud of Ralph, watching how tenderly he helped his wife into her coat. Between them, the two men basically lifted her down the front steps and tucked her into the front seat of Ralph's truck. She seemed only half-conscious as she settled back, her head drooping against the closed window.

CHAPTER SIXTEEN

Y

" . . . FEAR DEPARTS WHEN FAITH ENDURES"

Ralph followed the bishop's truck into the emergency room parking lot, then stayed with Linda, looking around protectively while the bishop ran to get a wheelchair for her.

"Hurts so bad," she whispered as they lowered her into the chair.

"Here comes Dr. Lanier," Ralph told her, as Scott hurried toward them and bent over Linda, asking her questions as they wheeled her toward the building. She answered weakly.

The emergency area was all too familiar to Bishop Shepherd, and superimposed over the present emergency was the memory of Christmas night and the battered, chilled body of Thomas Rexford, his parents' anxious faces blurring with those of Ralph Jernigan and Scott Lanier. Scott introduced them to a Dr. Copeland, assuring Ralph that this was an honest, capable physician whom they could trust. Ralph nodded curtly, his eyes still worriedly examining the premises.

"I'll wait right here for you, Ralph," the bishop said, patting the man's shoulder as Linda was whisked into an examination room. Ralph nodded again, looking like a condemned prisoner as he followed Linda and the doctors.

The bishop sank into the same orange vinyl chair he had occupied while waiting for word of Thomas, bowed his head briefly in a silent prayer, then tried to occupy his mind with a magazine. After a few minutes, Scott rejoined him.

"It probably is her gall bladder," he said. "They have to rule out a few other potentially more serious things, but that's what it's looking like. She may need surgery. In any case, they'll give her something for nausea, get her rehydrated, and make her more comfortable."

"Thanks, Scott, for stepping in. I don't know if you're aware, but Ralph has so many fears that sometimes they tend to paralyze him. He knew you from your testimony, though, and felt he could trust you."

"The poor guy's really paranoid, isn't he?"

"He is. He's been through some super-tough times—things that would shake any strong man—and this is how he's reacted. It's hard for him to venture out into any situation where he feels out of control, such as this one. So he and I both appreciate your help."

"Oh, no problem. It's good to be of use."

"By the way, I saw Marybeth yesterday," the bishop mentioned casually. "She was buying stuff for a fund-raising luncheon today—she and Dugan Winston."

"Oh, right—the Youth Sports Association lunch. She wanted me to go, but for some reason, I didn't feel I wanted to. Maybe it's because I would be needed here. Anyway, I gave them a donation."

"That's what I'm doing, too." The bishop fought his normal

inclination to avoid anything resembling gossip, but he felt a strong need to warn Scott. "Do you know Winston?" he asked.

"Dugan, known as 'Dugie'? Met him a time or two. Why?"

"What's your take on the man?"

"I don't know. Kind of a high-energy, supercharged type. Rah-rah for the cause, and all that. Why do you ask?"

The bishop shrugged. "I don't know him very well, but his wife is Trish's best friend from high school, and she's told Trish some pretty unsavory things. Their marriage is apparently over."

Scott sighed. "So many are. I'm not real sure about mine." He looked up. "Are you suggesting that he might try something with Marybeth?"

"I hope not, but I'm afraid he's not above it."

"And she does seem to admire him. Talks about all his good works for the community and so forth."

"Right. And it's hard to fault a man for that."

"Exactly. But I never thought—I guess I'm naive, in some ways."

A long silence ensued. Finally the bishop spoke.

"He wouldn't be good for her. Wouldn't make her happy. But I reckon I shouldn't judge him because I hardly know the fellow—just what his wife says."

"Well, she should know."

"That's how I see it. And she's a nice woman. Good mother. Well, Scott—I hope there's nothing to it. But just be aware."

"Thanks. But how can I say anything to warn Marybeth? She's so doggoned bound and determined to do whatever pleases her! Nothing I say holds much water these days."

"Me, either—obviously. And of course, since she removed herself from the Church, I no longer have any kind of jurisdiction or influence over her."

Scott sighed again. "Who does?"

An answer to that question popped into the bishop's mind, but it wasn't one he wanted to articulate to this sorrowing husband. It would be no comfort at all.

Y

By the time he met with his first appointment that evening, the warm breezes had fulfilled their promise and blown in a cold front that dropped the temperature a good twenty degrees and flung an icy, slanting rain-mixed-with-snow across the landscape.

"Hang on just a second, Pratt—I just need to tell Sister Reams something before the ladies start their Enrichment meeting," he said to soon-to-be-Elder Pratt Birdwhistle, holding the door to his office open for the young man.

"Ida Lou?" He took her aside in the hallway. "I wanted to let you know that Linda Jernigan's in the hospital with a bad gall bladder attack. They're planning surgery for tomorrow morning. I'll be going over there about eight o'clock to sit with Ralph for the duration, and I thought you'd want to alert the sisters. Anyone who's close to Linda at all might want to check on her afterward. I wouldn't have anyone call tonight, though—she's sleeping now, and exhausted from three days of misery."

"Oh, pore little thing! I had that gall bladder business onc't, and it's no fun at all. I was glad enough to part company with that little rascal. I thank you for letting us know. Anything else we should be aware of?"

"I don't think so, but I also wanted to thank you and Barker for taking that tape recorder up to Hazel Buzbee. How'd she do with it?"

"Well, she cottoned onto it pretty quick, and I b'lieve it'll be a pure pleasure to her. We're recording all our Relief Society lessons for her, and different sisters are bringing in other tapes they think she might enjoy."

"Wonderful. Thank you all—I really appreciate it."

He went back to his office and his meeting with Pratt with a smile on his face. Ida Lou was one of the people in the ward who helped to sustain and comfort his soul—and the souls of many others, he realized, if the truth were known.

His smile remained throughout the interview. Pratt was an excellent, cheerful, hard-working young man with a strong testimony and desire to serve—a typical product of the large Birdwhistle family, with their pioneer attitudes and practically self-sustaining log home and farm up in the hill country.

"Hey, and guess what, Bishop?" the young man said, pausing as he turned to exit the office. "We got us a computer for Christmas, and we're all learning to use it—even the little kids! They get to use it as a treat—after their other work is done. Sometimes we get stuck, though. Seems like even the manual doesn't have all the answers to the dumb things we pull!" He laughed.

"Well, don't come to me for help," the bishop advised, laughing with him. "But as I said before, my guru is Buddy Osborne. The kid's a natural—and I'm sure he'd be glad to help."

"You know what we oughta do? We oughta invite him up for a weekend, let him show us a few things. We could bring him back down for church on Sunday. But d'you think he'd even come? He seems awful shy."

"He'd come. He's shy, all right—but not so much, once he gets to know you. And I know he'd enjoy seeing how your family lives. It'd be something new and different for him. Ask him."

"I'll talk to the folks, and I bet they'll go for the idea. Thanks, Bishop!"

Y

Trish was seated at the kitchen table, looking through the latest copy of the *Ensign,* when he let himself in the back door, dripping with sleet. He slipped out of his jacket and hung it on a peg in the laundry room

"Some storm, huh?" he commented. "Glad you got home okay. Hope everybody did. How was enrichment meeting?"

She smiled. "It was good, but now say it right: Home, Family, and Personal Enrichment Meeting. If we have to say the whole thing, so do you!"

"Can't get away with anything, can I? How about HFPE? I mean, we have PEC and FHE and BYC and BSA and—"

"And think how confusing all that must be for investigators and new members! But hey—try this one on for size—TJU."

"TJU?" he repeated, unable to think of any phrase so designated.

Trish waved the copy of the Church magazine. "The jig's up," she said. "Or maybe, WFO—we're found out."

He sat down across from her and crossed his arms on the tabletop. His wife usually made sense, and he couldn't decide if she was teasing him by being deliberately obscure or if his long day had taken more of a toll on his brain than he realized.

"Sorry to be slow, babe, but I'm a couple of steps behind you here."

She relented. "It's the neighbors. They know the bitter truth, now. We're Mormons."

"Oh?"

"You know how the *Ensign* comes in a plastic wrapper?"

Had he known that? "Umm—okay."

"Well, today it didn't—and it was delivered this afternoon by Mrs. Maxine Lowell, who slapped it into my hand in a state of high dudgeon, whatever that means. I read it once in a novel, and it seemed to fit her mood. She said, 'Here's your church's publication, Mrs. Shepherd. It was delivered to our house by mistake—if you believe that the good Lord makes mistakes. I think it happened for a reason!' Then she stomped off, muttering something about wolves in sheep's clothing. Obviously she had taken the wrapper off, peeked inside the magazine, and discovered the awful truth about us."

"Whoa. Well . . ." He reached over for the magazine and looked through it. "'We Believe in Him,' 'Preparing the Way,' 'Gifts of the Spirit,' 'The Lord Is among Us,'" he listed. "Sounds like a pretty Christian concern, to me. Don't know what she's worried about. Listen to this: 'The message is clear. We believe in Jesus Christ. We believe in doing what He taught. We believe in Him as Savior of all mankind and as the Head of the Church.'"

"Right, but didn't I tell you she was one of those people who see Mormons as among the worst of the heathen hordes? I could just tell."

"You had her pegged, all right. It's too bad. I reckon she'll just have to think whatever she chooses to. But it's just ignorance, honey—and misinformation."

"I know that. But I hate it. I hate to be thought of as bad, when I try so hard to be good!"

"I know, babe, and you don't deserve it. It happens a lot, though. Certainly happens to the missionaries. Happened to Joseph Smith. Happened to the Lord, Himself, for that matter, and his Apostles. It's nothing new."

"True, but I haven't had to deal with it that much. I suppose it'll be a growing experience, if nothing else."

He grinned. "Well, it's not like the lady was all that inclined to be friendly, anyway. She wasn't likely to become your bosom buddy."

"Nope. But now she thinks we tried to deceive her. Or that poor Hestelle did. I bet now she'll be filling Hestelle's head with all kinds of poisonous nonsense."

"Miz Hestelle's known us for a long time. I don't think she'll be swayed."

"I hope you're right." Trish sounded dubious, and he didn't dare let her know how dubious he felt. People like Mrs. Lowell could do a lot of harm, if they set their minds to it.

"Sure I am. All we have to do is keep being kind to her and her family, and her hostility will melt away."

Trish's nose crinkled in disbelief. "I don't think we'll be given many chances to be kind," she stated. "We've already been turned away in practically everything we've offered."

"There'll be something," he promised. He hoped he was as right as he sounded.

Promptly at 8:00 A.M. the next morning, he presented himself at the surgical waiting room to be with Ralph, who looked about as distraught as the bishop had ever seen him.

"Hate to lose sight of her, Bishop. Doesn't feel right. Anything might happen."

"It is scary to see a loved one go into surgery," the bishop agreed. "But this is a pretty routine procedure, and Scott Lanier tells me it's a much simpler, less invasive technique than they used to have. Much quicker recovery period. She'll be home and good as new in no time."

"That's good, but I should be there with her. The enemy can take advantage, when we're separated, or unconscious. She can't watch out for herself. And they won't allow me . . ."

"Ralph, the enemy in this case is Linda's diseased gall bladder. The medical folks in there are your friends, and they're fighting the enemy for you. They're the ones with the weapons. Now, what did the ultrasound show?"

"Bunch of small stones, one trying to slip into the bile duct. Doctor said that was what was hurting her so bad."

"Right. And in order to deal with that, we have to trust the doctors and nurses long enough to let them do their job in peace and in a sterile environment. Everybody's all scrubbed and masked to keep germs out. We're doing them—and Linda—a favor by staying out here."

Ralph leaned forward, looking at his hands—strong, capable hands with black hair on the backs and bitten nails. "Know you're right, Bishop," he admitted softly. "Just can't—can't deal with the thought of maybe losing her. Things happen. You know."

"I understand. It's unthinkable. But you know what? I don't think the Lord would have prompted me in the blessing we gave her to advise you to seek medical aid if it wasn't in her best interest. We just have to hang on to our faith that things will work out right."

"Yes, sir. Stay by me till it's over? Till we know she's all right?"

He did.

Y

On Wednesday evening, Bishop Shepherd and his first counselor, Bob Patrenko, emerged from an enjoyable visit with Tashia Jones and her grandmother, Mrs. Martha Ruckman.

Bob chuckled. "Mrs. Ruckman's quite the lady, isn't she? You can tell she's strict with Tashia, but you can also plainly feel the love they have for each other."

"Strictness and love, that'd be Mrs. Ruckman," agreed the bishop. "You know she was my fifth grade teacher?"

"Believe you mentioned that. What's the story on Tashia's parents? How come Grandma's bringing her up?"

"I asked Mrs. Ruckman about that, and she said they were both deceased. I got the feeling that the less said about them, the better, so I haven't brought the subject up again."

"Well, the girl's in good hands."

"She sure is. I just hope Grandma'll keep allowing Tashia to come to church. And I pray she'll see fit to let her be baptized. She wants to, so badly."

"I'd like to see the grandmother come into the Church, for that matter," remarked Bob.

"Boy! You and me, both. Can you picture her teaching Primary? She could handle those Valiant-11 Boys with one hand tied behind her."

"Now, we wouldn't want to drive her out of the Church," Bob cautioned with a laugh.

"Let me tell you something. Nothing and nobody could drive Mrs. Martha Ruckman out of any place she wanted to be! She's tough. She used to have us boys begging for mercy when all she'd done was look at us."

"How'd she do that?"

"She'd say, 'Look at me,' and her expression would be all sad and stern and disappointed and unflinching. One of the guys, Carey Plimpton, used to say it was like facing Mrs. God. A little irreligious, I reckon, but I sure knew what he meant."

"And what would bring on that kind of look?"

"Oh—anything dishonest or mean, or way below the standard she felt you were capable of achieving. You just didn't want to disappoint Mrs. Ruckman."

Y

They dropped in on Buddy at the mobile home belonging to his mother, Twyla Osborne. Twyla admitted them, unsmiling, and yelled for Buddy, who came and invited them into his small bedroom. They sat on the edge of the bed, which was the only place to sit, and Buddy sat Indian-style on the floor.

"You see all this artwork, Brother Patrenko?" inquired the bishop, gesturing at the walls. "Buddy did all this. Can you believe his talent?"

"It's impressive, all right," agreed his counselor, while Buddy looked embarrassed.

"It's just a hobby," he said dismissively. "Passes the time, you know?"

"It's a wonderful use of your time—to develop the gifts Heavenly Father gave you," the bishop advised him. "The Lord loves you, Buddy Osborne—and so do we."

Buddy ducked his head. "Reckon I don't know why, but that's good."

Bob Patrenko smiled. "He loves you because you're his child, and he knows you inside and out. He knows what you were before you were born, and what your potential is, both in this life and in eternity. He knows the righteous desires of your heart, and he hears your prayers."

Buddy thought about that for a moment, then nodded. "That's what the scriptures say, huh? Reckon it takes a while, though, for some prayers to be answered."

The bishop nodded. "It can. Sometimes the answer is, 'Just wait awhile,' and sometimes it's 'No, that wouldn't be right for you,' and sometimes it's 'Yes, my child, I'm happy to bless you in that way.' Our challenge is to be patient and to learn to be sensitive enough to hear the answer when it comes."

Buddy frowned. "Well, so how's it sound, when He answers? I'm not sure I know how to recognize when it's Him and when it's just me, you know? My own mind. That make any sense?"

"Sure it does," Bob Patrenko replied. "We all face that challenge, like the bishop said. And it's easy to fool ourselves into thinking we've had the answer we want to get. For me, though, over the years, I've learned that the answers that come into my mind from the Lord feel a little different from the things my own mind conjures up. And the way I've learned that, is that sometimes I've received answers that I didn't want or didn't expect, and I've compared how that felt with other occasions when I suspected it was my own mind answering me, and there was a difference in intensity, somehow. What's been your experience, Bishop?"

The bishop nodded. "Very similar. And I've also noticed that I don't forget the true answers. It's kinda like they're stamped on my mind indelibly, word-for-word. Not that they're necessarily wordy. Sometimes it's just brief, like 'Have faith,' or a simple 'Yes' or 'No.' And sometimes it's just a prompting, such as 'Talk to her,' or 'Go see him,' or 'Turn right.' I may never know, in that case, what would've happened if I turned left at a given intersection—maybe I would have had a wreck and hurt someone. But it's enough to know that I was directed. 'Course, that doesn't happen all the time. Most of the time He expects us to find our own way, based on what he has revealed in the scriptures and to our leaders."

"And I s'pose you know, Buddy, the pattern we follow when we're praying to make a correct decision, don't you?" Bob queried. "How we study it out in our own mind, and make the best decision we can, and then present that plan to the Lord for His confirmation? He doesn't want to have to do all the work for us. But if we make a choice that's displeasing to him, he'll cause us to feel confused or doubtful about it, or to forget all about it, or maybe we'll get a clear, 'No.' It just takes practice in learning to follow his promptings and answers. The more we follow them, the easier it gets to recognize them."

The bishop spoke. "I think, too, if we're uncertain about an answer, it's just fine to ask for a clarification, like 'I thought I had a confirmation from Thee that this was the right choice. Is that really what I was feeling?' Because I believe He understands how distracted and weary we can be, even when we're trying really hard to discern his answers. So—does that help, my friend?"

"Reckon it does. And I reckon I've got a ways to go."

The bishop wondered what prayers Buddy was sending up and listening for the answers to. He hoped those answers would come.

CHAPTER SEVENTEEN

" . . . STRENGTH TO DARE"

Thursday on his lunch hour, he sped to the hospital and visited Linda Jernigan, who was sitting up in bed, still pale but with an expression of weary peace. A vase of assorted flowers stood on her bedside table and another on a shelf. He knew one of them had arrived the night before with Ida Lou Reams and Rosetta McIntyre.

"Hi, Bishop," she said. "I want to thank you for everything you did—helping us get here and then staying with Ralph, and all. He told me how good you were to do that."

"You're most welcome, Sister Jernigan. I hear your surgery went very well, and I'm so glad."

She nodded. "Me, too. I feel tired and sore and bloated, but I don't hurt like I did, and I'm real glad the worst is over with. They say if I keep doing okay, I can go home tomorrow."

"That's super. Where's Ralph?"

"He just stepped out to the restroom. He'll be right back."

"Linda, I just want to tell you that Ralph's a good man, and he loves you with all his heart. That's been plain to see, through all this."

A faint blossom of color began to bloom on her cheeks.

"Well," she said. "Thanks. I know he's good, but I also know that some folks think he's plumb crazy. But he's just fearful, and cautious, is all. He got that way after we lost our Jodie Lee. He watn't never that way, before."

"I understand. We'll just try to help him be reasonable about things. I think he knows his fears overwhelm him, but it's not something he can just shrug off or set aside. I believe he'd need some really good professional help to get over his problem, and I suspect that right now, he wouldn't go for that."

Linda shook her head. "He wouldn't touch psychiatric treatment with a red-hot cattle brand," she affirmed. "He'd be afraid of being brainwashed and—what's the word? Manipulated." She looked up at him shyly. "But you know what, Bishop? You been more of a help to him than anything or anybody else, so far. You're like a voice of reason that he'll listen to. I'm real surprised how he trusts you. And you're about the only one."

"I'm happy to help, however I can. Feel free to call me, okay? Anytime I'm needed."

"I thank you, Bishop. *We* thank you."

Y

"So, guys," Tiffani began that evening when dinner was over and the younger children had repaired to the family room, "Claire and I've been thinking . . ."

"Guys?" questioned her dad, looking around. "What guys are you talking to?"

"Okay, okay—Mom and Dad. Anyway, Claire and I have an idea I wanted to run by you. See, the Girls Preference Dance is coming up at school, you know? And we thought it'd be fun to double date. She'd ask Ricky Smedley, and I thought I'd ask Pete. What d'y'all think?"

He and Trish exchanged glances.

"It does sound fun," Trish said cautiously. "But Dad and I were thinking that a good policy, at your age, might be to not date the same fellow twice in a row. Kind of break it up—date several boys so you'll have a chance to learn to talk and associate with different people."

Tiffani gave her mother a weary glance. "Right, Mom. Like I have all these cool LDS guys lined up just waiting to take a turn going out with me. Maybe in *your* day it was like that, but now? Get real! There isn't anybody."

"It's not that we have anything against Pete," the bishop began. "It's just—"

"I know. It's just that he's not LDS. He couldn't take me to the temple. But honestly—you think Lisa Lou Pope jumps ahead of herself and makes assumptions! I'm not talking about getting married. All I'm talking about is one double-date, in high school, when I'm sixteen! I'm talking about one fun evening with friends. Three of the four of us would be LDS, and Pete's not the type to do anything bad, anyway. He's a nice guy."

Her mention of Lisa Lou gave her father an idea.

"Hey, I know—why don't you ask Billy Newton?" he inquired.

"Dad! Tell me you don't know that he and Lisa Lou are practically engaged! Everybody else knows."

"Oh, I'm not so sure about that. Why don't you ask him and see?"

"*Because*—if Lisa Lou's already asked him, I'd feel like a dork. And if she hasn't, he's going to want to hem and haw around because he knows she's going to—and again, I'll be the dork. I don't enjoy being a dork."

Trish leaned over the table to remove a plate of bread. "I don't think it'd be automatic dorkdom to ask him," she said. "You could say something like, 'You've probably already been asked, but if not, would you like to go with me?' He'll be flattered."

"Mom, that's not even how it's done! You have to be creative. You have to do something spectacular, like put one word of your invitation inside each of a bunch of balloons or in wrapped candies and deliver them at school or a game or someplace, so that he has to pop all the balloons or unwrap all the candy to get your name. You don't just *ask*. That's way old-fashioned."

"Seems simple and straightforward, to me," her dad said, scratching his head. "And then you know, right away, yes or no, so if you need to, you can move on to someone else."

Tiffani rolled her eyes. "How dull! Dork city. Sorry, Dad. So, may I ask Pete? I mean, if I really need permission about who I ask."

He and Trish looked at each other, seeking to communicate. Finally, he spoke.

"Look, honey—humor us on this, okay? Try Billy Newton first, and if Lisa Lou or somebody else is taking him, then you can ask Pete."

"Why don't you just come right out and ask Lisa Lou if she's planning to ask Billy?" asked Trish.

"Why are you guys so determined to get me together with Billy Newton?" Tiffani asked, scowling. "I mean, he's a nice guy and all, but so is Pete, and I have fun with him. Besides, he asked me out first, so it's only fair for me to ask him now."

"Why don't you call Lisa Lou right now and see what her plans are?" suggested her father. "Then you'll know for sure if Billy's spoken for. If he is, by all means invite Petey."

Tiffani looked from one to the other of her parents. "Y'all are weird," she pronounced, but having won a conditional permission to invite Pete, she headed for the phone on the dining room desk, preferring that to the wall phone in the kitchen where her conversation would be overheard.

Trish closed the swinging door that separated the kitchen from the dining room. "We won't eavesdrop, will we?" she said virtuously.

"No, but we're weird. Us and the neighbors." He gestured toward the east.

"Oh! That reminds me. Hestelle came over this afternoon and brought a jar of her homemade picalilli."

"That was nice of her. How is she?"

"She's fine, since I didn't mention the symptoms of any dread illness for her to adopt as her own—like some people might do, just to torment the poor lady!" She gave him a significant look.

He grinned. "She's weird, too, huh?"

Trish tried not to smile. "In a way. We've always known that. But she's also a love. Of course she came to tell me that Maxine Lowell has been over to see her—already—to take her to task for saying we were Christians when we obviously are not."

"Oh, boy. Already?"

"Sure. Maxine couldn't waste one minute before trying to destroy our reputation with Hestelle. But Hestelle, bless her heart, took up for us. She said, 'I told her that if it looks like a Christian and walks like a Christian and quacks like a Christian, then it must be a Christian!'"

The bishop laughed out loud. "That's just ducky," he said, chortling. "That's classic!"

"It's pure Hestelle. She's priceless. But seriously, Jim—if Mrs. Lowell goes around and does that with all the neighbors and spreads who knows what kind of lies about us—what'll we do?"

He shrugged. "Reckon we'll just keep being the same people we've always been—the same neighbors, the same friends, the same Latter-day Saint Christians, as best we can. Most folks around here know us pretty well and knew my family. I don't think they're going to be taken in by that kind of nonsense."

"I hope not. I feel bad enough that Maxine, herself, believes it. I suppose I should try to talk to her—but I'm not sure it'd do any good. Her mind's obviously made up, and she doesn't seem the type to change her thinking easily."

"Well, we'll see what opportunities may arise. So—are you in agreement with me about Tiffani asking the Newton boy, this time?"

"Sure, he seems like a great kid—but Lisa Lou does appear to have dibs on him. Or do you know something I don't?"

"I might. I'm not sure. But I thought it was worth a try."

Tiffani pushed through the swinging door and pointed a finger at her father. "You knew," she accused. "Lisa Lou obviously already told you that she broke up with Billy."

"Um, not exactly. But I figured it wouldn't be long in coming."

"Then you knew that she's already invited Pete MacDonald to Preference."

"No! She did? Honestly, I had no idea about that."

"And he accepted. Oh! That steams me! Lisa Lou only wants him because she knows I like him. Kind of, that is. Boy, I'm so glad I didn't go to all the trouble to invite him! How embarrassing would that be?"

"So—do you think you'll invite Billy, then?" Trish queried carefully.

"Of course. And I'll have to do it quick, before everybody at school finds out Lisa Lou dumped him. I've gotta call Claire!"

She headed back for the dining room desk, and the bishop looked at his wife, eyes wide and hands spread.

"I don't know about you," she said suspiciously. "Are you sure you didn't know about Lisa Lou and Pete?"

"I promise I did not. Lisa Lou confided that she didn't want to go steady with Billy, that's all. He's a nice boy and a new convert, and I wanted the other kids in the ward to rally around and keep him feeling welcome at church. What better way than to be asked out by another LDS girl—and one with a bit steadier head on her shoulders than Lisa Lou has?"

"Should be a win-win situation, if it works out. It might distract Tiffi from her crush on Pete."

"M-hmm. *And* keep Tiff from lighting into Lisa Lou for pre-empting her choice."

"What if Billy's already accepted another date?"

The bishop looked at his wife with horror. "That's something I don't even want to contemplate," he said.

Y

Friday night basketball games were not quite the major sporting and social events that football games were in Fairhaven, but they ran a close second and were well-attended by students and townspeople alike. Collecting Buddy, the bishop and Jamie knocked on Twyla Osborne's door, which was opened by Jeter, her current boyfriend, whose chain-smoking habit had thickened the air with a grayish haze that floated visibly between the visitors and the television screen.

"Who is it?" called Twyla from the hallway.

"I dunno," replied her friend, giving the man and boy a quick glance. "Couple of guys."

"We're here for Buddy," the bishop said. "For the basketball game."

Buddy hustled into the room, carrying his backpack. "Bye, Mom," he called. "See you Sunday, sometime after church."

"Are we dropping you at your dad's, then, after the game?" the bishop inquired, as Twyla sauntered into the room.

"No, sir. The Birdwhistles want me to come up to their place to help 'em with their new computer and all. Pratt and some of the kids are coming down for the game, and I'll ride home with them. Said they'd bring me back down to church with 'em, on Sunday."

"Oh, you'll enjoy that," the bishop told him. "It's fun, up at their place."

"You're just gettin' to be a real little nerd, aren't you, Bud?" his mother commented. "Shoulda known you would, when your father bought that dang machine. I don't see what use they are, in people's houses. Stupid waste of good time, if you ask me. 'Course, your dad was always good at wasting time—and money."

Buddy didn't answer but looked at his shoes.

"Oh, Buddy's good at this stuff, though," the bishop told her. "He taught me what I know. He's real bright and knowledgeable. You can be proud of him. Well—ready to go?"

"Yessir."

"Okay, then. See you folks!"

Neither Twyla nor her friend answered. She shut the door firmly behind them.

Y

The basketball game was fast-moving and interesting, but the activities at half-time were of even more interest to the bishop. Pratt and Moroni Birdwhistle and two of their younger siblings spotted them and came to sit beside Jamie and Buddy. Tiffani, of course, pointedly avoided them all until half-time, when she and Claire Patrenko came bouncing up and addressed Jamie and Buddy in a stage whisper.

"We've got a little job for you guys," Tiffani whispered. "If you'll do it, I'll buy you each a bag of caramel corn. It's real easy."

"What?" Jamie asked, suspiciously.

"All you have to do is take a bunch of balloons over and hand them to Billy Newton. He's sitting right over there, see? With his brother and some other guys. Okay? Will you do it?"

"Nope," stated Jamie with conviction. "I don't want any caramel corn. I'm stuffed."

"Jamie, please? For me? I'll do something else for you, later. I'll do one of your chores. I'll get you whatever you want—as long as it doesn't cost more than the caramel corn."

"No thanks."

"A-agh! Brothers! Buddy, I don't suppose you'd . . ."

Buddy blushed and shook his head. "Sorry," he muttered.

"What is it?" asked Pratt Birdwhistle. "I'll do it for you."

"Would you? That's so cool! All we need is a bunch of balloons taken over to Billy Newton. You know who he is?"

"Kid that just joined the Church? Sure. Where're the balloons?"

"Come with us. We've got somebody hiding them under the end of the bleachers."

Pratt followed Tiffani and Claire—and so did the bishop, Moroni, Buddy, and Jamie—at least with their eyes. Soon Pratt emerged, holding aloft a bunch of blue and white balloons as he marched along the front of the bleachers and climbed up to where Billy Newton sat with his group. Pratt said nothing to Billy, but grinned and bowed ceremoniously as he presented him with the balloon bouquet. Billy looked totally taken aback and rather alarmed. Pratt proceeded back to join the group, while

Tiffani and Claire hid at the end of the bleachers, peeking around to watch Billy's reaction.

The bishop peeked, too. Billy's brother reached up to capture one of the balloons, drawing Billy's attention to the fact that there was a word printed on it in black marker. Quickly they ascertained all the words, which the bishop assumed added up to something like, "Will you be my date for Preference?" One balloon apparently had nothing written on it, and one of Billy's friends indicated that it should be popped. Billy produced a key from his pocket and after a few pokes, the balloon disintegrated with a satisfying pop. A tiny piece of paper fluttered downward. Billy and his brother made grabs for it, but it found its way through the open part of the pull-out bleacher and was lost to view.

The bishop could hear Tiffani's and Claire's concerted gasp of "Oh, no!" as they realized what had occurred. He kept his eyes on Billy. The boy tried to peer down into the shadowy under-the-bleachers area, with little success. He conferred with his brother and their friends. They all looked confused. The bishop peered under his own bench. It was no use. There were strong expanding supports every so often, and they weren't constructed so that a person could squeeze between them. Only at the ends of the bleachers were there a few feet of open space. Billy wasn't going to be able to retrieve the paper that way. What would he do? And perhaps, more to the point, what would Tiffani do? Would she confess to having sent the balloons?

He glanced toward Tiffani and Claire. Tiffani was shaking her head, her hand over her mouth, while Claire was apparently trying to convince her of a course of action.

He read Tiffani's lips. "Not now!" she said. Then she and Claire began to giggle at the absurdity of it all. The bishop smiled, too, as the basketball teams ran back onto the floor. *Too bad,* he thought. *Half-time was definitely more interesting.*

Y

Tiffani and Claire were able to persuade Pratt to deliver another slip of paper bearing Tiffani's name to Billy, just as the crowd was breaking up after the Mariners' close loss on the hardwood. This he did with less ceremony, handing it to him with a smile and "Looks like you might need this," as the boy made his self-conscious way outside with his fistful of blue and white balloons. The bishop paused in place to watch Billy's reaction, which was a surprised grin when he read Tiffani's name. His friends and brother crowded in then, peering to see the name and teasing Billy good-naturedly. The bishop drew a sigh of relief. This might actually work out.

Y

Tiffani got her answer the next evening at Ward Game Night. The party was one of LaThea Winston's less-imaginative efforts, she still being in a semi-depressed state after VerDan's precipitate marriage and the embarrassment that had accompanied it, but it was still a fun occasion with various table and party games going on simultaneously. The bishop and his wife kept a discreet eye on Tiffani, who had started to fret because she hadn't received an answer. She had threatened to boycott the party, saying she preferred to stay home and read a good book rather than take part in such childish activities. Claire, however, had prevailed, telling Tiffani that if *she* had to go, then so did Tiff. Plus, Claire reminded her, it was entirely possible that Billy might be there and planning to give her his answer. Billy indeed was there, but he was totally involved in a game of Foosball that someone had lugged in, and he acted as though none of the girls in the ward existed.

Come on, guy, the bishop encouraged silently. Be a gentleman! Don't ignore my daughter. Be man enough to tell her yes or no!

About halfway through the evening, Billy's brother and one of his friends strolled in. His brother carried a bouquet of multicolored balloons. They stood at the entrance to the cultural hall, looking around until they spotted Tiffani. She saw them about the same time, and her face suddenly flamed. They marched over and silently presented her with the balloons, then turned and left with barely a glance in Billy's direction. They evidently had their instructions.

Several girls gathered around Tiffani, chattering excitedly, and a number of adults looked on curiously as well. Lisa Lou joined the group, peering over Tiffani's shoulder. Once again, the balloons were read. The bishop learned, much later, that the message read, "Sure—I'd like to go—to Preference—with you. From . . ."

Again, the blank balloon had to be popped, but this time the slip of paper wasn't lost. It read, "B. Newton."

"Cool!" Lisa Lou's enthusiasm rose above the cheers and congratulations of the other girls. "Yay! Good for you!"

Tiffani threw Lisa a raised-eyebrow look that, as Trish said later, spoke volumes. Trish informed him that it should be interpreted, "Yes, you'd better be glad that I'm willing to ask the boy you just dumped, since you moved in on the guy I wanted to ask." In any case, the bishop was glad that it was only the look that was expressed and not the sentiment in spoken word. She also tossed a shy smile in the direction of the Foosball game, and shortly afterward, Billy Newton found a reason to exit the party.

The bishop stretched tiredly at home later that evening, after receiving Trish's interpretation of The Look. "You know what?" he asked. "It's fun watching them, but I wouldn't want to be that age again for all the balloons in the world."

CHAPTER EIGHTEEN

" . . . MORE LONGING FOR HOME"

The new deli counter at Shepherd's Quality Food Mart was shaping up nicely. The proprietor watched with satisfaction as the refrigerated, glass-fronted display case was being set in place and an area of dark red and green vinyl tile-flooring laid around it. The colors set it off nicely and would call the shoppers' attention to the new wares.

"What d'you think, Mary Lynn?" he asked as she stood nearby, chewing on the end of one lengthy strand of brown hair and watching the floor bloom in color.

"It's way spiffy," she commented. "Onliest thing is, it makes the rest of the old gray floor look dull."

"We'll give it a good shine once they're done with all the construction."

"I think maybe—what about having a coupla nice leafy plants on top of the case? Green stuff always makes a place look friendly. And we're puttin' out a platter of different samples every day, ain't we?"

"We are," he agreed. "And I've taken out some ads in the

Lookout, to let people know about our new products. I'm hopeful it'll be a success. We're not as fancy as the big guys, but that was never our intention."

"You know, I ain't sayin' you should do this, Jim, but lots of folks shop the big places purely because they can get their booze and smokes there, same time they shop for food."

He nodded. "I know. But that's something we haven't done since I took over the store. You know me, Mary Lynn—I figure it's a matter of conscience. I don't condemn anybody who smokes or drinks, but on the other hand, I don't want to contribute to anybody's lung cancer or death by drunk driving."

"Uh-huh. Figured it was that. Lady was in here the other day, fussin' about it, and Yvonne told her something along those lines. She was real snippy, this lady, and she says, 'Well, then, he shouldn't oughta carry anything with preservatives or saturated fats, either! He doesn't advertise to be a health food store.'"

"Wow. What'd Yvonne say to that?"

"Somethin' like, 'Well, we specialize in good, fresh food—locally grown, in season. There are other stores in town that do carry tobacco and alcohol. In fact, there's a liquor store just around the corner, there.'"

"Good for Yvonne!" He made a mental note to give that checker a little bonus for good customer relations.

"She's real nice, Yvonne is," Mary Lynn agreed. "Oh, hey—I'm sorry, I plumb fergot! That guy—the one who abused his wife? He was in here the other day, askin' fer you. It was when you was at the hospital with that one lady."

"Oh—Jack Padgett? Thanks. I'll try to get in touch with him."

"He seemed a little nicer, or somethin', than the last time he was here. Perliter, or somethin'."

He smiled at her. Mary Lynn was a perceptive person. "I'm glad," he said.

Y

Saturday morning, the Relief Society was hosting a brunch at the bishop's home in honor of the visiting teachers in the ward. Tiffani, the proud owner of a new driver's license, carefully pulled away from the curb in Trish's car, bearing the precious cargo of her younger siblings off to an early children's movie. The bishop stood at the window, his arm around his wife, as both of them took deep breaths. He squeezed her shoulders.

"We prayed," he reminded her. "And she's been a good, careful driver, so far. She's real precise and smooth, just like I tried to teach her. The weather's nice, roads are dry. I believe they'll be just fine."

"I sure hope so. It's just . . . she's still so inexperienced."

"Only way for her to get experience is to drive."

"With Mal and Jamie, though . . ."

"I know. All our dear little eggs, so to speak, in one moving basket."

"I'll try to have faith. Oh, good—here's Ida Lou, and it looks like she's brought Hilda and Sister Mobley. I hope everybody carpools—we'll be taking up a lot of street parking as it is."

"Hello, all!" called Ida Lou as she held the kitchen door for the older ladies. "Hope y'all don't mind us comin' in the back. It's closer to the car. Is that okay, Trish, that I pulled right up to the garage?"

"It's fine. Jim's already got his truck out on the street, so we could get as many cars in the drive as possible. How are you, ladies?" Trish gave each of them a hug and escorted Hilda to a chair.

Ida Lou went back to her car and brought in two covered baskets of muffins.

"I made these here oat and fruit muffins. I hope people like 'em. Barker and me, we think they're real good. Countin' the applesauce, they got five kinds of fruit."

"Sounds yummy to me. Thank you! I made some blueberry and some cranberry orange, and I've got the juice and cocoa ready to go. Sit down, everybody."

"And, hey there, Bishop, how're you this mornin'?" Ida Lou greeted, vigorously shaking his hand.

"Doing just fine, Sister Ida Lou," he returned and went to shake hands with Hilda and Nita. "Nice to have you ladies here."

He reached to scoop up a curious Samantha who was eyeing the muffins on the counter with interest.

"Oh my, y'all have got you one of them cute Siamese kitties!" Ida Lou exclaimed. "We used to have us one of them, and I'll tell you what, he was the smartest thing I ever did see. Is this one real smart, too?"

"She's smart enough to think she should be in the middle of everything we do," the bishop confirmed. "I can't compare her to other cats 'cause she's the first one I've ever owned."

"Or been owned by," Trish said wryly. "Sometimes I feel like she thinks it's her house, and we're allowed to live here and be her servants and playmates."

"Well, yes, that's about right. But let me just tell you what my cat did, one time. Two young missionaries had stopped by the house to visit. They did that a lot—still do, for that matter, on account of they know I'll feed 'em at the drop of a hat!" Ida Lou chuckled. "But, speakin' of hats, this was back when the elders had to wear a straw hat in the summer months, and one warm day these two fellows come in to have a cool drink and rest their feet for a spell, and one of them boys—he watn't the brightest star, let me tell you, and he watn't the sort should've been out teachin' the gospel, either, 'cause he had no manners nor testimony neither, that I could see—well, anyway, he comes in and grabs my Siamese cat—ol' Sultan, we called him—by the tail and holds him up in the air! Well, you can imagine how many points that won him, with Sultan and with me. I says, 'Elder, put that cat down! That hurts him, and hurts his dignity, too. You oughta know better'n that! Where's your manners?' And he says, 'I got no use for cats. Where I come from, we shoot 'em on sight.' Well—that tells you his mentality.

"I didn't say no more about it, and poor old Sultan, he goes off a-shiverin' his fur and switchin' that tail, and I knew he was fit to be tied. I was, too, but I served them boys some lemonade and cookies, and they sat on the sofa and put their straw hats up behind 'em, on the back of it. Well, purty soon, here comes Sultan, sneakin' around the other way, real quiet. And he leaps up on the back of the sofa, so's they don't see him, and goes and sniffs each hat. Then he picks the one that belongs to that elder, takes it in his teeth, and drops to the floor, quiet as you please. I'm watchin' this, mind you, and not sayin' a word, on account of I figure it's well deserved. Time comes for them to leave, and the one says, 'Where's my hat? I put it right up here.' And I says, 'My goodness, I don't know. Let me look around.' So I track down ol' Sultan, and he's got that hat under the bed, just plumb chewed and ripped to smithereens! I whisper 'good boy!' and take it back to the elder. He says, 'That blasted cat done this!' and I say, 'I'm afraid so, Elder. I reckon he didn't 'preciate your treatment of him.' And I didn't offer to pay for that hat, nor nothin', ain't that awful? Reckon I oughta repent of that. But land, it was funny!"

The bishop laughed heartily. "Cover your ears, Samantha,"

he advised. "Don't get any ideas of revenge just because I put you in timeout."

"And you know what else, about that missionary?" Ida Lou added. "Not too long after, he got packed off home in disgrace, for somethin' or other, I never heard what. I don't reckon it was for mistreatin' animals. But I watn't at all surprised."

When more sisters had arrived and the brunch was well underway, the bishop slipped out to his truck and ran a few errands—one of which just happened to take him by the movie theater where his children were supposed to be in attendance. Sure enough, there was Trish's car, appropriately parked and locked. He drew a sigh of relief.

"You big fake," he chided himself as he drove away. "You were just as worried as Trish."

When he had completed his errands, he drove to the town of Oneonta, where he had arranged to meet Jack Padgett for lunch at a small café. Jack was already there, seated in a booth and reading a newspaper when the bishop entered and slipped in across from him. They shook hands across the table.

"How are you, Jack?" the bishop inquired.

Jack shrugged. "I'm getting by. Well, actually—I'm kinda having a tough time, if you want the truth."

"I'm sorry to hear that, but you bet—I always want the truth. What's going on?"

Jack glanced away, out the window to the parking lot, where the winter sun was glinting off windshields. He blinked at the glare and turned back. "Been eight months, you know. Since I've seen them. Except for that one time, by mistake, when they were shopping on the south side of town and I was on the way to my store. That's been six months—and we didn't talk or anything, then. I don't think Andi even saw me. Mel snatched her away real quick."

"You've been real faithful about obeying the restraining order."

"Yeah. It's okay, you know, during the week, because I stay real busy, going from store to store. Opened another one, did you know? In Gadsden."

"That's good."

"Yeah. Business is real good. But weekends—man, they're the pits! Nothing to do, nobody to be with. I see every movie that comes out, whether it's something I'm interested in or not. I go to church on Sunday, but it's not like I'm a permanent part of the ward. Went to a ward dinner over there one time and swore I wouldn't do that again. I mean, everybody was nice and all—but that was the problem. They ask questions, you know what I mean? They see my wedding ring, and it's 'Where's your wife, Brother Padgett?' Or, 'Do you have any kids?' Or, 'How long do you expect to be with us?'" He shook his head. "I don't know how to answer any of that! What do I say? 'Well, my wife and daughter live over in Fairhaven, but I'm here because I'm not allowed to go near them. See, I was so rotten and abusive the police issued a restraining order.' Yeah, that'd go over real well, wouldn't it?"

"The bishop there knows, though, doesn't he?"

"Right. He said he wouldn't tell anybody the situation, so that I could feel okay about coming to church. And I appreciate that. You know what's funny? I feel closer to Mel and Andi at church than anywhere else. I s'pose that's because it's something we did together—going to church, hearing the same teachings and all. It kinda makes me feel good, to hear those things now. Except, you know—guilty as hell, too."

"Hey!" said a young waitress brightly. "Y'all ready to order?"

They gave their orders, the bishop taking Jack's word that the chicken-fried steak was the best thing on the menu.

"And see, that's another problem," Jack said, watching the slender, swaying retreat of the server. "I'm starting to look at women. I mean, I think about Mel all the time—but she's untouchable. There are women available, all over the place, who're very touchable. Man, I mean—the Lord was right when He said man shouldn't be alone. I haven't done anything, though, Bishop—no dates, nothing. But I'm afraid I'm looking—with interest."

"It'd be tough not to," the bishop agreed. "I understand how it is—you're in limbo. Married, but with no access to your wife—not even allowed to communicate with her. Anybody'd find that frustrating. Anybody with morals, anyway—and a belief in the sanctity of marriage—and I know that includes you."

"Yeah, I guess. Well, sure—I believe in those things." He glanced out the window again. "And Mel always wanted to go to the temple. Oh, well—guess that's a forgotten dream."

"Not necessarily. It may take a while, but it's still in the realm of possibility. If, of course, you folks both want it and are willing to work for it."

"I am, honestly, Bishop. If I can just get through this. I thought it'd get easier with time, but I was wrong. It's getting harder. That's why I contacted you. Any suggestions you have, I'd be grateful for."

The bishop sent up a quick and silent prayer for wisdom. He was given a brief reprieve as their food arrived and they buttered their rolls and settled into eating.

"Jack, how did you come to join the Church?" he asked. "I'm pretty sure you weren't raised LDS, were you?"

Jack snorted. "Not hardly! No—I joined when I was in the Marine Corps. One of my buddies was a member, and he used to take me and another guy to church activities with him. Funny, now that I think of it, that I actually enjoyed going. It was so different from anything I'd ever done—and the girls were so cute, and so nice—there was a good feeling there. I guess you'd even say a homey feeling, although that word didn't have the same meaning to me that I s'pose it does to most people. But it was all light and friendly, and I thought it was so cool that people could laugh and dance and have a good time without hangovers the next day!

"Anyway, finally I started going with my pal on Sundays. I'd never had any kind of religious training, growing up, and at first I thought it was all pretty weird and hard to swallow. Then I got into a Sunday School class that was taught by a really great guy. He was a test pilot in the Navy, and he was sharp and very knowledgeable about a lot of things, the gospel included. He convinced me that I could find out for myself if the Book of Mormon was true, if I would sincerely read and pray about it."

"So you did?"

Jack looked at his plate. His voice, when he answered, was hoarse. "Yeah. I did."

"And you got an answer?"

"Yeah. And I think it was real. But over the years, I kind of forgot about it. I started to think, 'Nah—all that's a bunch of bunkum.' But I still went to church because it meant a lot to Mel, and I thought it was okay for Andi to learn all that stuff about Jesus that I'd never known about as a kid. But I'd begun to be a doubter. I'd listen to people bear their testimonies, and I'd think, 'Yeah, right. Tell me another one.'"

"I see. How do you feel about it now?"

"I've been trying—my therapist, Brother Tappan, he's been helping me—to get back in touch with what I felt back then—when I first joined the Church and when I first met Mel. It's hard." He chuckled, but it was a choking sound with an overtone of unshed tears. "I guess you could say I've come a long way, baby—in the wrong direction."

"That can be reversed," the bishop said quietly.

Jack drew a ragged sigh. "Man, I sure hope so. Looking back, that's the only really happy time in my life. I'd sure like to feel that way again."

"You know, Jack, repentance is a great blessing. It's the only way back to that clean, free, happy feeling. God'll forgive you, when you've truly gone through the repentance process. In fact, He says He'll forget all about your sins."

"Yeah—but how can I? And should I?"

"Yep, you'll need to do the same. Forgive yourself—and others."

"Brother Tappan says I need to make peace with the memory of my folks. That's pretty nigh impossible. "

The bishop nodded. "Just try to let them go. They did their damage to you and your brother, but then, they didn't have the benefit of the gospel in their lives, either. Maybe they had no faith, no belief, no understanding of their relationship to God— or yours. It's hard to say, now—but they might've done differently if they'd had that understanding."

"Hard to imagine either one doing any different."

"I know. But according to our belief, they're in a place now where they can learn a happier way, if they will. They may already be aware of the truth and wishing they'd done better by you boys."

Jack raised his eyebrows. "I've always pictured them roasting in hell, yelling and cursing and blaming each other, just like back home."

The bishop smiled faintly. "That'd be a temptation, all right. I'd imagine they're in the spirit prison, from what you tell me of their character, and I suppose that's not always the happiest place, or the best company. But real hell—I believe that comes later, after the final judgment, for those who won't repent in this life or the next or who've committed unpardonable sins. But even that apparently isn't a permanent situation, except for those who are cast into outer darkness. Most who suffer in hell and pay for their sins themselves are eventually saved in a kingdom of glory."

Jack snapped his fingers. "Shoot! And here I was hoping they'd suffer forever." He smiled sadly. "I'm kidding—I guess."

"Well, one thing you can be sure of—that the Lord knows exactly how to handle your folks. But the important thing right now is you. Getting yourself back on track, emotionally and spiritually. Breaking the abuse cycle, letting that part of the family heritage be stopped forever."

"I know that if Mel and I ever get back together, things'll have to be totally different. And I realize now that controlling her doesn't work. It wasn't even what I needed to do—I just thought it was the only way to keep her. Like I've said before—I thought she'd take Andi and leave if I didn't watch her every minute and control where she went and who with. I s'pose I knew, deep inside, that was what I deserved to have happen. Them leaving, I mean."

"I'm no therapist, as you know, but I wonder, Jack, when did you start that kind of controlling behavior? Was it early on, when you were dating Melody or first married?"

Jack thought. "I know I felt jealous when we were dating and she'd talk to other guys. I mean, she was so gorgeous, and she was this sweet, innocent little Mormon girl, and a lot of guys were attracted to her. I felt incredibly lucky that she liked me back. But I didn't do anything about my jealousy then. After we were married, I told her I didn't want her talking to other men, especially not alone. Not at church or anywhere. One time I really embarrassed her when she was talking to a guy who stopped by the house. I kind of threw her back into the living room and told him to get off the premises and stay off. I thought he was making a pass at her. Turns out he'd been assigned to help with the Church magazine drive, is all. So it all just kind of grew—and then, when Andi was born, I was so crazy about her I got kind of paranoid about losing her. I was jealous even of Mel getting to spend time with her without me. Now, look at me—I don't have either of them, and haven't even seen them for months. Great job, huh!"

"We all make mistakes. Yours are more serious than some, that's true. But I still think with complete repentance and therapy to help you realize the whats and whys of your behavior, you can get through this in good shape."

"Bishop, I sure hope you're right. But what do I do about looking at women? About the thoughts and temptations?"

"Same thing any single LDS man has to do. Distract yourself with acceptable things. What do they call it? Sublimating. That's it. And it might sound kind of simplistic, but it really does work to replace negative thoughts with positive ones. Keep good reading material handy, including the scriptures and the *Ensign*. And other good books, on whatever you're interested in. Get yourself a hobby. Learn to tie flies or build furniture or play the guitar. Something you've never had the time to try. Take a night class. Learn a new language. Get into genealogy—maybe see what you can find out about your mother's parents. Maybe you'll come to understand her better. Stuff like that can help to pass the time for you and make you a stronger and more interesting person at the same time." The bishop sat back. He felt, suddenly, as if he were counseling Lisa Lou or T-Rex or VerDan.

Jack was nodding thoughtfully. "What hobbies do you have?" he inquired.

"Me?" The bishop sighed. "Certain things have developed a new value for me, this last year. Sleep. Spending time with my kids—and time alone with Trish. Hobbies? I like Nascar racing. Love truck races, 'cause that's what I did as a kid—souped up my old pickup and raced it on Saturday mornings. I like to read—mostly history and Church books. Like country music— the old style, not so much all the hybrid stuff they play now, the so-called 'new country.' Give me Hank Williams and Loretta Lynn. Come summertime, I don't mind working outside in the yard and garden, though I complain about it. Really like to go hiking and tramping around up at my great-grandpa's old place up in the hills. Best thinking place I know. Enjoy taking my boy fishing and camping and to ball games. And I like working with people. I've pretty much enjoyed all my Church callings." He grinned. "Maybe some of those things qualify as hobbies."

Jack was pensive, gazing out the window again. "I used to like building model airplanes," he said softly. "I'd be so careful to do it just right, and put extra touches on 'em, like they were real planes that I was personalizing. My old man smashed most of 'em one day, in one of his drunken rages. I didn't do it anymore, after that. But it's funny—it wasn't my planes I missed so much—it was the making of 'em. That make sense?"

"Whole lot of sense. In lots of things, I think it's the process that counts, much as the end result. It's good to enjoy the journey. Maybe life's like that, when you think about it. So allow yourself some pleasures along the way, Jack. Life needn't be all work and struggle. Just keep away from the forbidden pleasures. You know what they are."

"I'll do it, Bishop. I swear to you, I will."

The bishop believed him.

CHAPTER NINETEEN

" . . . SHOULD YOU FEEL INCLINED TO CENSURE"

And then, she had the nerve—the unmitigated gall—to say that we were violating a city ordinance by having so many extra cars parked along the street! Have you ever heard such a thing?"

Bishop James Shepherd looked at the sparkling eyes and flushed cheeks of his beloved wife, thinking that such a display of temper was, thankfully, rare with her—but also that it was undeniably becoming, something he didn't dare say while she was in the heat of battle—or, in this case, the rehash of a battle.

"So what'd you say?" he asked.

"Well, I pointed out to our dear neighbor that no one's driveway was blocked and that there was plenty of room for people to back out into the street and for two-way traffic, so I didn't think she had cause for alarm."

"And she said . . ."

"She said that we had no business hogging all the street parking, no matter what kind of Mormon meeting we were having over here, and that we shouldn't invite more people over than we can accommodate in our own driveway."

"That's absurd. There's street-side parking all along this street, both sides, and everybody has access to it, whenever they need it. Always been that way."

"I know! She just wants to cause trouble. Any excuse will do. And you should have seen her craning her neck to get a look at the sisters in the house! I stood back and asked if she'd like to come in and discuss things, and she said, 'Certainly not! I'll take the matter to the proper authorities. I'm just giving you fair warning.'"

"My goodness. Did any of the ladies hear all this?"

"Most of them were in the dining room, but Ida Lou caught a little of it, and Rosetta could see that I was upset and took me aside to ask about it. She thought it was outrageous, too. I didn't tell anybody else because I was afraid people would leave early. Oh! That woman! I wish she'd never moved here."

"Sounds like she's determined to try our patience and our faith," he agreed. "Reckon we'd better be up for the challenge. Maybe I'll step over and have a word with her."

"Do you think you should? She'll probably call the police and say you're harassing her."

"Hmm. Too bad we can't take over a pie or something, with a nice note, apologizing for causing her any inconvenience. Turn the other cheek, you know?"

This was not a concept his wife was ready to entertain. "Jim Shepherd! You think *I* should apologize to *her*? I can't believe you said that!"

"Babe—I don't mean that you *ought* to have to apologize. You did nothing wrong. But sometimes a soft answer really does turn away wrath."

"I doubt it would, in her case."

"Well, maybe not. Did the kids get home all right?"

She nodded. "Thankfully. The poor things saw the state I was in, banging things around the kitchen when they came in, and scattered to their rooms for the duration." She allowed herself a tight little smile. "I haven't been this mad in a long time."

He held out his arms, and she came into them, but stiffly, and still trembling with indignation. "No, you haven't—not since I tried to break our date."

"I wasn't even this mad, then. Just a little hurt. But honestly, this woman brings out the worst in me."

He nodded against her hair. "Some people have a gift for that," he agreed.

A sound of building, hammering, worked its way into his consciousness. He realized that it had been going on for some time.

"What's going on? Who's building?" he asked, lifting his head.

"I have no idea. I've been too upset to notice."

"Think I'll check." He squeezed her arms, released her, and went out the kitchen door, his ears attuned to the direction of the sound. It seemed to be coming from behind his garage. He went around that building and found two workmen constructing a six-foot-high board fence just inches east of his own three-foot pickets.

"Hey, there," he greeted. "You fellows putting up a fence for the Lowells?"

One of the men squinted at him in the summer sunlight. "Yessir, that's what they hired us to do. Six foot high, clear to the sidewalk. Didn't check with y'all first, huh?"

"No, indeed. We've always kind of enjoyed having an open

view between our yards—at least when Mr. Jenkins lived here. But I reckon the Lowells feel differently."

"Seems like it, all right. The lady seemed in a big hurry, told us she needed it up on the first day the weather would allow."

"I see. Okay, thanks."

He stalked back into the kitchen, feeling a bit warm under the collar himself.

"A fence," he told Trish. "Lowells are putting up a board fence, just the other side of ours—except theirs is six feet high, all the way out to the sidewalk."

"You've got to be kidding! Why would they do that? Is that even legal? Do the codes allow it? Did Mr. Jenkins give permission? They're only renters!"

"I don't know, but you can bet I plan to find out."

He called a friend from high school, Rand Ezell, who served on the Fairhaven City Council. Luckily, Rand had just returned from a round of golf in the winter sun.

"Yep, Jim, I'm afraid they're within their rights, long as they have permission from the owner," he confirmed. "If it was a corner lot, they'd only be able to put up three feet of fencing for the first five yards back from the street or sidewalk, so the fence wouldn't block the view of drivers. But between inner lots, like yours, six feet is the allowed height, all the way front to back. Now, it'd only be common courtesy for them to visit with you about their plans before they carried them out, but it's not required. Sorry, chum!"

He thanked Rand and sat back, thinking for a minute. Then he flipped open the phone book and searched for a number—that of Margery Roane, a friend of Mr. Jenkins's daughter Rosemary. He called and asked Margery, whom he knew slightly, for Rosemary's number, telling her he wanted to contact Rosemary's dad.

"You know what?" Margery replied. "I had a call from Rosemary the other day. Her dad passed away very suddenly, just over a week ago. They went ahead and buried him down in Talladega, by his wife, with just a graveside service. He didn't have any family left up this way, so they didn't plan a funeral or anything here. I didn't even see a notice of it in the paper."

"Is that right? Well, that's too bad. But there should have been something in the paper—he still has lots of friends here, I'm sure. My problem is, I wonder if Rosemary gave the renters of her dad's house, which is next door to mine, permission to put up a six-foot fence?"

"Well, I don't know about that, of course, but it seems like she said the renters were actually planning to buy the place, on kind of a rent-to-own basis for a while, so she's prob'ly told them to do whatever they want to it. I have her number, if you'd like to ask her."

"Would you mind giving it to me? I just might decide to check with her."

Margery supplied the number, and he thought for a few more minutes. Finally, he picked up the phone and dialed. He offered his sympathies to Rosemary Jenkins Beade, told her that her father had been missed since he moved away and had been a fine neighbor, then asked his question.

"The Lowells? Right—they're renting with an option to buy. They asked if they could do some fixing up, and I thought sure, why not? A little painting, landscaping, a new fence—it all sounded like it would improve the property. I'm sorry if they're annoying you folks, though."

The bishop was curious. "D'you mind if I ask if they had references, when they accepted your offer?"

"They had one, from their preacher. It was glowing. Good

Christian family, totally responsible and dependable and honest—all positive."

"Uh-huh. I see. Okay. Thanks—oh—did you meet them, in person?"

"Just the wife. Kind of a no-nonsense lady, I thought."

"M-hmm, that'd be Mrs. Lowell. Thanks so much." He hung up.

It looked as though the fence couldn't be stopped. What was it the poet had said? "Good fences make good neighbors." Well, maybe so. His personal feeling was that good neighbors shouldn't need such good fences.

Y

The ward choir sang in sacrament meeting. Bishop Shepherd was gratified at both the quality and the quantity of the singers and how well they blended—although he did think he could detect LaThea Winslow's soprano above the others. By and large, considering their reluctant origin as an organization, he thought they were great and complimented them extravagantly in his remarks. He was pleased that six of them were participating in the stake choir for the upcoming conference in Birmingham.

He was also pleased to see in attendance, for the first time since the Sunday before Christmas, Tom and Lula Rexford. He had greeted them in the hallway before meeting, where they were mobbed by a crowd of well-wishers and inquirers about T-Rex.

"He told us to come," Lula had proclaimed happily. "He says, 'Y'all, get on out of here and go to church! You been slackin' too long, hangin' around this boring old place.' Besides, now that he's in rehab, they won't allow us to stay there twenty-four-seven."

Tom added his bit. "Boy's doin' real good; they've got him up walkin' around the place. He's still kind of dizzy and off-balance, and his vision's kinda fuzzy, but his mind seems clear, and he's gettin' better every day. We're just real grateful—to the good Lord and to all y'all folks."

The bishop was just real grateful, too. This was the most he'd ever heard Tom Rexford say at church.

Y

He caught up to Buddy Osborne as the boy was mounting his bicycle to ride home—home probably being "Deddy's" place, this weekend.

"Hey there, Buddy—been wondering how your weekend up with the Birdwhistles went."

"Way cool," Buddy said, standing over his bike. "They got the neatest place. You seen it, Bishop?"

"I have, just once. Lots of space, and animals, a big, nice log house, and plenty of company, right?"

"That's about it. Had a good time showin' them some stuff about their computer, and then them kids pulled me all over the place, showed me ever'thing. And their mom—she's just about as good a cook as Sister Shepherd! She makes ever'thing from scratch, Pratt said. I hatn't eat that much fer a long time." He glanced wistfully away. "They sure know how to have fun, them Birdwhistles. I mean, they work hard, and all, but it's like they— they *like* each other."

"Exactly. Well, I reckon they need to because it's a long way to any neighbors, except deer and rabbits."

"So cool," Buddy repeated. "Didn't know anybody around here lived like that."

The bishop stood and watched as the boy rode off in the cold breeze. Was it a blessing to Buddy, to see what a happy family life could be—or was it a cruel reminder of what his own was not?

Y

In the bishop's own home, there was a flurry—nay, a frenzy—of activity of a new kind over the next few days. Trish and Tiffani were doing some building of their own—hammering out an agreement as to what Tiffani should wear to the Preference Dance on the tenth of February. If Billy Newton had been her second choice of escorts, that fact was long forgotten in the effort to find exactly the right dress for the occasion—her first formal dance. Claire was wearing red, so that was obviously out, even though the occasion was close to Valentine's Day. Lisa Lou had mentioned light blue, and that took one of Tiffani's best colors. Trish was opposed to black. They searched the local stores, even made an after-school expedition to Birmingham but found nothing that they could agree on with regard to cost, modesty, degree of sophistication, or flattery of Tiffani's figure or coloring.

"Tiff, I don't see anything for it. We're going to have to sew you a dress," Trish said wearily one night at the supper table.

"Homemade! I might just as well wear flannel pajamas or jeans and a sweatshirt," Tiffani wailed and burst into tears.

"Home-sewn doesn't have to mean tacky," her mother said patiently. "I'm not all that bad at sewing; it just isn't my favorite thing to do. And Ida Lou will help me if I get stuck. She made her girls' wedding dresses. She made a dress for Sister Buzbee, that fit her just right, just by looking at her. She's amazing. She even makes up her own patterns."

"And I'm just so sure they're wonderful—for Sister Buzbee! Mom, I'm sixteen!"

"Oh, baby, I'm well aware of that."

Tiffani sniffed. "What exactly does *that* mean?"

"It means that I'm knocking myself out trying to help you find the perfect dress, and I don't think it exists around here. It means that you're going to have to come down off your high horse and cooperate with me, or there won't be a dress, perfect or otherwise. We have to work within a framework of reality here!"

"High horse! How can you say that? I thought moms were supposed to enjoy helping their daughters get ready for special occasions! All you do is gripe and criticize me."

"And all you do is ask for unsuitable dresses and ignore my wishes."

"There was nothing wrong with that black lace dress—it was darling!"

"Tiff, it made you look like a thirty-two-year-old cocktail waitress."

Predictably, Tiff threw down her napkin and stormed off to her room. "I just won't *go* to the stupid dance, then, if I'm that much trouble!"

There was a moment of deep silence at the table.

"Wow," said Jamie reverently. "That was the best one yet. She's getting good."

Trish sighed. "Guys, I'm sorry," she said shakily. "I shouldn't have brought the dress thing up during supper."

The bishop looked at his wife with concern. She looked worn out, hollow around the eyes. "Try not to stress too much over this, sweetheart," he counseled. "You know how Tiff is. Kind of volcanic. She erupts and lets off steam, and then she settles back into being her sweet, reasonable self."

"She'd better settle soon," Trish said. "Because I sure haven't seen much sweetness or reason, lately."

They ate quietly for a minute, and then Mallory asked plaintively, "Where's Samantha?"

"Samantha?" her mother repeated. "I don't know, honey. She was around, earlier. She's probably sleeping somewhere."

"She never sleeps when we're eating."

"Well, I don't know. Maybe Jamie'll help you look for her after dinner."

"I'll bet that weird Marguerite next door's got her," Jamie said. "She's always calling her over when she's outside. Even that stupid, ugly fence doesn't stop her. She peeks around the front of it and looks for Samantha. I see her, all the time."

"Mom!" Mallory looked ready to erupt next. "Mar-greet likes Samantha. Let's go see if she's over there."

"Um—no, honey. We're not going over there. Samantha knows the way home. But I bet she's here, tucked up somewhere, snoozing away."

"No she's not!"

The bishop felt he should say something wise—that the currents of family conflict were swirling around him faster than he felt comfortable with. He tried to think what that wise something might be.

"Why don't we have a family prayer?" he suggested.

"Dad," Jamie said patiently, "we just had a blessing on the food ten minutes ago."

"Right, my man, we did. But we didn't pray about Tiffani's dress or getting along in our family or finding Samantha."

"You'd better say it," his wife advised. "I'm not quite in the proper spirit to pray right now."

"Brigham Young said that when we don't feel like praying, we should get down—"

"Jim," his wife warned, "I know what Brother Brigham said.

Pray till you do feel like it. It's good advice, but I don't think we want to take that long in the middle of a meal."

The bishop said a prayer and, subdued, they finished their supper in silent thought.

Y

By nine-thirty that night, the cat Samantha had not been found, and Mallory was in a state of desperation. They had called her inside and out, searched the house from top to bottom, and the bishop had, without announcing it, gone out for a walk with a flashlight and looked for a still heap of beige and brown fur along the street, mentally trying to prepare something comforting to say to his little girl in case he found it. He reviewed the dogs he knew of in the neighborhood, wondering if any of them had chased her away or even caught and mauled her. Chilled, he went back into the light and warmth of his home with a hope that the cat had been found, but it was not so. Mallory was hunched in a corner of the family room sofa, sniffling and red-eyed. Jamie sat on a hassock nearby, earnestly trying to make her feel better.

"She'll be back in the morning, when she gets hungry," he assured her. "She's probably just out running around, having fun."

"It's dark and cold," Mallory objected. "She hates to be cold. She sleeps under the covers with my feet when it's cold."

"Well, maybe when you wake up in the morning, that's where she'll be."

"Nuh-uh! How could she, unless somebody lets her in?"

"I'll try to listen and hear if she's meowing, if I wake up during the night."

Mallory sniffed. "You never wake up. Neither does Tiffi."

"Well, Mom and Dad do, a lot. And they'll hear Samantha if she meows."

"Nuh-uh."

Mallory's dad could see sleep creeping up on his youngest, even as she struggled against it in her concern for her pet. He lifted her in his arms.

"Let's go up and say a special prayer for Samantha," he said. He carried her up the stairs to her bed and snuggled her in it. "Fold your arms, sweetie, right where you are, and talk to Heavenly Father about things."

"H-heav'nly Father, I don't know where my kitty Samantha is, and I'm scared. Please help us find her, 'cause she hates to be cold and she wants me. Please give her back to me. Please . . ." Her breathing grew even, except for one little gasp of a sob that touched her father's heart. He whispered a prayer that her faith would be rewarded and that she would be comforted if it turned out that her cat was forever gone.

Trish came out of Tiffani's room as he emerged from Mallory's, and they went back downstairs with their arms around each other.

"A dance dress and a missing cat," Trish mused. "Small, unimportant things, you'd think, in the big scheme of things. But, boy! What a tempest they stirred up. What strong feelings!"

"How's Tiff? Feeling any better?"

"Kind of repentant about how she talked to me at dinner but still certain that I'm going to make her wear something dowdy and tacky."

"What'll you do?"

"Shop for patterns and look at fabric, first thing. Talk to Ida Lou. Pray."

"Sounds like a plan. What do you think really happened to Samantha?"

Trish shook her head. "I can't imagine. Well, I can, but . . . I'd rather not. Poor baby Mal. Did she settle down?"

"Said a sweet little prayer and dropped off in the middle of it."

Jamie walked through the kitchen, headed upstairs. He pointed toward the house east of them.

"They've got Samantha over there. I'll bet you anything," he said quietly.

"You really think so, Jamie?" his mother asked, smothering a yawn. "Mercy, I'm exhausted."

"I wasn't kidding about that Marguerite lady. She's always out there, calling 'kitty, kitty, come here, kitty.'"

"Well, if Samantha hasn't shown up by morning, I'll go ask if they've seen her," his dad promised.

They put the house to bed and went upstairs themselves. It was funny, the bishop reflected, how the absence of such a small creature as a family cat could cast a pall over everyone's spirits. There had been times, when Samantha was being too boisterous or obstreperous, that he'd regretted allowing Mallory her pet. But he had to admit that Samantha was also funny and affectionate and made herself very much a part of any family gathering or project. He had to admit that he missed her, too. She should be curled up under the covers, warming herself and Mallory's little feet.

He lay awake for a time, half-listening for Samantha and half-pondering the unpleasant feelings being engendered in himself and all of his family by the Lowells. He didn't like harboring such feelings and knew that they were harmful to the others as well. There had to be a way to make friends of those foes—and if not, to deal with their own feelings. He prayed for wisdom and patience and forgiveness. Finally, he slept.

CHAPTER TWENTY

Y

" . . . OUR HEARTS BEAT HIGH WITH JOY"

T he bishop dawdled the next morning, putting off going to work, hoping that his little girl's missing cat would show up alive and well and expecting breakfast. Mallory herself couldn't eat hers. She toyed with it, mouth drooping, saying little. Jamie, standing behind Mallory as he hoisted his book bag onto his shoulders, caught his dad's eye and again pointed significantly toward the house next door. His father nodded and winked to show that he understood.

"Jamie, how about I give you a ride to school this morning?" Trish asked. "I'm going over to Sister Reams's house first thing, before she heads down to the temple. Dad can take Mallory to school on his way to work." She looked questioningly at her husband, who agreed.

"Soon as Mal and I finish our breakfast, we'll spend a little time looking for Samantha before we have to take off," he affirmed. Mallory began to eat with renewed purpose.

Trish hugged and kissed them both, whispering, "Good luck," in her husband's ear.

"I'll let you know," he whispered back.

He and Mallory presented themselves at the front door of the Lowell house promptly at nine o'clock—the earliest hour that it was considered polite in Fairhaven to knock on someone's door. He knocked twice. Finally, the door swung open, and a small, bent man leaned forward to peer at them. He had rheumy blue eyes and wisps of white hair both above and in his ears.

"Yes?" he asked, in a cracked voice. If this was Mr. Henry Lowell, the bishop thought, he was obviously older than his wife. Or perhaps, a cynical part of his mind suggested, living with her had aged him beyond his years.

"Good morning," he said cheerfully. "Mr. Lowell? I'm Jim Shepherd from next door. We wondered if you folks might have seen my little girl's cat. It's missing."

Mr. Lowell peered through the screen at Mallory. His expression seemed kindly enough.

"Well," he said. "Let me get my wife. Mother!"

He turned and shuffled away. The bishop looked at Mallory and gave her what he hoped was an encouraging smile. After what seemed a rather long time, Maxine Lowell came to the door.

"Yes?"

The bishop repeated his question.

"I don't know whether I've seen your cat, or not. I didn't know you had a cat."

"Surely you noticed Mallory playing with her out back, before your fence went in," he said. "It's a Siamese—beige and brown."

"I don't have time to watch the neighbors' children. And I don't know where your cat is." She started to close the door.

"Could we ask Mar-greet?" ventured Mallory. "She knows Samantha. She likes her."

"Marguerite is busy. She has work to do." The door did close, then, and they were left standing on the porch. The bishop did not feel satisfied that Maxine Lowell's response had been entirely forthcoming, and he raised his hand to knock again, when they heard a whisper from the edge of the porch.

"Mallory!" It was Marguerite, crouching where she couldn't be seen from any windows in the house. "I didn't take your kitty," she whispered. "I didn't put her in a box."

"Who did?" asked the bishop, also in a whisper.

Marguerite fidgeted, her lips tight as she fought with herself. "Mother," she admitted.

Mallory, fortunately, also spoke in a whisper. "What'd she do with her, Mar-greet?"

Marguerite shook her head. "I don't know. Took her off in the car. She wouldn't let me go. I'm sorry." She turned and made her way to the back of the house, ducking under windows.

"Daddy! That lady took Samantha away!" Mallory's whisper-voice was getting louder, and her father quickly led her back around the tall board fence to their own yard. "Mar-greet said! But her mom said she didn't know where she is. Was she fibbing, Daddy?"

"I believe she might have been, sweetheart. Let Daddy make a phone call, okay? I'm going to see if she took Samantha to an animal shelter."

Mallory stood by, trying to be brave and quiet, but with sniffles beginning again, as he looked up the local number for animal control. He knew there was a small, temporary shelter in Fairhaven, but that the main shelter was at the county seat, some twelve miles away. He caught up to the animal control officer on the man's cell phone and asked if he'd seen a Siamese cat in the last twenty-four hours.

"It's a female, brown and beige," he explained. "We believe our neighbor may have dropped her off."

"Um—records show we did receive a Siamese cat, yesterday about one P.M.," the man agreed. "Mondays and Thursdays are the days the truck from the county rounds up animals and takes them down to the main shelter, so she would've gone out about four P.M. yesterday. Let me give you that number."

The bishop winked at his young daughter and took down the county shelter's number, which he immediately dialed.

A woman's voice answered, and with trepidation, he asked his question.

"Well, sir, it's possible we may have your cat. We have two Siamese at the moment, a seal-point female who was brought in—let's see—last evening, from Fairhaven, and a lilac-point male from Blountsville. If you'd like to come and see, we're open to the public from nine to two on weekdays, and from nine to noon on Saturdays. We're closed on Sundays. If you'll bring your cat's papers from the vet showing that her shots are current, we can release her to you for a fifteen-dollar boarding fee. If she hasn't had her shots, then she'll have to be given them before she's released, and that'll be forty-five dollars. Has she been spayed?"

"She has. And I'm pretty sure she's current on her shots. I'll look for the papers. Thank you!"

"She's there? She's there?" Mallory was dancing up and down.

"Well, there's a kitty that sounds like it might be Samantha," he told her. "We'll go see, okay? Let me just call the store and tell Mary Lynn I'm taking the morning off."

He also called Trish at Ida Lou's and apprised her of the situation.

"That witch!" she said, with an indignant squeak in her

voice that reminded him of Tiffani. "Jamie was right, wasn't he? Jim, what are we going to do about her? She's just plain mean."

"I honestly don't know. I'm frankly puzzled, at the moment— and pretty mad, too. But, tell me, babe—where do you keep the cat's immunization papers?"

She told him where they were filed, and he was lucky enough to find them all by himself, which was not something he could take for granted without Trish's presence and sure memory for detail. She also reminded him to take the cat carrier, to trans- port Samantha safely home—if, indeed, it was Samantha. He tried to stifle the fear that Maxine Lowell had simply taken Samantha "for a ride" and dumped her in some out-of-the-way place, and that the cat at the shelter wouldn't be Samantha at all. All the way to the shelter, while Mallory bounced on the truck seat in anticipation of being reunited with her friend, he tried again to think how to comfort her if it was some other cat.

He needn't have worried. He was certain he recognized Samantha's distressed contralto yowls as soon as he opened the door to the shelter office. There was a deeper cat voice, as well as assorted other meows, barks and howls, but Mallory also heard Samantha.

"It's her! I can hear her voice," she said, running to peer through the glass window in the door that led to the cat cages. "Samantha! We're here!"

The volunteer worker who had taken their call examined the immunization papers, retrieved the cat from the holding cages, brought her back and set her on the desk. Samantha shook her- self, took one look at Mallory and her dad, and told them in no uncertain terms what she thought of her ordeal. Mallory picked her up, and the cat clung to her young mistress's coat for dear life, rubbing her chin against Mallory's and beginning a loud purr. The bishop stroked her fur, too, immensely grateful to have found her.

"Apparently she's yours, all right," the volunteer said with a chuckle. She proceeded to take the fifteen dollars and obtain the necessary signature, then counseled them about the advantages of having pets wear collars, or even better, have an identification chip implanted so that lost pets could be immediately identified. "Especially when they're prone to wander," she added, with a significant look at Samantha.

"Actually, she isn't all that given to wandering," the bishop told her. "She kept being called into the neighbor's yard by their daughter, and then the mother trapped her and hauled her off to the shelter."

"Oh, my. Didn't she recognize her as yours?"

"I think she did. I believe she has some kind of grudge against us."

"Be grateful, then, that she chose the shelter," the volunteer said. "Some do much worse. And you might want to keep a close eye on your cat from now on."

"We sure will." With an effort, he removed Samantha from Mallory's shoulder and put her in her carrier, where the yowls began again.

He was relieved, he told himself as they headed back toward Fairhaven. He was also very angry because he was certain that Maxine Lowell was perfectly aware of whose cat she had captured and hauled away. He imagined the things he would like to say to her regarding the stress and pain she had caused his little daughter—and, in fact, the whole family—and he pictured the bill he wanted to send her for the boarding fee, gas and oil, and damages. He wanted to demand an apology. He wanted to know exactly what she had against his family, when they had done nothing but try to welcome hers into the neighborhood.

Then his conscience caught up to him, and he realized how uncharitable such thoughts were—how un-Christian, just as Mrs. Lowell suspected him of being. Jamie's family home evening lesson on charity toward those who persecute sprang into his mind, and he recalled counseling Tiffani to try to pray for people who insulted her. He winced and tried to form a silent prayer in Maxine Lowell's behalf.

"Daddy, can't I let Samantha out? She's sad," begged Mallory. Indeed, the cat's multi-syllabic cries continued unabated from the carrier on the floor by Mallory's feet. Normally, the sound would have set his nerves on edge, but he was so glad for the happy outcome of the incident and for Mallory's joy that he almost welcomed the din.

"Sorry, sugar. She's safer in her carrier and actually probably feels more secure than she would bouncing around loose in the truck. It's kind of like her seatbelt. Just keep talking to her, and maybe she'll calm down." She didn't, until they pulled into their own driveway again and the bishop lifted her carrier out of the cab of the truck. Then she quieted, sniffing and peering through the openings in the carrier, obviously aware that she was home. In the house, she shook herself again, and after a brief tour of the kitchen, settled in a sunny spot on the family room floor and began to bathe herself, washing away all the scent of fear and of alien surroundings.

"Tell you what, Mal-pal," the bishop said. "Now that Samantha's safely home, you and I have to go back to school and to work. But first we need lunch, and since Mom's still not home, why don't we head for the Dairy Kreme to celebrate?"

"Daddy, don't you remember? I'm out of school at lunchtime. I don't go in the afternoons!"

"Oh, that's right. Well, then, we'll go have lunch, and by then, Mommy will probably be back."

"Why don't we wait for Mommy, and she can eat lunch with us?"

"Because I don't know how long she'll be, and I need to get to work."

She dimpled. "I think it's 'cause Mommy won't let you get fries and onion rings."

He leaned over and whispered in her ear. "You are far too smart, young lady!"

Mallory giggled. "I won't tell."

Y

He had stewed about the Lowell situation and prayed about it for two days. Finally he decided he needed to say something, so once again he knocked on the door of the house next door. No one came. There were lights on; he knew they were there. Their car sat in the drive. He knocked again, louder. Finally, Marguerite opened the door.

"Hi, Marguerite," he said pleasantly. "Is your mother here?"

Her eyelids flared as if with fear, but she nodded, and turned away from the door without a word. A few minutes later, Maxine came bustling forward, wiping her hands on a towel.

"What is it now?" she asked, frowning.

"I just wanted to let you know that we found our cat," he said. "Someone had taken her to the animal shelter. We had to drive down to Oneonta to get her. From now on, she'll be wearing a blue collar, with our name and address on the tag. If she wanders over into your yard, I'd appreciate it if you'd let us know, and we'll come get her. I wouldn't want her to bother you folks, or get lost again. It's too upsetting to our little girl."

"Cats don't stay home. They wander by nature. Anything might happen to them."

"Well, ours is pretty much a homebody, and she's never

disappeared before. If you aren't sure it's our cat, ask Marguerite. She knows her. Thanks."

"Mr. Shepherd! Are you accusing me of taking your cat away?"

"No, ma'am. I didn't ask the folks at the shelter who brought her in—if they even know. I'm just letting you know that she's back and that we'll try to keep her out of your way. We want to be good neighbors, and in that spirit, I feel it's best if we give one another the benefit of the doubt and treat each other with good, Christian charity, don't you? You have a nice evening, Mrs. Lowell." He smiled when the door slammed as he stepped off the porch.

Y

On Sunday afternoon, the bishop drove his son, Jamie, and Buddy Osborne down to Birmingham to visit T-Rex at the rehabilitation center. The boys were excited to see their hero, and although they were suddenly shy in his presence, they grinned continually. T-Rex was sitting up in a chair, his left arm still in a cast and sling, also smiling widely at his young friends.

Buddy nodded toward the helmet. "Last time I saw that thing, it was still on your head," he commented. "I was scared your head was split open the same way."

"Naw, reckon that didn't happen till I got down here and the doctors went to operatin' on me," T-Rex replied, reaching to explore the scar on the side of his head with his fingers. "Reckon I'm grateful for that there helmet, though. I didn't always like to wear one, but I'd just got it for Christmas, and it must've been cold enough that night that I thought it was okay. I don't remember, yet, anything past Christmas mornin'."

"Yeah, you were real proud of the helmet, and the new seat

and handlebar grips and stuff. I'm sure sorry, though, that you got hurt after takin' me home. Felt like it was my fault."

Jamie spoke up. "It wasn't your fault, Buddy! It was just the road was bad, with holes and all."

"That old Post Hole Road? *Pot Hole* Road, my dad calls it. I was real dumb to take that road at night. Ain't no way it's your fault, Bud. 'Sides, I'm told I invited you to go for a ride—told you I'd take you home. Ain't that right?"

"Well, yeah. But I made you late, and that's why you took a shortcut."

T-Rex chuckled. "Wadn't much of a shortcut, was it? I ain't made it home, yet!"

"How soon do you think they'll release you?" the bishop asked.

"They say iffen I keep doin' this good, and can keep my balance a little better, maybe by next week. I'll still have to go to therapy, but I figger, what the heck? Half the NFL players spend most of their spare time in therapy!"

As they were preparing to leave, T-Rex motioned the bishop over and said, "Bishop? Reckon I could have a few minutes with you, just us? There's a snack bar on the second floor that the guys might want to check out."

"Sure, Thomas," he replied. He ushered the boys out with a ten-dollar bill and instructions to get themselves something good, saying he'd join them there in a few minutes. Curiously, he went back into the room and pulled a chair close to T-Rex, whose roommate was out at a therapy session. "What can I do for you?" he asked.

"Um—it's just there's this thing been botherin' me, and I figgered you'd be the one to ask about it. It's probably just a crazy dream, on account of my head injury and all, but I don't know, 'cause it seems awful real, and I cain't get it out of my mind."

The bishop nodded. "Tell me about it."

"Well—it's like I dreamed I was somewheres else, someplace I never seen before, walkin' on this little old path that run beside the bank of a river. It was just a real purty place, and had these flowers growin' alongside the path that weren't like none I ever seen before—they, like, glowed from inside, you know? And the grass moved, like with a little breeze, and man! I felt so good there, and so happy. And then this guy—this dude in white clothes—comes walkin' along the path towards me, and he smiles at me and says, 'Do you like it here?' I kinda felt like I oughta know him, but I couldn't quite come up with his name. I says, 'I sure do, it's great.' And he says, 'Around that bend in the path is a bridge. If you cross the bridge, you won't be able to go back home to your parents. You'll stay here. They really want you to come back to them and finish your life, but it's up to you. What do you want to do?' Well, I wanted to stay there in the worst way, 'ceptin' I felt bad for my mom and dad, and I dithered around and couldn't make up my mind. Then he says, 'Look.' I looked where he was pointing, and Bishop, I swear, it was like all of a sudden I was in our chapel in Fairhaven. Only thing was, people wadn't sittin' on the benches like normal. They was all kneelin' down, between the benches, like they was prayin.' I seen old Buddy there, kneelin' down, and Sister Tullis, and you and your family and a whole bunch of people. I couldn't hear nothin' that was said, but all of a sudden I knew they was all there, prayin' for me, that I'd come back. So right then, I decided I would, and—well, that was all there was to it. Next thing I knowed, I was startin' to come around, and ever'thing hurt. It was real hard to open my eyes the first time. Now, is that crazy, or what?"

The bishop leaned forward and squeezed the young man's hand. "Thomas, that was not crazy. And it wasn't a simple, everyday dream. That was a real and very sacred experience. I reckon it's what some folks would call a near-death experience. The reason I know it was real is that when I blessed you, out at the accident scene, before the ambulance got there, I had the distinct impression that you could recover and be just fine, *if you chose to be*. I knew you'd have the choice to live or die—that it was in your hands. You can ask Brother Patrenko, or my wife, or—come to think of it—your own folks. I told them about it, too. And you can ask anybody you saw kneeling in the chapel, Thomas, because we did that. We had a special ward fast for you, and we all met at the chapel at the end of it, and had a kneeling prayer. Sister Tullis was there, and so was Buddy—among lots of others. Jamie even fasted for you—it was his first time. So you see, son—you had a true and sacred experience. You were very blessed."

The mighty T-Rex, tough, popular football player, sat with tears running down his cheeks. "I . . . I kinda died, then, didn't I?"

"I believe you must have been out of your body, briefly. And now you know, for certain, that there is life after death."

"Yeah—I do, don't I? I was there, huh? Not all the way, I reckon—but almost to the bridge. Who d'you reckon that fella was?"

The bishop shook his head. "I don't know. Could've been an angel, or maybe one of your own ancestors. Somebody you once knew, certainly—maybe in the premortal life, before you were born."

"Wow. I'd've known if it was the Lord, Himself, wouldn't I?"

"I expect so. My guess is he was a representative of the Lord, and spoke the truth to you, and showed you a true vision, too. Did he say anything else?"

"Iffen he did, I don't remember. All I remember is what I told you. What should I do now, Bishop?"

"Live to be worthy of your second chance, Thomas. Pray. Learn all you can about the Savior and His gospel. Honor your priesthood. Be clean and true. And first of all, when you get a chance, write your whole experience down in a journal. But it may not be something you want to tell everybody about. Sacred things like this should be kept mostly personal, unless you feel a strong prompting to tell somebody, like you did today. Mostly, just keep it in the back of your mind and ponder it. Let it guide your life."

Thomas nodded. "I don't see myself tellin' nobody about it, 'ceptin' maybe my folks. Reckon that'd be okay?"

"Very much okay. Thank you so much, Thomas, for sharing it with me."

The familiar grin returned. "Well, sure, Bish. Um—Bishop. I mean, you da man!"

The bishop hugged him gratefully. T-Rex was back.

"What if the rain gets on it? Won't it spot?" Tiffani fretted, turning around before the dining room mirror to gauge the effect of the light on the off-white, pearlized sheen of her gown.

"The only evening wrap I have is velvet, and that'd spot, for sure," her mother replied. "You'll just have to wear a regular coat, and remember to pick up the hem, and be careful getting in and out of the car so you won't splash on your skirt. It would be raining, wouldn't it! But at least it's not icy. You look absolutely delicious, Tiff! Like vanilla ice cream."

"Exactly," her father agreed proudly. "With strawberry cheeks and butterscotch hair."

"You guys are weird," Tiffani said, as she had said before—

but her voice was soft and pleasant. Her father was grateful and knew his wife was, too—perhaps more than he—that the problem of the dress had been solved, with the expert help of Ida Lou Reams. Working together, she and Trish had altered a pattern to make it a little more modest, and the result was stunning—a slender column of a dress that made Tiffani look like the living statue of a graceful Greek maiden. Lucky Billy Newton tonight! How could he possibly appreciate all that had gone into this evening? Boys had no clue.

Billy did, however, look properly appreciative when he arrived, wearing his suit and carrying a corsage of pink rosebuds for Tiffani, who had a matching boutonniere for his lapel. The flowers had been arranged for by Ruth MacDonald, who had called Trish to ascertain the colors the girls were wearing. After some discussion, Lisa Lou and Pete had been included in the group date, and Pete's dad, Big Mac himself, had volunteered to chauffeur the three couples in his capacious car. They would be a little crowded, but that didn't seem to bother the young people. After the dance, Mac would pick them up, drive them to his home for a midnight feast, and then take them each home—girls first, of course. Tiffani's dad was grateful to his old friend. He also hoped that the presence of the five LDS young people in the MacDonald home would be a good example of their faith to Pete and his parents.

He and Trish stood at the door and watched Tiffani pick her way daintily down the walk, holding Billy's arm. A few raindrops glinted on her amber curls in the gleam of the porch light.

At the wheel, Mac leaned over to give them a big wave, which they returned.

The bishop put his arm around his wife.

"She's gorgeous, babe," he said softly, as the car eased away from the curb. "Almost as beautiful as her mother."

"Well, she has her father's coloring, which is nice." Trish turned in his arms and looked up at him affectionately. "By the way, there's something I need to discuss with you. Would now be a good time?"

"None better," he said cheerfully, keeping his arm around her as they turned back into the house.

Y

Later, when Trish had reluctantly gone to bed, citing weariness, he sat at his desk in the dining room, organizing some receipts for their income tax files, forcing his eyes to stay open and his brain to keep functioning until he heard Tiffani's key in the front door.

She skimmed in, her cheeks flushed and a small, happy smile on her lips. He breathed a sigh of relief on two counts: she was safely home, and evidently the evening had gone well.

"Well, hey, Tiff! How was it?" he asked, stifling a yawn with a fistful of papers.

"It was great! We had tons of fun," she replied. "How come you're still up?"

"Oh . . ." he gestured with the papers. "Income tax. Takes lots of preparation."

"Uh-huh. Well—you can work on that tomorrow. Better get some sleep now, hadn't you?"

The look she gave him told him that she understood exactly why he was still up after a tiring day and a long evening. He'd better learn to be more subtle. She was developing a way of reading him that was uncannily like her mother's.

Y

Ironically, even after he was in bed, he couldn't sleep right away. Trish, lying on her side, turned slightly, murmuring, "Tiff home okay?" He reassured her, and she sank back into contented slumber. His mind was still processing a whole line of subjects, the young men of his ward figuring prominently among them. He thought of Elder Rand Rivenbark, flourishing now in his new mission assignment, of T-Rex and his venture into the spirit world, of Buddy Osborne, being such a stalwart little soldier amid the war between his parents, and of VerDan Winslow, for-mer ward heartthrob and candidate for missionary service, now turned newlywed husband and expectant father. He was proud of—no, grateful for—all of them, even VerDan, who was at last standing up to his responsibility. Growth experiences were not always easy, but it did seem they were always personally tailored for maximum benefit, if we will only allow the Savior to guide us through the process.

Reflecting on growth, he thought of Jack and Melody Padgett, ever-so-slowly moving, perhaps, toward reconcilia-tion—or, at least, toward healing of their wounded souls. He thought of Tom and Lula Rexford, humbled and refined by their son's accident and the ward's response. Necessity had instigated a good deal of stretching and growing outside their restricted comfort zone for Ralph and Linda Jernigan, and he was grateful for that. He thought of his own Tiffani and her sometimes painful progress toward maturity. He felt the pangs of stretching and expansion in his own soul, as well, from going through these varied experiences with the people involved.

Another kind of growth was occurring, too. A warm glow of gratitude suffused his heart as he snuggled closer to Trish and slipped an arm around her in the winter night. He relived the moment earlier in the evening when, sitting close beside him on the living room sofa, she had informed him that she was expecting—that another child was on the way for their family. He had held her hands, hardly able to credit it.

"Babe, are you sure?"

She nodded, her eyes brimming. "Just today, I found out for certain. I've suspected for a while, but I didn't want to disappoint you if I was wrong. You know, I've hoped before and been disappointed. But this time, Doctor Jennings agrees with me!"

"Oh, honey, that is so—I'm so tickled! I know how you've wanted another baby!"

"Well, you have, too, haven't you, Jimmy?"

"You bet I have. I had just kind of reconciled myself to its not happening, and this is . . . this is flat-out amazing!"

"Well, she said with a demure smile, "it's not as though we don't know how it happens."

He took her into his arms. "I'm grateful for both the process and the result," he told her. "When are we going to tell the kids?"

"I was thinking Sunday dinner—if you'll be home for it?"

"I wouldn't miss it. Not a chance."

"Tiffi will probably be embarrassed."

"Why?"

"Well, it's not quite like the old Mormon joke you hear, about 'how can you tell which one in the reception line is the mother of the bride? She's the one that's eight months pregnant!' But, still, Tiff probably thinks we should be beyond all that by now. Teenagers don't like to think of their parents—you know—being intimate."

"Well, too bad for them. But she'll love the baby, won't she?"

"I'm sure of it. And she'll be a big help. Once she gets over rolling her eyes."

Lying in bed beside Trish, listening to her softly breathe, he grinned in the dark. Growth was good, even if painful. Growth implied life, and life was good. It was good to be a husband and father. And it was good to be a bishop, the symbolic father of the living, stretching, growing Fairhaven Ward. Murmuring his thanks for such blessings, he gave himself up to sleep.